'Hello, Norville,' she said warmly. 'Have you been a good boy while I was away?'

As Amanda spoke, her fingers moved almost absently to the buttons of her crisp, white blouse. She began to unpick each button slowly, tantalisingly, exposing first the slender hollow of her throat and neck and then the shadow of the deep and enticing valley between her breasts.

Norville understood, suddenly. He knew this game. They had played it before, many times, but it never failed to excite him, set his old heart pumping yet again with the throb of hot blood from his wild youth . . .

Passion in Paradise

Anonymous

First published in 1993
by HEADLINE BOOK PUBLISHING

A HEADLINE DELTA paperback

10 9 8 7 6 5 4 3 2

ISBN 0 7472 4208 9

Typeset by Avon Dataset Ltd, Bidford-on-Avon

Printed and bound in Great Britain by
HarperCollins Manufacturing, Glasgow

HEADLINE BOOK PUBLISHING
A division of Hodder Headline PLC
338 Euston Road
London NW1 3BH

Passion in Paradise

Chapter One

Norville Clements was already in bed as Amanda let herself into the apartment using the pass key he had given her four months previously.

In bed — far from asleep. Laying passively beneath the white silk sheets, Norville felt an involuntary shiver of anticipation ripple across his naked flesh at the faint sound of the key turning in the lock.

The slight movement produced an immediate and erotic tingling in his body, like static electricity. Norville felt the hairs on his chest and legs tickle and tingle at the smooth and sensuous caress of the shiny material.

The tingling moved down his body, to centre itself in his swollen balls and vibrate upwards into his rising prick.

The pounding of his expectant heart threatened to stifle him, but he managed to croak out a greeting.

'Mandy . . . is that you?'

There was no answer for the moment, but then Norville had hardly expected one. The question itself was irrelevant — for who else could it be but the beautiful and exciting Amanda letting herself into his apartment at this time of night? No one else ever came to visit him. A lifetime of amassing riches by cheating and conniving on every business deal, using

1

the least acquaintance as an excuse for a quick profit, had left him few friends to ease the loneliness of his old age. He had never married, happy to use and abuse a thousand different women when his body was lithe and vigorous and pulsing with the hot blood of youth.

So the nocturnal caller had to be Amanda, and his pleasure was yet to come.

Norville's anticipation increased at the continued silence. No doubt Amanda was outside the bedroom door at that very second, preparing herself for the passion ahead. Norville imagined her slipping out of her tight skirt, her fingers straying to the crotch of her thin panties, rubbing the material against the lips of her cunt until it was moist and reeking with the overpowering heady smell of her juices.

Only then would she push open the bedroom door and tiptoe across the floor towards him, holding the soiled panties aloft in the air like an incense burner.

Kneeling by the side of the bed, she would gently peel back the top sheet until she had exposed his throbbing manhood. Then, as gently as a baby's nurse, she would wrap the warm and moist knickers around its rigid shaft, wipe them under his bulging scrotum and down the insides of his thighs until her smell was on him, her damp juices slowly cooling against the burning of his flesh.

Or perhaps she had some other treat in store tonight. Suddenly Norville could take the suspense no longer. His prick was twitching spasmodically, dancing like a candle flame in the wind. His throat was dry, the pounding of his excited heart throbbing like a jungle drum inside his chest. He feared that at any moment his cock would start to spurt, wasting his precious spunk on the pristine sheets instead of inside the burning lava flow of Mandy's cunt, where it belonged.

Norville ran his wet tongue over his dry lips.

'Mandy,' he managed to cry out. 'Please don't make me wait any longer.'

The bedroom door sighed open. Norville pushed himself up in the huge king-sized bed, raising his head on the soft pillows to get a better view of the sexy vision about to enter the room.

He was not disappointed. As Norville had anticipated, Amanda had stripped off her skirt, making her long, shapely legs the focal point of attention. Norville feasted his eyes upon those legs — powerful, young legs which could wrap themselves around a man's waist and hold him in a vice-like grip while the pulsing contractions of her hot pussy milked the last drop of juice from his love-shaft.

His eyes moved upwards as Amanda came closer, and his momentary disappointment that she was not carrying her knickers was quickly swept away by the sight of the skimpy black split-crotch panties which adorned her creamy thighs. Through the gaping, lace-trimmed split of the panties, Norville could clearly see the soft golden curls of her pussy hair framing her beautiful pink slit.

Amanda stopped a couple of feet from the end of the bed, smiling gently.

'Hello, Norville,' she said warmly. 'Have you been a good boy while I was away?'

As Amanda spoke, her fingers moved almost absently to the buttons of her crisp, white blouse. She

3

began to unpick each button slowly, tantalisingly, exposing first the slender hollow of her throat and neck and then the shadow of the deep and enticing valley between her breasts.

Norville understood, suddenly. He knew this game. They had played it before, many times, but it never failed to excite him, set his old heart pumping yet again with the throb of hot blood from his wild youth.

Amanda's deft fingers flicked open the last button. She peeled the sides of her blouse apart slowly, revealing the swelling creamy mounds of her magnificent tits straining against the enclosing restriction of her white bra.

The blouse slipped away from Amanda's smooth shoulders as she reached behind her back to unclip the restraining brassiere. It fell to the bedroom floor, finally allowing her perfect, large breasts to swing free.

Norville felt the comforting warm moisture of saliva ease the burning dryness of his mouth and throat as the thought of sucking on those stiff pink buds came to him. The very tips of his fingers tingled as he imagined them beneath the milky softness of those beautiful pleasure orbs, lifting them gently, feeling the weight of them, marvelling at each delicate, quivering movement of their soft flesh.

Amanda took another step closer to the bed, her fingers dropping now to hook inside the split-crotch panties — now the only thing which hid the full beauty of her nakedness from him.

Slowly, smoothly, she began to pull out the secret

pleasure tool she had been hiding from him. Norville's lips trembled and his whole body was convulsed with a tiny shudder of excitement as Amanda drew out a thin skein of silken threads, each individual strand bearing a small, tight knot at the end.

Amanda dangled the silken lash from her fingertips as a quizzical smile curled the corners of her lush, red lips.

'Well,' she asked again. 'Have you been a good boy?'

Norville giggled nervously, like a schoolboy caught wanking in the toilets, as he warmed to the game. He shook his head sheepishly

'I had dirty thoughts. Last night . . . and the night before. I touched myself.'

Amanda's face was immediately stern. 'Where? Where did you touch yourself, you wicked man?'

Norville was too weak with excitement to lift his hand from the bed to point to the offending part. Instead, he managed a faint nod of his grey head.

'We'd better take a look,' Amanda said curtly, striding the last couple of paces to his bedside and reaching down to grasp the silk top sheet in her left hand whilst brandishing the lash threateningly in her right. With a single savage tug, she pulled the covering sheet away from Norville's naked body.

Amanda's eyes blazed furiously as they fell upon the unmistakable evidence of his wicked thoughts. Her mouth dropped open in a mock expression of horror.

'Oh, Norville — you really are a wicked, wicked,

filthy minded man,' she chided him. 'I really don't know what I am going to do to cure you of these disgusting thoughts.'

'I suppose you'll have to punish me,' Norville suggested helplessly. Although he was trying hard to play the game in a way which pleased her, it was difficult to keep the smile from his wrinkled lips.

Amanda nodded, her expression one of concerned pity. 'I'm afraid you're right, Norville. And punish you I shall.'

Suiting her deeds to her words, Amanda lifted the silken lash high above her head and brought it down with all her force across Norville's bare belly.

The tiny silk knots eating into bare flesh caused only a slight stinging sensation – but to Norville it was the most excruciating and ecstatic agony he had ever endured. Waves of pain and pleasure tore through his body and into his mind. Tremors of delicious torment rippled down from his stomach into his thighs, and down his spindly legs until even his toes tingled.

Amanda struck again – and a second thrill of anguish and excitement pulsed into his loins, making long-forgotten bunches of tiny muscles around his balls contract tightly, adding to the sensual agony of his torture.

The total effect of the combined assault on flesh and spirit was not lost upon his excited cock, which jerked and throbbed at every stroke. Nor, indeed, was this effect lost on Amanda, who stared at the pulsing prick in shocked awe.

'Oh, Norville . . . now you're being so naughty you're making me feel naughty too,' she exclaimed, forming her perfect lips into a tight 'O' of disapproval. 'I've never seen such a monstrous thing. It's huge . . . and frightening . . . but just looking at it is making me go all funny and hot inside.'

Norville bit nervously at his lower lip in sheer excitement, fuelled by every ounce of his once-justified masculine pride. He, Norville Clements, still had the power to make a beautiful woman go weak with lust at the sight of his massive, throbbing prick. Even now, in his eightieth year, the stiff magnificence of his mighty cock could start a young girl's blood racing, pumping through her body to make her lips hot and red, the tiny pink bud of her clitoris stiff and burning, the walls and lips of her cunt swollen and moist with love-juice.

Norville's heart surged. He had won the game. The sheer force of his masculinity had overpowered this woman who had wanted to punish and humiliate him, and turned her into a quivering, helpless jelly of lust whose only desire now was to feast herself upon the thick shaft of his mighty manhood.

Flushed with happiness and passion, Norville waited for the next move in the game.

Amanda sank to her knees beside the bed, her eyes riveted upon the twitching, glistening shaft which once more proudly announced its sexual dominance to the world. A tiny, shiny bead of lubricant oozed out of the purple, swollen tip like a miniature translucent pearl, catching and refracting the light of the bedside lamp.

Like a small helpless mammal mesmerised by a snake, Amanda continued to stare openmouthed at the tantalising cock inches from her face. Then, slowly, as though savouring every precious moment, she flicked out her pink tongue from between her full red lips and licked up the small globule of seminal fluid with delicate precision.

Amanda retracted her tongue into her mouth, rolling it around inside as if to spread the salty tang of it over every single taste bud. Finally, her lips formed into a soft, red, fleshy pout as she prepared to suck the whole organ into her hungry mouth and throat.

'No — not yet.' Norville's voice had a new strength, his tone forceful and commanding.

Amanda looked upwards, her eyes torn from her expected feast by the powerful presence of this new Norville.

'You will have to contain yourself and be patient, my darling,' Norville told her somewhat patronisingly. 'I want you to get yourself good and ready for the treat in store for you.'

Amanda's eyelashes fluttered submissively. 'Anything you say, my dearest.'

Norville beamed expansively. He was enjoying this new and unexpected round of the game.

'I want you to go into the bathroom and put on lots and lots of fresh lipstick,' he instructed. 'Put it on really thick — so that when I let you suck my cock I will be able to feel the gooey stickiness of it against my throbbing shaft. Then, when you have licked it all over and sucked it deep into your throat until you start to choke, I'm going to give you the biggest mouth-fucking you've ever had.'

Amanda forced a look of enthusiasm. 'I can't wait.' she murmured, wondering momentarily whether she had gone a little over the top.

But any trace of sarcasm in her voice was lost on Norville, now completely immersed in his male dominance fantasy.

'And when I've finished fucking your mouth, I'm going to ram my still-rigid prick into you hot dripping cunt,' he went on. 'I'll thrust it so far into you that you'll think I'm going to split your belly in two and break right through into your womb. And just when you think you've been fucked like no man has ever fucked you before, I might just fuck your arse for an encore.'

Amanda rose from her knees submissively and headed for the bathroom, picking up her handbag and purse from the floor where she had dropped it. 'I won't be a moment,' she called, over her shoulder.

'You take your time. Take all the time in the world,' crowed the exultant Norville. 'And don't forget – put it on really thick. I want to see my cock slipping between the brightest, stickiest and reddest lips a man has ever seen.'

Norville slumped back against the pillows, delighted with himself. Amanda headed for the bathroom, smiling gently to herself.

Amanda regarded herself in the bathroom mirror. She had to admit that she was pleased with what she saw. A heart-shaped face, with high, prominent cheekbones and large green eyes and thick, full lips – topped off with a mane of fine, light golden hair which owed its colour and lustre purely to nature and not any bottle from a chemist's shelf.

Extracting the brightest shade of lipstick from her

handbag, she pursed her lips and prepared to smear it on. Suddenly she paused, thinking of Norville waiting for her in the huge bed and wondered if it was all worth it.

His new-found virility wouldn't last, of course. By the time she returned, his proud prick would be in a semi-flaccid state again and she would have to wank him gently until he finally reached a state of half-hearted orgasm.

It was always the same. Sometimes Amanda wished that the poor old man really could rediscover the passionate fires of his youth, so that she could give him a really good fucking to add to his store of memories. For memories were all he had, Amanda was sure.

Thinking about him. Amanda realised that her feelings went way beyond mere pity. In a strange way, she was genuinely fond of the old man. Despite his years and the frailty of his body, there was a youthful eagerness in him, a sense of fun and mischievousness which was missing in many a younger and more virile man. And although he had a reputation for being grasping and ruthless in business, he had always been more than generous to her — a fact which Amanda had gratefuly accepted over the last few months, as her beloved business slipped further and further down the tube of recession.

Five years ago, when she had first set up the Amanda Redfern Escort Agency in London's plush West End, it had been a little goldmine and a source of almost constant pleasure. Rich American and Arab clients, a list of some of the most attractive young girls in the City and a constant round of parties, expensive restaurants, nightclubs and nights of real passion in luxurious hotel suites.

Amanda had enjoyed her work — and the fact that she was making a small fortune at the same time was merely a bonus.

But the Americans weren't coming to London in such numbers anymore. The Arabs seemed to have more interest in a spouting oil well than a spurting prick — and the increasing number of Japanese tourists seemed to prefer petite, dark-haired girls with small breasts to the busty blondes which made up the bulk of the agency's regulars.

So the agency, which had been the source of so much pleasure and profit to her, had run down to the point where it was little better than a door-to-door call girl service. With clients like Norville Clements.

It wasn't that Amanda was purely mercenary, although she appreciated her comforts as well as the next woman. But bread was bread and head was head, as Amanda had often said to herself. Given a free choice, she probably preferred a big thick cock to a big thick bankroll — but when times were hard and the pricks weren't, Amanda was sensible enough to compromise.

Which brought her thoughts back to the waiting Norville. Amanda finished slapping on yet another coat of lipstick and headed back towards the bedroom, determined to give the old man a good time. He deserved it, Amanda told herself — and not just for the £200 he would tuck between her breasts as she left. It was the look of sheer gratitude in his rheumy old eyes as he said goodbye which invariably got to her. In fact, the only thing which really irritated her about Norville was his habit of calling her 'Mandy'. It was an abbreviation which Amanda had hated ever since her schooldays, when the boys had taunted her with cries of 'here comes randy Mandy'. The jibe, although perfectly true then as it was now, had somehow always managed to make her feel cheap and common, when she really wanted to think of herself as one of the great courtesans of history — a mistress or femme fatale on the lines of Nell Gwyn, Madame Pompadour or Jezebel.

Most of Norville's bravura had evaporated by the time she returned. His massive erection lost, he was once again faced with seeing his body as it was, not how it had once been. But the fire still burned in his loins, and the sheer heat of it could still put a glow in his eyes.

'I think you will have to be gentle with me again, my dear,' he said bluntly, as Amanda swept back into the bedroom. His eyes flickered down to the collapsed member, which now coiled upon his stomach like a strangled snake.

A new wave of compassion flowed over Amanda. She smiled at him roguishly as she knelt once more beside the bed.

'Be gentle with you? What nonsense,' she murmured. 'An old roué like you? Why, you've still got enough lead in your pencil to write a whole textbook on the art of fucking.'

She reached down to take the flaccid prick in the palm of her hand, massaging it gently. 'We'll soon have you back on form again . . . and then I'll use up a whole tube of lipstick just sucking the last drop of come up from the bottom of your balls.'

At the mere mention of the lipstick-smeared blow job, Norville's prick gave a convulsive little jerk and stiffened perceptibly.

Knowing that she had hit upon the right note, Mandy began to trace the tip of her fingernail across the helmet of his prick, talking all the while.

'You don't know how good it is to feel your thick shaft sliding between my lips. The sheer pleasure I get running my tongue up and down its pulsating length before I take it deep into my throat and feel that huge bulbous knob make me start to gag. To feel myself drooling so much that it runs out of the corners of my mouth and starts to trickle down your cock on to your thighs. To imagine that my mouth is really a hot, juicy cunt, and that you are fucking it like a satyr, a sexual demon whose lust is unappeasable, beyond all human power.'

Amanda broke off, suddenly aware that Norville's former erection had returned with a vengence, and that there was more pressing work for her mouth than mere talk.

The swollen, rigid gland which had a moment before been laying meekly in the palm of her hand was now a pulsing, living rod of flesh sheathed in her clenched fist.

Amanda was more than impressed. In this stage of arousement, Norville's cock was a good eight inches long, knobbled and veiny in a way that would put many an oriental dildo to shame.

Amanda was suddenly aware that her earlier sense of compassion was gone, to be replaced by a genuine desire to feel this mighty member throbbing away between her lips. She bent over him, cupping his swollen balls in her hand and squeezing them gently so that the entire unholy trinity of his equipment reared up like a phallic fertility symbol.

The swollen head was hot and dry. Amanda ran a wet tongue under and over the purple helmet, lubricating it with her saliva until it glistened enticingly.

Norville gave a little moan as Amanda's tongue slid down the blood-engorged underside of his cock and began to deliver a light, moist massage to the hairy balls she still held cupped in her hand.

The stiff prick began to twitch — at first spasmodically but then quickly, becoming a more rhythmic pulsing. Amanda realised that Norville was fast losing control over his unexpected erection, and that he just didn't have the sexual stamina to withstand any prolonged foreplay.

It was now or never, Amanda told herself. Taking a deep breath, she opened her mouth and sank down on the full length of it until her lips were almost brushing the wiry bush of his pubic hair. She fought the first reaction to gag, remembering the strict rules of self-control which made the 'Deep Throat' technique possible. Using the muscles of her neck and throat, Amanda began a series of little contractions which gripped the sides of Norville's cock, and sucked at it like a milking machine.

Norville came almost at once. Amanda felt the mighty piece of equipment give one powerful throb inside her mouth, and then a series of minor ripples, which slowly subsided. Deep in the back of her throat, Norville's ejaculation was already gone, swallowed without a thought.

Amanda pulled her head back slowly, until Norville's rapidly shrinking prick plopped out of her wet mouth. She looked up at him, laying back on the pillow with a satisfied smile on his face. Amanda smiled too, sharing his obvious pleasure.

'Good?' she murmured.

Norville's eyes twinkled with an inner fire. Suddenly his whole face looked twenty years younger. He sat up in the big bed.

'My dear . . . that was better than good. It was bloody marvellous,' he said, in a voice rich with youthful resonance.

Their eyes met, sharing a deep and wonderful joke for several moments. Gradually, the light which burned in Norville's eyes dimmed to a faint glow, finally fading to no more than a faint ember. He looked old again. Old, and tired, and something else which Amanda couldn't quite identify.

Exhausted, Norville let his head drop back on to the thick, soft pillows and managed a faint smile. Suddenly, Amanda knew what that elusive expression on his face had represented.

It was resignation.

Norville's eyelids fluttered weakly, as though fighting some terrible and utter fatigue. His lips moved faintly.

'Thank you, my dear,' he murmured.

The fluttering of his eyelids ceased abruptly. The last dying glow in his now fully open eyes sputtered and was extinguished for ever. The tiredness fell away, to be replaced by a look of absolute and total peace. Norville Clements was dead.

Amanda sat on the side of the bed. For a moment she was in complete shock. Then she reached for the phone and rang for an ambulance.

'At least the poor old sod died happy,' she said to herself as she dressed.

On the way home, she cried.

Chapter Two

The bedside telephone rang. At the fourth jangling note, Amanda propped herself up in bed and reached out for the offending instrument, trying to shake the remnants of a hangover out of her head. As she lifted the receiver to her ear, she managed to take a quick glance at her watch. It was 9.30 am.

'Hello?' she managed to croak out from between thick, dry lips.

The voice on the other end of the line sounded disgustingly chirpy.

'Miss Redfern? Miss Amanda Redfern?'

'Speaking,' Amanda said, without enthusiasm.

'Ah . . . my name is Peter Blake. Of Blake, Blake and Watts, solicitors.'

'Really?' Amanda tried hard to clear her befuddled mind. Those last seven vodka martinis must have been spiked with something, she thought to herself. 'And which Blake are you?'

'I beg your pardon?' Peter Blake sounded confused.

'Which Blake are you?' Amanda repeated. 'The first one or the second one?'

'The second one,' Blake said, falling in. 'The first one is my father.'

Amanda swung one leg out of bed experimentally. The wave of giddiness and nausea which followed the movement lasted only a couple of seconds, encouraging her to go the whole hog and attempt to stand up. On the third attempt she made it, and picking up the portable phone, padded towards the kitchen to make a cup of coffee.

'So, Mr second Blake. What can I do for you?' Amanda asked as she staggered across the bedroom. 'Blonde, brunette . . . redhead? Straight sex, or do you require special services . . . something kinky?'

There was a slightly strangled gulp from the end of the phone. 'I think we might be talking at cross purposes here, Miss Redfern. This is legal business.'

'Oops, sorry,' Amanda said, feeling rather foolish. She had assumed that the caller was a client. 'So what's this all about?'

'I'd rather not discuss it over the phone,' Blake said. 'Shall we just say that if you would care to drop into my office you will learn something of great advantage to yourself.'

Who could resist a line like that, even at 9.30 in the morning, Amanda thought to herself. She put down the coffee percolator she had been about to fill.

'Put the kettle on for coffee,' she instructed Blake. 'I'll be there in fifteen minutes.'

A pretty brunette secretary regarded her with a look of bored disinterest as Amanda bounced into the office.

'Can I help you, love?'

'I'm here to see Mr Blake. He's expecting me,' Amanda announced.

The secretary made no move to get up from her

18

desk, but merely nodded towards one of the doors
off the reception area.

'Go on in, I don't think he's busy.'

Amanda pushed her way between the corner of the
secretary's desk and a couple of filing cabinets and
walked over to the door. Reaching for the brass
handle, Amanda twisted it, opened the door and
started to walk in.

Behind her, Amanda thought she heard the
secretary start to say something, but she was already
through the open door and starting to close it behind
her.

Had Amanda not been in quite so much of a hurry
to discover this matter of great advantage to herself,
she just might have heard the secretary's words,
which actually were: 'Oh Christ, that's the wrong
office.'

But, of course, it was already too late.

At first glance, the office appeared to be deserted,
with just a large, empty wooden desk with a chair
either side of it. Amanda was about to turn on her
heel and leave when two distinct sounds alerted her to
the fact that the office was inhabited after all.

The first sound was a regular and rhythmic wet,
smacking noise. The second was a series of sporadic
and noisy grunts. Both seemed to come from behind
the desk.

Intrigued, Amanda tiptoed forward, skirting the
chair and the right-hand end of the desk until she had
a clear view. The source of the strange sounds
became immediately apparent.

Amanda had blundered in on a particularly hot

and active little sex session, for, on the carpeted floor, kneeling down like a pair of rutting dogs, were a couple in an advanced state of copulation.

Neither seemed to have noticed Amanda's presence, and the scene was interesting enough to dissuade Amanda from making an immediate and discreet retreat. So she watched, fascinated, as the canine-style copulation built up towards its floor-fucking finale.

Oblivious to their observer, the couple went at it with a single-minded fervour which would have put their four-legged counterparts to shame. Amanda wondered, fancifully, if she should go and get a bucket of water to throw over them, so intense was their dedication to the job in hand.

Both the partners were old enough to have learned more decorous and perhaps delicate techniques of lovemaking, Amanda thought – but then her admiration for the sheer joy of their coupling took over.

The woman, a plumpish brunette in her middle forties, had both hands splayed out on the carpet at an angle of ninety degrees – spaced out far enough to support her against the savage battering she was receiving from the rear. Behind, her middle-aged partner had his arms outstretched to cup her large, pendulous breasts in his hands while he used her chubby white buttocks as a fulcrum for a see-sawing motion which must have taken a layer of skin off his knees at every stroke.

The source of the strange sound effects became clear. The woman was doing most of the grunting, with each frantic forward stroke which set the cheeks of her arse quivering like oversized blancmanges. Each animal-like grunt was immediately preceded by the wet smacking sound which Amanda had noticed earlier, as a thick, rigid piston of flesh plunged deep into her soaking, dripping cunt and a pair of huge hairy balls sloshed against her wet thighs.

The man was obviously near to his climax. His rhythmic forward lunging took on a slower, more forceful cadence as he plunged harder, deeper and more desperately into the creaming slit of his partner.

She too was fast approaching the second plateau of carnal delight. Her grunts rose in pitch to become little screams of sheer pleasure as the column of tumescent flesh tore into her fanny, fighting its way towards her very belly.

Words and finally whole phrases began to find their way out between the screams and the grunts, and the rasping, grasping of her breath.

'Yes . . . fuck . . . oh yes, fuck . . . fuck me . . . oooh yes, fuck me . . . fuck me you animal bastard . . . bang it in . . . shove it up to my womb . . . fuck my guts, fuck me inside . . . poke it right up to my throat . . .fuck, you bastard, fuck, fuck, fuck meeee . . .'

Amanda was aware of two distinct sensations as the sexual marathon approached its inevitable climax. One was that her own cunt was tingling and burning with excitement, and the second was that somewhere behind her an interconnecting door had opened and there was someone else in the room.

The second sensation was confirmed first, as a large and powerful hand descended on her shoulder and pulled her backwards. A second later, Amanda was in another slightly smaller office and the door had closed on the final, shuddering climax of the woman on the floor.

Amanda felt a distinct sense of disappointment. Unintentional as it had been, she had found her first trip into voyeurism extremely exciting — and to be torn away at the crucial moment somehow robbed her of her own, however vicarious, sexual pleasure.

She turned to identify the owner of the hand which had so abruptly pulled her from the room, and was pleasantly surprised. The tall, athletic young body built on to the hand was surmounted by a head crowned with dark, curly hair and a handsome face wearing a rather sheepish and embarrassed smile.

'You walked into the wrong office,' said the face. 'I'm Peter Blake, by the way. I take it you are Amanda Redfern?'

Amanda nodded. 'You take it right.' She nodded towards the interconnecting door. 'So who was that?'

'That was the first Mr Blake — my father,' Peter explained. He coughed nervously, unsure of whether to offer any explanation for his father's behaviour.

He finally decided not to, and fell silent. Partly to break the embarrassed silence, and partly to satisfy her own curiosity, Amanda asked: 'Does he usually screw his clients on the office floor?'

Peter Blake looked slightly shocked. 'Good Heavens, no. That wasn't a client — that was mother. She used to be his secretary before they got married, you see. They like to relive the good old days from time to time. Quite romantic, really . . . don't you think?'

22

Romantic wasn't quite the word which would have sprung to Amanda's luscious lips, but she nodded anyway.

'So what is this matter which could be of great advantage to me?' she asked, getting the conversation back to basics.

Peter Blake motioned her to sit in the swivel chair by his desk. As Amanda sat down, he perched himself on one corner and picked up the bulky file which had been laying on it. From this elevated position, he had a superb view of Amanda's considerable cleavage down the front of her V-necked sweater. With something of an effort, he tore his eyes away and began to pull sheets of paper out of the file.

'Norville Clements,' Peter said bluntly. 'You knew him, I believe?'

Amanda nodded. 'Intimately.'

Peter gave another little nervous cough. 'Yes . . . quite. You know that he died the other night, of course?'

'He died a happy man,' Amanda confirmed.

Peter stole another quick glimpse at Amanda's breasts. 'I'm sure he did,' he murmured fervently. 'Anyway, to get to the point, he left you something of considerable value in his will.'

Amanda's pert face brightened with a sudden smile. 'I always wanted to come into money, as the nudist shopkeeper said when he caught his dick in the till.'

'It's not exactly money,' Peter warned. 'Although, of course, it is *worth* a great deal of money. Actually, it's a property — a large country club in quite

23

spacious grounds, in fact. At the last estimate, the estate was valued at just over one and a half million pounds − but that was before the recession and the plunge in property values of course.'

Amanda drew in her breath with a noticeable gasp. 'And that's all mine?'

Peter nodded. 'The property is, yes,' he confirmed. 'But there are certain restrictions and complications under the terms of the will.'

Amanda came down to earth with a bump. 'Restrictions?' she asked, in a disappointed tone.

'Basically, you can't sell or dispose of the property. You have to run it as a going business. Mr Clements was very fond of the country club. He went there a lot in his younger days,' Peter told her.

Amanda digested this information for a few seconds. 'You mentioned other complications.' she pressed Peter Blake.

Peter looked slightly shifty. 'Nothing which can't be sorted out, of course. As Mr Clements' solicitors for many years, we are in an ideal position to deal with all matters relating to his estate − so it would make things a lot easier if you empowered us to deal with things.'

'In other words − you would like to handle my assets,' Amanda said.

Peter Blake gazed on the swelling voluptuousness of her magnificent tits again. 'Oh yes . . . please,' he breathed, absently.

Amanda caught the direction of his unashamed stare, and added one more tiny piece of information to the complicated thinking process which was going on inside her head. Like father, like son, she thought, finally concluding that being as amenable as possible to Peter Blake could have distinct advantages.

At the same time, she was still acutely aware that the doggie-style fuck marathon she had witnessed earlier had most definitely tripped her switch. Amanda could feel the warm juices from her pussy soaking into the material of her panties.

It would be a terrible waste for all that hot and lubricating juice not to ease the passage of a good thick cock into her aching slit. And if the good-looking Peter had inherited some of his father's sexual stamina and prowess, then being nice to him could be a distinctly two-edged sword.

Acting on sheer impulse, Amanda reached under her skirt and slipped off her warm and slightly steaming panties. She tossed them across the polished top of the desk to where Peter was sitting.

'Here — you're a solicitor . . . so hold my briefs,' she said with a slight giggle.

Peter's eyes widened in delicious anticipation.

'Does this mean that you're going to give me your business?'

Amanda flashed him a dirty look. 'Oh, I'm going to give you the business, all right. More to the point — what sort of a business have you got to give me?'

Amanda began to peel off her V-necked sweater. As it came off over the top of her blonde head, Peter noticed with utter delight that she wore no bra. Her full, lush breasts swelled out proudly, needing no artificial support. Like a final piece of decoration on each creamy, fleshy orb, each masterpiece of mammary perfection was crowned with a small, stiff pink bud.

Amanda stood up and leaned across the top of the desk, parading the twin delights for Peter's closer attention. Pausing only to run the tip of his tongue over his lips, Peter needed no second bidding. He bent down to bury his face between Amanda's tits, marvelling at the delicate smell of her expensive perfume and the smooth, soft texture of her flesh.

His tongue flicked out again − but this time to trace a moist line down the valley of her cleavage and under the swelling softness of each breast in turn. Then, as he felt the growing tightness inside his well-tailored trousers, he abandoned himself to sheer pleasure, taking first one and then the other firm nipple right into his mouth, sucking gently on them as though they were the most delicious and delicate sweetmeats he had ever tasted.

Amanda moaned softly at the warm, wet feel of his mouth on her nipples. She could feel them stiffening, swelling as her blood warmed, rushing to flush every part of her sexual being with the heat of passion.

Withdrawing his mouth, Peter stared in fascination as each pink flower bud blossomed out, gradually becoming more erect and changing in hue to more of a reddish-brown, like the darker aureoles which surrounded them.

Amanda could feel the juices from her frothing cunt beginning to bubble out and run down the insides of her soft thighs. She shivered deliciously with the tide of rising lust which welled up from that centre of orgasmic pleasure to every other part of her body.

Finally she could take no more. Her cunt was yearning to be filled, her stiff and throbbing little clitoris aching to feel the rough passage of a thick prick rubbing against it.

It was time to find out what Peter had to offer in that department, she thought to herself.

Putting her hands on either side of his head, Amanda pushed him away from her breasts. Caught suddenly off balance, Peter fell backwards to sprawl full-length on the desk top.

With an eager, and surprisingly athletic bound, Amanda was up on the desk as well, straddling his legs. With deft fingers, she unzipped his fly and slipped her hand inside to seek out his hidden treasures.

Initial contact was very promising indeed. Amanda's hand closed over a hot, throbbing column of flesh which was rapidly swelling and stiffening to peak performance levels. Encouraged by the promise of delights to come, Amanda set both hands to the job, struggling to free the trapped cock from its boxer-shorts prison and pull Peter's trousers down to his knees.

With her prize fully exposed, Amanda sat back on her haunches to admire it. Although not particularly long, the erect appendage was incredibly thick, and stood out proud and straight from a mass of dark, crinkly hair. For some strange reason, it reminded Amanda of a much loved soft toy she had always taken to bed in her childhood, and she immediately felt a strong urge to stroke it, cuddle it, play with it.

Slowly and delicately, she ran the tip of her fingernail up and down the pulsing underside of the playful beast, delighted at the way in which it jerked and twitched at her touch. Reaching the burning, glowing helmet, Amanda inserted her longest nail into the tiny hole at the top, forcing it open and exposing the highly sensitive and delicate flesh inside. Her ministrations were immediately rewarded by a particularly strong muscular spasm, which made the whole thick shaft jump like something electrocuted.

Peter, meanwhile, was doing his own bit of exploring. He slid his cupped hand under Amanda's crotch to feel the hot and slippery juices from her fanny against his palm. Rubbing his hand against the silky curls until it was thoroughly lubricated, he spread his fingers until his thumb was pressed against the very lips of her cunt and his longest finger was poised against the tiny, tight hole of her anus.

Then, with slow and deliberate precision, Peter manoeuvered each digit into its chosen orifice and began to probe deeper.

Amanda wriggled her arse in pleasure at the dual thrill of Peter's fingers. Although the idea of anal sex had never appealed to her, she was surprised to discover how erotic the feel of something hard and stiff massaging the inside of her arsehole could be. And with Peter's thumb now starting a sensuous circular movement against her throbbing clitoris, the sensation of sheer pleasure was doubled.

Squealing with delight, Amanda pressed her buttocks down harder, as if to impale herself more deeply on both intrepid explorers. Peter's thumb slipped off the slimy button of her clit and plunged deep into her oozing love canal. Amanda felt her first delicious ripple of pre-orgasm shiver through her body.

But a thumb was no longer enough to assuage the yearning hunger of her greedy cunt. The aching emptiness of it went deep inside – perhaps even deeper than the longest and fattest cock could possibly reach.

Amanda flexed her knees and raised her buttocks. Peter's finger popped out of her arse with a faint plopping sound. Wiggling herself along the smooth surface of the desktop, Amanda moved up Peter's body until she was poised directly above his thighs. Then, grabbing his stiff prick in her hand, she guided it into position so that its blunt, bulbous head was between her swollen labial lips and began to sink slowly on to the entire pulsating length of it.

Peter let out a throaty groan as Amanda's tight but slippery pussy engulfed his manhood. He thrust his hips up to meet her as he felt the hot wetness of her cunt against the smooth skin of his belly, but Amanda bore down on him, urging him to submission. Like an expert horsewoman, she rode her proud stallion with a whip hand, dominant yet appreciative of his raw animal power, the as yet unreleased energy of the beast.

Now in total control, Amanda used the muscles of her knees and thighs to urge her steed onwards – at first to a gentle trot, then to a canter and finally into a full-blooded gallop. The race was on, the winning post was in sight . . . and the prize was the shuddering, all-consuming release of orgasm.

Peter came first, pumping his hot ejaculation deep inside her as Amanda continued to urge him on, grinding her pelvis down upon his body to coax every last ounce of stimulation and sensation from it. Then, finally, she too was past the post and the race was won.

Amanda flopped down to sprawl full-length upon him, as she exploded wetly around Peter's thick shaft still embedded deep inside her.

They lay, exhausted, for several minutes. Finally, Peter spoke.

'I suppose you'll be wanting to go and take a look at your inheritance?'

Amanda shrugged. 'No rush — tomorrow will do. Right now I have other plans.'

She sat up and wiggled herself back down the desk until she was in eye contact with Peter's spent prick, laying flat and limp against his belly.

'Looks like I've got some work to do if I want a ride home,' she murmured.

Peter groaned softly as she lowered her head and took the soft cock into her warm mouth and began to suck wetly upon it.

The interconnecting office door sighed open. Blake senior, who had come in to discuss a business matter with his son, froze with embarrassment in the doorway, his hand still upon the brass handle.

Alerted by the flash of movement out of the corner of her eye, Amanda glanced up, her mouth still clamped around Peter's rapidly rising prick.

'My God . . . I'm terribly sorry,' Blake senior stammered. He backed out of the office hastily, closing the door behind him.

Amanda worried, briefly, if she had made a bad first impression. It was, on the one hand, terribly bad form not to offer at least some sort of introduction to one's lover's parent. Then again, it was extremely bad manners for a well brought up young lady to talk with her mouth full.

So, on balance, Amanda reflected that she had acted with the proper decorum. And of course, it sort of evened up the score between them.

Satisfied, Amanda returned to the job in hand.

Or, rather, in mouth!

Chapter Three

'Well, this is it. We're here,' Peter announced.

Amanda shook herself fully awake. For the last two hours of the drive down from London, she had dozed fitfully in the passenger seat of Peter's Volvo, exhausted from the sexual exertions of the previous day and night.

After trying every possible configuration of sexual position in Peter's office, including spiral screwing with a swivel chair, they had returned to his apartment and the more leisurely and comfortable pleasures of a large double bed.

Amanda had to admit that Peter Blake was quite a find. He had certainly knocked any ideas she might have had about solicitors being stuffy and prudish out of her head. He was a lusty, full-blooded man — more than willing to plunge himself whole-heartedly into any carnal adventures his partner could conceive. And with Amanda as that partner, he had discovered a rich and fecund breeding ground of unborn delights.

For his own part, Peter was more than smitten with the beautiful and exciting woman which fate had seen fit to throw, quite literally, into his lap. However, his enthusiasm for the pleasures of her lush, ripe young body were slightly tempered with a fear that he might have bitten off rather more than he could chew, and that his powers of sexual stamina would be tested to the full in her company.

This fear had been reinforced several times on the drive down to the wilds of Hampshire. In between her little snatches of sleep, Amanda had taken great delight in unzipping his fly and playing lovingly with his balls and prick as he tried to concentrate on the road ahead. It had not been easy — and getting a blow job at eighty-five miles an hour on the Andover by-pass was definitely not a traffic hazard covered by the Highway Code.

But they had made it safely — and were now at the very portals of Paradise, so to speak.

'Welcome to the Paradise Country Club,' Peter said, as Amanda sat up in her seat to gaze out through the windscreen. She took her first look at her inheritance.

From the end of a long gravel driveway, it looked a most impressive establishment indeed. Obviously once a grand old stately home and country mansion, the building itself had a respectable, ivy-covered gothic facade, several more modern looking out-buildings and was set in some twenty to thirty acres of grounds.

Looming in the foreground were a pair of huge, tall wrought-iron gates which controlled entry to the driveway and estate proper. Glancing up, Amanda saw that the name of the place was written in huge iron letters worked into the metalwork of the gates themselves.

And here was the first sign that things might not be all that they appeared. On closer inspection, the gates were old and rusted, sagging drunkenly on broken hinges. The iron letters had corroded too, and leaned against each other at crazy angles. The letter 'O' had dropped off completely, so that the title of the establishment now actually read: THE PARADISE CUNTRY CLUB.

Amanda took this to be something of an omen — quite rightly, as it turned out.

'Shall we go in?' Peter asked, and without waiting for an answer he put the car into gear and began to cruise up the gravel driveway.

The nearer they got to the mansion, the more obvious it was that the whole place was badly run down. The huge, expansive lawns were neatly trimmed, but riddled with patches of moss and weeds. They passed what had once been an ornamental pond with erotic statues and fountains, but time, neglect and the droppings of a million birds had taken their toll. The once-clear waters of the pond were now an algae-covered greenish-brown slime, and the four naked women whose granite breasts had once spurted crystal plumes were dry. Only the central statue of Eros still fulfilled its original role as a fountain, but this only made matters worse. As a young, and virile god, his stone penis had spurted forth a shining jet of clear water. Now, discoloured and bird-shit stained, the broken stump of his dick merely pumped out an erratic ejaculation of yellowish-brown gobbets — making him look for all the world like a ravaged old debauchee in the tertiary stages of syphillis.

It was not a pretty site.

'Of course, there's a certain amount of maintenance work to be done,' Peter offered, helpfully. 'But

I'm told that the interior of the buildings are in good order.'

Peter pulled the car up outside the main entrance to the mansion house.

'Tell you what . . . why don't you go and take a look around the grounds while I go in and find the couple who have been managing the place,' he suggested.

Amanda accepted the suggestion gratefully. Her initial enthusiasm for the place had already turned to disappointment, and she was in no hurry to have that reduced to the level of despair. And something told her that things inside the building could well be as bad as the outside.

Apart from which, it would do her good to stretch her legs after the confines of the car.

'Right — I'll meet you back here in fifteen minutes,' she said, climbing out of the car. She set off across the lawn towards what looked like the shattered remains of a greenhouse as Peter went inside the house.

Peter was relieved to find that the interior of the house was not quite as bad as he had been dreading. Like Amanda, he had feared the worst on the drive up through the grounds, and had suggested that they split up mainly to spare her feelings while he costed up the necessary renovations. That Norville Clements had also left a sizeable amount of cash for the upkeep and running of the club was a fact he had not mentioned to Amanda — and he had no intention of doing so unless he had to. For Peter, although perfectly straight in terms of his sexual orientation, was more than a little bent when it came to business matters.

The vast, cavernous entrance hallway was deserted as he walked through towards the evening lounge and bar. The large and luxuriously decorated room was also empty, but at least showed signs of recent use. There were several brandy and whisky glasses both on the bar top and on some of the tables, indicating that at least a couple of dozen people had been enjoying the facilities within the last couple of days or so.

Peter lifted up the bar flap and walked behind it, helping himself to a large scotch from a row of optics. Swilling the amber liquid around in the tumbler, he looked around about the room.

Here, at least, there had been reasonable effort made to keep the place in order. The furnishings were clean and reasonably smart, even if some of them had seen slightly better days. The room boasted a plush, rich blue coloured carpet, with perhaps eighteen to twenty mock-antique tables with matching chairs upholstered in heavy tapestry cloth. Ornate embossed wallpaper and heavy brocade drapes over the windows lent the room an air of opulence, only slightly marred by the many gilt-framed pictures of nude women and orgiastic scenes which hung around the walls.

The overall effect was basically that of an up-market bordello. With little difficulty, Peter could visualise it as the setting for a movie about a German Officers' brothel in France during World War II.

Peter downed the last of the whisky in his glass and went to help himself to another double. Old Norville's estate could afford it, he thought to himself, remembering the five-figure sum lodged in a building society account to which he held the pass-book number. The scotch, and thoughts of money, combined to create a rosy glow inside him. Things were looking up. The country club obviously wasn't quite as run down as he had feared, still attracted customers and he had Amanda taking him at face value, for the present at least. His dream of a nice little villa on the island of Mustique got closer to reality by the minute.

It was time to explore further. Pausing only to replenish his glass, Peter walked to the door off the bar which led to the beer and wine cellars.

As he opened it, Peter was surprised to find that the expected gloom of the cellars was punctuated by bright, flashing pulses of coloured light. Somewhere beyond the bottom of the wooden steps which led down into the depths, he could hear a faint whirring sound.

Intrigued, he made his way down the steps, lurching slightly as the rather large and sudden intake of alcohol found its way into his bloodstream.

As he reached the cellar floor, the source of the flashing lights became apparent – playing on the ceiling was a silent, but full-colour Swedish porno movie.

Peter sat on the bottom step and bent his head back so that he could get a clearer view of the sexual saga unfolding above him.

A startlingly beautiful blonde-haired Scandinavian girl was into some real heavy stuff with three men — two white and one black. A zoom-in close up of her cunt made it graphically clear that Peter had missed some of the previous action, since the thick fleshy lips of her slit were already glistening and dripping with love juice and spent sperm. The three men were moving around her prone body, seeking out some new sexual configuration.

Peter took another deep swig at his glass, feeling a rising wave of heady excitement. He had never actually seen a really blue movie before. A few soft-core videos from the top shelf of his local hire shop was more or less the extent of his dirty movie watching — but what he was seeing now was the real thing.

The three naked men closed in around the blonde girl, with some new plan clearly in mind. The camera tracked in on each man in turn, blowing enlargements of their sexual equipment into gigantic, grotesque images upon the cellar ceiling.

Peter felt an odd sense of guilt and self-doubt as his own prick began to stir and stiffen inside his trousers in response to the distorted images of three gigantic cocks. Mentally, he tried to will the camera to return to safer images which he could feel more comfortable with. The girl's tits . . . her red mouth . . . her wet and swollen labial lips.

Peter drained the whisky tumbler, aware that even as the fiery liquid passed his lips they had already become dry and burning. Part of his brain told him to tear himself away from the strange compulsion of the film, go back to the bar and indulge in the more normal and acceptable masculine pursuit of getting steaming drunk.

Instead, he continued to watch the film as it unfolded above him.

One of the men had bent over the girl, lifting her up into a sitting position. As she obeyed his unspoken commands with total submissiveness, he sat down on the floor behind her and spread his legs out on either side of her buttocks. Reaching over her thighs, the man slapped both hands against the inside of her soaking crotch, kneading and stroking them together until they were wet and slimy with her secretions.

He moved his hands back to his own genital area, smearing the glistening love-juice up and down his huge, distended shaft. Satisfied that his cock was well lubricated, he lifted the girl's bottom from the floor and wiped his hands over her arse.

The man lifted the girl again, pulling the cheeks of her arse apart. The camera homed in on her tight, brown little arsehole as the man positioned the tip of his cock against the puckered orifice and then dropped her, heavily, on the full length of his shiny prick.

A second camera took up the story, closing in on the girl's face as it registered first a shock of pain and then the reality of pleasure as the huge cock buried itself deep in her rectum. The man reached out to grasp her hips firmly, rocking her forwards and backwards upon the fleshy spike which impaled her.

The girl's red mouth was open in a wide 'O' of sensual pleasure – a tempting, pouting target at which the other two men were only too happy to aim their meaty weapons. Closing in on her, they presented their massive cocks to the painted lips as the man beneath her continued to fuck her arse vigorously.

The girl's mouth fastened upon each tool in turn, first gobbling upon the purple, swollen helmet and then sucking the throbbing shaft deep into her throat. First a white, then a black cock passed the girl's lips — then white again, black again. Finally the girl reached up and grasped both throbbing pistons in her hands, and pulling them together, began to lick them both at once with a furious, darting tongue.

Both men urged forward, seeking the hot wet pleasures of her mouth beyond the flicking tongue. The girl stretched her mouth open wide to accommodate both bulbous heads, her cheeks bulging out as a double-barrelled weapon slid between her lips.

'Certainly makes you feel horny, what?' a cultured voice said suddenly.

Peter jumped with shock as the film seemed to have come to life around him. Standing in front of him was a completely naked man, who seemed to have popped out of nowhere.

'Thought you lot had all gone home,' the voice went on, as the naked man bent down for a closer look at Peter's face. 'Oh, I say . . . you're not one of our regular bunch. Who are you, then?'

Peter shook his head, stupidly, as though to clear this impossible fantasy from his mind. Waves of alcoholic giddiness swept over him, but the naked man didn't disappear. Instead, he reached out a hand in greeting.

Peter succumbed to the insane logic of the situation. He grasped the proffered hand and allowed its owner to pull him up from the cellar steps into a standing position.

'Andrew Baines . . . I'm the bar manager here,' said the man by way of introduction.

'Peter . . . Peter Blake,' Peter managed to mumble. 'I brought the new owner down to take a look around the place.'

Andrew looked disappointed. 'Oh, what a pity. Thought you might be hanging around for a few more fun and games, eh?'

Andrew didn't seem in the least embarrassed by the weird situation. Somehow, Peter got the impression that he regarded being totally starkers in a beer cellar and greeting a total stranger like a long-lost friend as perfectly normal and acceptable behaviour.

'So where is this new owner?' Andrew asked.

Peter waved a weak hand vaguely in the air. 'Somewhere out in the grounds,' he slurred.

Andrew's face brightened. 'Ah . . . so there might be time for some fun, after all? Jolly good.'

Andrew clapped an arm around Peter's shoulder, hugging him. He pressed his mouth to Peter's ear in a conspiratorial fashion.

'Look here, old man . . . I don't suppose you'd be a real sport and come over and fuck my wife for me, would you? The thing is, we've been at it for over two hours now, and quite frankly, I'm absolutely shagged out. But I think she could do with going round one more time.'

Without waiting for an answer, Andrew began to lead Peter across the cellar to a darkened corner. Here, Peter became convinced that he had died of alcoholic poisoning and gone to Heaven. Or the other place!

Straddling a huge oak beer barrel, with her legs splayed wide open, sat an equally naked woman. She was plump, dark-haired, and smiling broadly, as if enjoying some secret pleasure. She showed absolutely no sign of surprise or even concern as Andrew led Peter up to meet her.

'Sally, old girl . . . this is Peter,' he said cheerily, by way of introduction. 'Damned decent chap, actually. He's volunteered to give you a good old rollicking, if you fancy it.'

Sally's chubby, but not unattractive face registered delight at the prospect.

'Super,' she said, enthusiastically. 'I was wondering what to do now that the movie is finished.'

Peter's befuddled mind had not even noticed that the porno movie was no longer playing on the ceiling. For him, the celluloid fantasy had blurred into reality several minutes previously.

'I'll just watch, if you don't mind,' Andrew announced to no one in particular. 'Perhaps seeing you getting a grade A shafting will put some of the poke back into my pecker.'

Sally began to wriggle off the barrel, with some difficulty. There was a loud and liquid slurp as she lifted herself off the large wooden bung in the top of the barrel which had been jammed up her sopping fanny. She slid down the rounded side of the beer keg.

'Well, don't stand on ceremony,' she urged Peter. 'Get your clothes off, there's a good chap.'

'Here, old man, let me give you a hand,' Andrew offered, reaching out to start pulling Peter's shirt-tail out of his trousers.

Dimly, through a fog of booze and bewilderment, Peter got the message that something seemed to be expected of him – and he wasn't too keen on the idea of being undressed by another man. He pushed Andrew away and started to fumble with his zipper, finally managing to drop his pants to the floor.

'Oh, I say – that looks jolly promising,' Sally exclaimed, as she saw the large bulge in Peter's underpants for the first time. 'Come round here and take a look, Andy – I think Peter is about to show us what a *real* cock looks like.'

'Steady on, old girl. Dashed bad form to cast aspersions on a chap's undercarriage in mixed company, don't you know,' Andrew muttered in a peeved tone. Nevertheless, he walked round in front of Peter to confirm his wife's opinion. 'Yes, well, it's not so much what you've got, it's what you do with it,' he said grudgingly, as Peter peeled off his shorts.

Now completely in the buff, Peter stood feeling slightly foolish, with his cock dangling at half mast. His earlier hard-on from watching the film had collapsed like a burst balloon when Andrew had surprised him. Now, the sight of Sally's huge pendulous tits and the thought of plunging into her well-used and well-oiled cunt was enough to raise a semi-hard, but not quite exciting enough to get his prick really throbbing. And the whisky wasn't exactly helping matters, he realised.

So, with his cock just managing to stand out at about forty-five degrees, Peter waited for Sally to make the next move.

It wasn't long in coming. Obviously a raving nymphomaniac, Sally's mouth had already started to drool at the mere thought of another stiff prick up her cavernous hole. She glanced hesitantly at Andrew.

'You don't mind if I suck it, do you?' she asked.

Andrew shrugged carelessly. 'You go ahead and do anything you want, old girl,' he said generously.

Sally didn't bother to extend the same courtesy to Peter. Dropping to her knees in front of him, she began to slaver at the semi-flaccid weapon like a dog with a new and meaty bone. Saliva dripped from the corners of her mouth as she used her tongue, lips and teeth to worry at it, play with it.

The warm and wet caresses started to have their effect. Peter's cock began to inflate again, until once more he could feel the pulsing of hot blood engorging the column of soft flesh into a rod of stiff muscle and sinew. Sally moaned with delight as she felt the growing stiffness between her soft lips. She reached up and grasped his hanging balls in the palm of her hand, kneading and massaging them gently as their proud soldier attendant rose to stand at full attention.

Erect again, Peter's prick stood ram-rod upright, pressed against his belly. Sally turned her attention to his testicles, first licking the outer sac and then taking each swollen sphere in turn right into her mouth like giant gobstoppers, sucking on each with relish.

Peter began to feel the thrill of real excitement coursing through his body. Sally might not be a raving beauty, but she was certainly a highly skilled and sensuous fellatrice. Even Amanda's sweet mouth had not managed to make his cock throb quite so violently. The pleasure was intense to the point of pain. Peter groaned as Sally let his balls pop out of her mouth and ran a wet tongue slowly up the pulsing underside of his prick until she reached the swollen purple head. She licked and kissed it for a few moments with a consummate sense of timing. First she would flick her tongue over the glowing knob, then pause for just a fraction of a second before pursing her full, thick lips into a pout and delivering a slow, sucking kiss.

Peter desperately wanted to thrust the entire rigid length deep into her tantalising mouth, but now Sally had other ideas.

Rising to her feet, she took the stiff weapon in her hand and led Peter back over to the beer barrel. Leaning over it, she braced herself and spread her plump legs wide. Pushing Peter into a position behind her, she wiggled her fleshy buttocks suggestively then rubbed her hand hard against her overflowing fanny.

Her hand came away glistening and wet with juice and lubricant, which she smoothed on to Peter's dry shaft with a gentle massage. Then, grasping it firmly, she slipped it between the cheeks of her arse until the tip rested against the hot wet lips of her slit.

Peter could feel the sheer heat which boiled out of her horny organ like a lava flow. His cock gave one last eager twitch and it was inside her, sloshing around inside the sopping, steaming cavern of her cunt.

Sally let out a little squeal of delight as Peter's entire length rammed into her. He thrust deeper still, until his balls were squashed against the sides of her quivering buttocks and his prick was like a tight cork, sealing in the running fluid which had been dribbling down them from the leaking vessel above.

Sally leaned further forward over the barrel to allow him even more penetration, and began a slow, rhythmic movement of her pelvis whilst rocking her hips back and forth at the same time.

Again, Peter was pleasantly surprised. He had expected Sally's cunt to be loose and flaccid – but she was using inner muscles to clamp tightly around his stiff member like a fleshy vice. Peter marvelled at the intensity of the sensation. With his eyes closed, he could easily have imagined that he was fucking the tight pussy of a sixteen-year-old virgin, and not the cunt of a slightly overweight woman in her middle thirties.

Peter felt the warning flutter deep in his balls which told him he was about to spurt his passion. Somehow sensing this, Sally relaxed her inner grip on his shaft and let the stiff cock slide in and out more loosely.

'I say, you two. Guess what? Watching you at it has given me a real boner again,' announced a voice from behind.

Peter had completely forgotten about Andrew –

47

but now the man was very much back in the game, and wanting to play.

He strolled forward proudly, gently stroking his stiff member to show it off. It was an oddly shaped weapon. Short — no more than four or five inches long — it had a tapered, almost conical shape. Although the glistening head was more or less average size, the shaft thickened out to the circumference of a man's wrist where it met his extraordinarily large testicles.

'So, what say old girl? Can Randy Andy join in?'

Without waiting for an answer, he climbed up on to the barrel and dangled his legs over the side. Shifting himself gently so as not to slide off, he worked into a position where his balls were tucked under his wife's fleshy chin.

'Come on, old girl . . . blow the hunting horn,' he bellowed out, and began to bounce up and down on the barrel like a galloping horseman as Sally's slobbering mouth closed over his dormant volcano.

As his wife sucked furiously on his cock, Andrew reached down to start playing lovingly with her huge breasts, bouncing them up and down like a pair of under-inflated basketballs. Sally's whole body was a mass of soft and quivering flesh as the two men fucked her mouth and cunt at the same time. The jowls of her chin and throat wobbled from side to side as she worked on Andrew's prick and the fleshy meat of her thighs shook like jelly as she slammed her plump arse back against Peter's pulsing length.

Peter could hold back his imminent explosion no longer. He began to thrust back against Sally's bucking arse, slapping his meat deep into her creaming slit with a shuddering impact which made her buckle at the knees. Suddenly, Sally tensed, her inner muscles clamping against Peter's driving shaft in one last, quivering spasm. It was enough to release Peter's passion like someone flipping the top off a shaken-up fizzy drink bottle. His legs turned to jelly as his orgasm exploded into her, spurting deep into the juicy recesses of her fanny.

Sally came with him, pushing her arse back on the gushing fountain inside her. Peter felt the hot geyser of love-juice splash out against his balls in scalding liquid waves.

'Oh no . . . don't stop now,' Andrew screamed out in panic, as his wife's body seemed to melt with spent lust. He wrapped his arms around the back of her head, pulling the sucking mouth deep on to his throbbing cock. Wriggling his arse frantically, he fucked her slack mouth for several more seconds until he too shot his bolt into her throat.

Peter sank to the cellar floor, completely fucked out. Sally collapsed beside him, moaning softly and contentedly and patting his limp dick gently as though it was a favourite pet. Andrew slid down the side of the barrel to join them, a happy smile on his face. He began to giggle. It was infectious. Soon the three of them were laying out on the hard floor, gasping for breath as waves of laughter shook their bodies.

'That was one hell of a fuck,' Sally said, after they had all composed themselves. 'We must do it again some time.'

'Rather,' Andrew agreed, with boyish enthusiasm.

Peter, perhaps wisely, said nothing. He had started

to worry about Amanda. She might have started to look for him by now, and it would probably not be a good idea for her to find him in his present compromising position. A fully liberated and broad minded girl she might be, but Peter suspected that she, temporarily at least, regarded him as her companion, and would probably not take kindly to having him sneak off to take part in sexual threesomes. And he had no wish to upset her. Not yet, anyway — while she was still of great potential use to him and his plans.

Peter started to get up from the floor. 'I'd better go and find Amanda,' he said by way of explanation.

'Andrew's face creased into a querulous frown. 'Amanda?'

'The new owner,' Peter informed him.

'Ah, yes . . . our new boss.' Andrew held the frown for a second, then his face brightened again. 'Perhaps she likes fun and games too,' he suggested cheerily.

'Ooh yes — that *would* be fun,' his wife agreed. She reached up to give Peter's dangling dick a loving squeeze. 'All four of us . . . how super. Now, where could we do it for a change, I wonder? On the billiards table? In the jacuzzi? How about in the freezer room? We could take plenty of blankets.'

It seemed a good time to make a discreet exit while the couple decided on the next bizarre venue for their sexual adventures. Peter started to get dressed, hurriedly.

'Well, what can I say? It's been nice meeting you,' he managed rather lamely as he finally zipped up his fly. 'I'm sure we'll hump into each other again sometime.'

Andrew laughed delightedly at the pun. 'Hump into each other . . . Oh, I like that. Jolly good, what?'

'I suppose you can't stay for a quickie?' Sally enquired wistfully.

'Fraid not,' Peter said quickly. 'Must go and find Amanda.'

'She's probably watching The Wanker by now,' Sally informed him. 'I watch him for hours sometimes. Quite fascinating . . . but such a waste.'

Peter shook his head at this latest piece of information. 'Who is The Wanker?' he asked.

'Young Phillipe, the gardener,' said Sally. 'Or rather, the supposed gardener. He really doesn't do anything except wander around the grounds masturbating. So we call him The Wanker.'

'A bit light up top,' Andrew added, tapping the side of his temple. 'Tuppence short of a shilling. Nobody living in the attic.'

Sally grunted. 'He may be a bit short up the top, but he's certainly well hung where it counts,' she volunteered. 'Really the most amazing prick you've ever seen. The only time I've ever seen a cock that size is on a stud stallion. The trouble is, he won't let anyone else touch it.'

For some strange reason, Peter found the thought of Amanda loose with a horse-sized cock quite disturbing. He remembered her expert ministrations to his own, comparatively modest, organ.

'Well, I really had better be going,' he said again.

51

'I expect she will want to see you when I find her. Perhaps we could get something to eat. I take it that you two do actually dress for dinner?'

'Good lord, yes,' Andrew said, sounding almost shocked. 'The Paradise is really quite a high-class establishment, dont'cha know.'

'Oh, I believe you,' Peter said.

He was lying.

Chapter Four

Despite her considerable and varied experience of the male genitalia, Amanda had to admit that she had never seen an appendage quite like this one before.

Nor, as it happened, had she ever crouched behind a large and overgrown rhododendron bush, spying on its owner stroking, petting and talking proudly to his cock.

But there's a first time for everything, Amanda rationalised to herself, continuing to watch a handsome, powerfully built young man carry on a strictly one-sided conversation with his prick.

'*Tu est belle, ma petite. Tu est magnifique,*' crooned the lad softly, as he slowly and lovingly slid his hand up and down the length of his incredible weapon.

Amanda vaguely remembered remnants of French lessons from her schooldays delivered by a large and extremely butch female teacher who had always worn tweed trousers and taken an especial interest in giving the pubescent Amanda her closest individual attention. So Amanda could still translate certain key words and phrases — and the adjective *petite* certainly didn't seem to fit in with the scene she was witnessing now.

Even from her secret vantage point, a good twenty feet away, Amanda could see that the object of the young man's attentions was a good thirteen inches long, and stood as straight and stiff as the proverbial pikestaff.

Amanda resisted the brief temptation to test her fifth-form education even further by attempting to convert into metric — but certainly in terms of length and thickness the mighty tool would have graced any delicatessen shop window as a more-than-passable garlic sausage.

Without realising it, and more by accident than intent, Amanda had stumbled upon Phillipe the gardener, a.k.a The Wanker, whilst pottering about in the potting sheds.

She had noticed him before he was aware of her presence, being at the time totally engrossed in watering some tall, spiky-leaved plants in a corner of the glass-roofed shed. Amanda had been about to make her presence known and introduce herself when three apparently unrelated facts registered in her brain.

The first was that the plants receiving the watering looked suspiciously like marijuana. The second was that the tall, muscular youth moved somewhat stiffly and awkwardly, in a manner which suggested retarded mental development. The third was that his large, limp tool was hanging out of the front of his dirt-stained trousers.

Making a mental leap to correlate these odd pieces of information gave Amanda a possible scenario in which they all made some sort of sense. In the absence of any harder information, it would appear that she had interrupted a physically strong, half-witted sex maniac in the process of raising highly illegal drugs. Having accepted this possibility, it did not seem the right time and circumstances in which a lone, defenceless young lady suddenly popped out of the woodwork and tried to start a light and cheery conversation about the weather.

So, deciding that discretion was the better part of valour, Amanda had retreated to the comparative safety of the rhododendron bush while the young man finished tending his potted plants.

Satisfied that they had received a good soaking, he had moved out of the potting shed to sit down on a small patch of grass. It was at this point that he demonstrated further evidence of his love for making things grow by turning his green fingers upon his wilted weapon.

Amanda watched with astonishment as the lad's dick quickly swelled and stiffened to its present gigantic proportions. Still trapped behind the bush, she could only gape goggle-eyed as the mighty cock twitched, throbbed and jerked its way into full erection.

Amanda reviewed the current courses of action. She glanced over her shoulder towards the mansion house in the distance. She supposed it was just over a quarter of a mile. A fair distance, but given the element of surprise and a standing start, it was more than possible that she could make a break for it and outrun the young man. A large stiff dick flailing about in the breeze would undoubtably slow him down considerably — if he decided to give chase at all.

The second option, of course, was to remain exactly where she was until he had finished whatever it was he was planning to do — and his loving ministrations to his rigid love-shaft left little doubt as to what that might be.

In strict terms of safety, this seemed the most sensible thing to do — and Amanda would have been untrue to herself if she had pretended that the wondrous weapon did not hold a prurient fascination for her. Already, she had wondered idly just what sort of a fountain such a piece of equipment might produce. As the young man warmed to his masturbatory intentions, Amanda realised that she could soon find out the answer first hand.

There remained the third option of making herself known, and Amanda was still undecided about this one. That the lad was less than the full ticket was self-evident — yet Amanda had seen nothing in his behaviour to suggest that he was in any way dangerous or even violent. Indeed, from the gentle and loving way he played with his prick, Amanda imagined that he could well be quite childlike and sweet-natured in temperament. And he was now safely away from the marijuana crop, with no way of knowing that Amanda had spotted him tending it.

She watched the young man grasp the pulsing thick shaft of his prick in a firm two-handed grip and begin to wank in earnest.

Seeing his two large hands wrapped around all that meat with plenty of space to spare more or less tripped the balance of doubt in Amanda's mind. Her curiosity had got the better of her. Throwing caution to the winds, she knew that she just had to get a closer look at that magnificent piece of equipment. It was a once in a lifetime chance.

Amanda stretched herself, rising from behind the rhododendron bush like a fully-clothed venus. Taking a deep breath, she began to stroll towards the furiously pumping young man.

Her sudden appearance hardly put him off his stroke, although he did slow down a bit. Amanda approached cautiously, on the lookout for any sign of hostility, but there was none. In face, the lad regarded her more with fear and suspicion than anything else.

'*Bonjour*,' said Amanda brightly, figuring that the use of the lad's native tongue would make him feel more at ease with a stranger. Now that she was closer, she could see that he was much younger than she had supposed − probably only seventeen or so.

He made no reply, continuing to stare at Amanda suspiciously.

'*C'est un tres bon après-midi*,' Amanda went on in her schoolgirl French, assuming that the Froggies, just like the Brits, accepted chat about the weather as international opening dialogue.

There was still no answer. Amanda began to wonder if the youth was dumb. She racked her brains for something else to say. For a moment, she seriously considered trying for the French equivalent of: 'Hi − that's a beautiful prick you've got there,' but realised that her translational capabilities just weren't up to it.

Instead, she just pointed at the object in question, smiled brightly and said, '*Tres bon*.'

Amanda realised that she had pushed the magic button of communication. The lad's look of suspicion faded, to be replaced by a beaming smile.

He nodded enthusiastically in agreement, still stroking his cock with obvious enjoyment.

Now that the ice was broken, Amanda had time to admire the massive meat machine more closely. It was, without doubt, the biggest weapon she had ever seen, and beautifully shaped. Amanda noted that it was circumcised, so that the long, thick shaft seemed to flow into the smooth rounded head like a seamless piece of sculpture – a work of art that might have been created by Rodin, Henry Moore, Aubrey Beardsley and a frustrated spinster working in collaboration. As a strictly side issue, Amanda reflected that they had probably cut off and thrown away enough to make most men weep.

Encouraged by the young man's response, Amanda sat down on the patch of grass next to him. 'I'm Amanda,' she said, pointing a finger at herself in sign language at the same time.

'Phillipe,' the boy muttered, still a little nervous.

Amanda felt a warm glow of satisfaction. Phillipe wasn't dumb, after all – and they were getting along famously. Now, if she could just get her hands on that beautiful prick . . .

She pulled herself up with a mental jolt. How, suddenly, had her friendly attempt at conversation turned into a burning desire to handle Phillipe's weapon?

For desire it most certainly was. Amanda could almost feel her palms itching to wrap themselves around that huge column of flesh. To feel the body heat of it, squeeze its stiffness, sense the pulsing of blood up the rigid shaft. Almost as though she had been hypnotised, Amanda was only half aware of her hand reaching out towards the throbbing weapon.

Phillipe, anticipating her intentions, let out a little yelp of panic. He threw both arms around his erect cock, hugging it tight against his stomach and chest in a protective gesture.

Amanda's hand froze in midair as she saw the look of sheer panic on the boy's face. It was obvious that the situation required far more delicate and subtle treatment. Very slowly and carefully, like someone reaching to pet a frightened kitten, she moved her hand forwards again inch by inch, until the tips of her fingers just brushed lightly against the warm, smooth knob atop the mighty column.

Phillipe yelped again, and tensed as though to pull away from her, to take his precious possession to a place of safety. Slowly, patiently, Amanda continued to stroke the shiny head with a delicate, feather-light touch, until Phillipe seemed to relax again.

Amanda continued stroking softly as the fear and tension evaporated from the lad's body. With trust established, he sank back to lay full-length on the grass, freeing his prick so that it sprang upright to point stiffly at the sky.

Amanda's mouth was dry with the sheer anticipation of fondling the beautiful thing. Some strange inner compulsion had taken over her, and she felt a wave of affection for this handsome man, his childlike mind and his superbly endowed body. Stranger still, she was not conscious of any really lustful feelings. Her desire to fondle and stroke the youth was oddly innocent, even what she might have described as maternal. It was, indeed, a strange mixture of seemingly clashing emotions which drove her to edge closer and closer to Phillipe's prone body, until she could feel his body heat through the thin material of her dress.

Finally, pressed against him, she lay down beside him, her fingers still gently caressing the tip of his prick. She felt Phillipe's hand stir beside her, pressing gently but firmly against her warm thigh. With her free hand, Amanda reached out to lift his, placing it lightly in her lap. She felt the boy tense and stiffen again, as though confused and unsure what to do.

Amanda began talking to him softly in English – not sure that he could understand but sensing that he needed some kind of reassurance and help.

'It's all right, Phillipe. You can touch me, stroke me. Haven't you ever touched a girl before, Phillipe? Have you never felt the soft flesh of a woman?'

Phillipe's hand moved, uncertainly at first but then growing in boldness as it slipped down the cleft of her thighs and over the slight bulge of her *mons veneris*. Slowly, hesitantly, his probing fingers began to pull up the material of her dress inch by inch, until he had finally exposed the creamy flesh of Amanda's inner thighs. Amanda spread her legs slightly, allowing his hand to drop into her crotch against the material of her panties, which were already hot and moist from her secretions.

Amanda let her fingers slide from the glistening knob of his prick and run gently down the pulsing underside of the blood-engorged tool. She marvelled at the feel of it, the sheer size and power of this virgin love machine. For Amanda now had little doubt that young Phillipe was a virgin, and that no woman had

60

ever been fortunate enough to feel the thrusting strength of his young and beautiful prick deep inside her belly. She felt a growing sense of awe at the realisation that soon she might well be that woman, experiencing a sensual delight such as few others were ever privileged to know.

Amanda felt the lad's questing fingers sliding into her damp knickers, seeking out the entrance to the secret chamber of love where his virginity might soon and finally be sacrificed.

Amanda clasped her hand firmly around the thickness of Phillipe's prick and began to massage it up and down, with slow, loving strokes. Although it seemed a physical impossibility, she was sure that she felt the rigid shaft stiffen even more as Phillipe's fingers parted the lips of her burning bush and sought the bubbling honeypot that they guarded. She felt a minor orgasmic ripple as the lad's fingers moved querulously against her throbbing clitoris and began to slide into her cunt like a hot knife into butter.

Amanda spread her legs even wider to let Phillipe explore her most inner recesses more easily. She continued stroking and rubbing his prick gently, knowing that she needed to lead him cautiously into the promised land. To panic the boy now by pushing him too far, too fast, would be a disaster.

But fate had other plans. Above the pounding of her own heart, and the sound of Phillipe's rasping breath beside her, Amanda heard her name being called, as if from a distance. She rolled her head sideways, and saw Peter walking across the lawns in their direction.

Amanda groaned softly to herself. 'Oh no, not now, Peter. Not now.'

But it was too late. Peter had obviously spotted the two figures laying on the grass, because he changed his original direction slightly and began to make a beeline straight for them.

Phillipe had noticed the approaching stranger too. His whole body jerked stiffly, like a frightened animal. His fingers withdrew hurriedly from Amanda's sopping cunt and he rolled away from her, scrambling to his feet.

Seconds later, without a word, he was running for the safety of the potting sheds leaving Amanda cursing with anger and frustration. She lifted herself up, smoothed down her dress and began to walk towards the approaching Peter. Glancing over her shoulder, she could just catch a faint glimpse of Phillipe, cowering in a corner of the shed and masturbating furiously.

What an utter waste, she thought, as Phillipe spurted his seed into the seedlings. She mouthed a silent promise in his direction.

'I'll be back Phillipe. Believe me, I'll be back.'

She waltzed up to Peter, covering her frustration with a smile.

Peter said nothing about Phillipe, even though he must have seen him running away. Instead, he greeted Amanda warmly, throwing his arm around her shoulders.

'You must come and meet the couple who manage this place,' he said. 'Only I suppose I'd better warn you that they're a bit weird.'

Amanda shrugged carelessly. 'Who cares,' she said

happily, still daydreaming about her next encounter with Phillipe.

Peter regarded her quizzically, a question forming on his lips. He repressed it, realising that now was not the time to start rocking the boat.

'You know something — I think you could be on to a big thing here,' he said, waving one arm expansively around the grounds of the club.

A wicked smile puckered up the corners of Amanda's lush lips.

'You don't know the half of it,' she said, mysteriously.

Chapter Five

Andrew and Sally Baines came out to greet them as they approached the front of the mansion house.

Peter was forced to do a quick double-take, hardly recognising them with their clothes on. Andrew was wearing flawlessly pressed black trousers, a white tuxedo and dress shirt with a black bow tie, and his wife was clad in a somewhat austere Courrèges two-piece suit. The pair of them looked the very epitome of genteel respectability. The only thing which slightly undermined the total effect was the faint but unmistakeable smell of come which hung in the air around them.

If Amanda noticed it, she showed no sign, apparently quite willing to take the couple at face value as Peter made the initial introductions.

'Mr and Mrs Baines — may I present Miss Amanda Redfern, the new owner,' he said formally.

Suprisingly, it was Sally who made all the running, fussing around Amanda like a mother hen ushering her brood of chicks back to the nest. She clasped Amanda in a rather overt gesture of feminine familiarity, hugging her like a long lost sister.

'Sally and Andrew,' she gushed. 'We don't like to stand on formality here. Welcome to the Paradise Country Club, my dear.'

Andrew remained stiffly formal and businesslike.

'Do come in, Miss Redfern. Perhaps you would care for a little drink before we have dinner and then show you around the place.'

'Yes, that would be nice,' Amanda agreed. She detached herself from Sally's continuing embrace and followed Andrew into the house. Minutes later, they were ensconced in the evening lounge with a freshly opened bottle of chilled Pouilly Fuissé.

'So, Miss Redfern — were you related to the late Mr Clements? His daughter perhaps?' Andrew started to say, conversationally. His short speech ended in a painful gasp of sharply indrawn breath as his wife kicked his shin viciously under the table.

'I'm sure Amanda doesn't want to talk about poor Norville,' Sally put in, hastily changing the subject. 'I do hope you like fish, Amanda. We have fresh local trout for dinner.'

'How local is local?' Amanda asked, guardedly, remembering the murky brown waters of the ornamental lakes she had seen on the way up the drive. Having inherited a million pound estate one day, she had no intention of following dear Norville into the great country club in the sky on the next from eating poisoned fish.

'Ah — don't you worry about that, my dear,' said Andrew, as if reading her thoughts. 'All good pukkah stuff — comes from the Colonel's trout farm a couple of miles from here.'

'I thought he was into chickens,' Amanda murmured.

'Good Lord, no. Nothing kinky about the Colonel,' Andrew protested vigorously. He fell sheepishly silent as Amanda's joke finally clicked in.

'Ah . . . yes . . . see what you mean,' he murmured eventually. 'The Colonel . . . fried chickens . . . trout. Get the picture, don't you know. Jolly good, eh, what?'

'The Colonel is one of our local patrons,' Sally explained. 'In fact, he's probably our only local patron, come to think about it. The local anti-vice squad have scared everybody else off.'

It seemed a natural intro to the question which had been framing itself in Amanda's mind. 'So what actually does go on here?' she asked.

Andrew's face clouded over. 'Umm, yes . . . good question,' he murmured lamely, glancing nervously across at his wife for rescue.

'We're just a nice peaceful country club,' Sally said. 'People come down from London, and places like Southampton to relax and use the facilities — especially at the weekends.'

'People?' Amanda prompted.

'Businessmen, mostly,' Andrew put in. 'With their wives, or even girlfriends, sometimes.'

'Or bimbos,' Amanda put in.

Andrew gave a slightly strangled laugh. 'Bimbos . . . such a quaint word. But, yes, some of our clients do tend to favour the younger woman.'

'So, basically, this place is mainly in the business of being a rustic shagging shop?' Amanda asked, somewhat rhetorically.

Andrew started to defend the accusation. 'There are lots of other facilities, of course. The health club, the sauna, jacuzzi, the riding stables, sports facilities . . .'

He tailed off as Sally patted him gently on the arm.

She turned to Amanda, her face serious. 'You have it in one, Amanda. Now — do you have a problem with that?'

'Good Heavens, no,' Amanda said. 'The point is — does it pay?'

Sally's face relaxed into a smile. She reached across the table to briefly clasp Amanda's hand. 'I think we understand each other perfectly,' she said. 'And, yes, annual subscriptions, takings over the bar and fees for little "extras" are more than enough to make Paradise a viable financial proposition. Which isn't to say it couldn't be improved, of course. Perhaps you will have some ideas of your own on that score.'

Peter, who had been sitting silently listening to the conversation, chose this moment to break in. He didn't like the way things were going at all, with all this talk of profits and improvements. A commercially successful club didn't fit in with his plans very well. He glanced at his watch and let out a gasp of feigned surprise.

'Oh dear, I didn't realise how late it was. Nearly six o'clock, and I have an important meeting back in town at eight-thirty. Going to have to miss out on dinner, I'm afraid.' He turned to Amanda. 'We have to go.'

Amanda was on her guard at once. Peter had not mentioned a business meeting to her previously, and his sudden hurry to leave didn't seem quite natural.

'Why don't you go back for your important meeting and leave me here?' she suggested sweetly. 'After all, I have nothing to hurry back for, and I'm sure Andrew and Sally can fix me up with a guest room for the night. I would like to take more of a look around.'

Andrew and Sally exchanged a quick glance, each registering the others delight at the prospect of a night with the delectable Amanda.

'No problem at all,' they both said in unison.

Peter cursed under his breath. This was one little development he had not forseen, and he wasn't too happy about it.

'How will you get back?' he asked Amanda, hoping to set up doubt in her mind.

'Again, no problem,' Sally said. 'I'll run Amanda into Southampton myself tomorrow, in perfect time to catch the express train to London.'

'Oh good, that's settled then,' said Andrew happily. 'I think this calls for another bottle.' He scurried over to the bar to pick it up.

'I'll just go and see Peter off,' Amanda announced, standing up.

Peter rose to his feet reluctantly. Having talked himself into an awkward situation, there wasn't much he could do about it. 'Look — are you sure you don't want to come with me?' he said, almost pleadingly.

'No, I'll be fine,' Amanda assured him. 'Besides — I'm rather looking forward to fish for dinner.' For a moment, thoughts of Phillipe and his king-sized cock sprang into her head. 'And perhaps a nice meat course afterwards,' she added.

She began to walk Peter towards the door. Sally waved cheerily after him.

'Come again soon, Peter,' she called. 'And don't worry about bringing a blanket — we've got plenty.'

Amanda gave Peter a quizzical look as they exited. 'What was that about blankets?'

Peter shrugged hopelessly. 'They want to fuck in the freezer, for Christ's sake. I told you they were weird.'

Amanda accepted the information philosophically. 'We've all got our own ways of having a good time. Anyway, they seem a normal enough couple to me — except that they both smell of come.' She gave Peter a testing sniff. 'So do you, come to think of it.'

'Ah, that's probably the blow job you gave me in the car,' Peter said, thinking quickly. 'Must have spilled some on my trousers.'

'No chance,' Amanda said emphatically. 'I never wasted a drop.' It suddenly occurred to her that she might not be able to get away from Andrew and Sally to go in search of Phillipe. It could be a long and lonely night. 'Talking about that — got time for a quickie before you go?'

Without waiting for an answer, she pressed him back against the wall, her hand diving for his zipper. No sooner was his soft cock in her hand than Amanda was kneeling on the floor, gobbling it up greedily between her red lips.

Peter's prick jerked and twitched into a full erection in seconds under Amanda's expert ministrations. 'This is crazy,' he muttered helplessly, flopping back against the wall as Amanda really got into her stride, alternatively licking the full length with a hot, wet tongue and sucking the swollen head with pouting lips.

Amanda mouth-fucked him until she was sure that his rigid rod couldn't get any bigger or stiffer. As the column of flesh began to pulse erratically between her soft lips, she rose to her feet and deftly slipped her panties off. Grabbing Peter around the waist, she lay back against the wall herself and pulled him round in front of her, thrusting her hips out provocatively.

Peter bent his knees slightly and reached down to grasp his stiff cock in one hand, guiding its smooth tip to the hot swollen lips of her fanny. With one thrust he was inside her, driving into the slippery recesses of her love canal which was already beginning to bubble and froth with lubricating juices.

Amanda let herself sink down the wall, impaling herself even deeper on his throbbing shaft. Awkwardly, urgently, Peter bucked his hips and pumped into her until he could feel the knob of his prick slamming against the constricted channel of her cervix.

It was indeed a quickie. After only a few seconds, Peter let out a long. shuddering sigh and shot his sauce deep into her insides. Panting, with his knees feeling as though they were turning to jelly, he let his prick flop out of her sopping cunt and slumped back against the wall to get his breath back.

Amanda grinned at him roguishly. 'Thanks — I needed that,' she said.

Peter shook his head, amazed at her capacity for almost instant lust. 'Do you know I haven't had a knee-trembler since I was seventeen,' he said.

Amanda gave his wilting cock a gentle, playful squeeze. 'Just like riding a bike,' she murmured. 'You never forget the technique.'

She reached down to hitch up her underwear as

Peter tucked his limp prick back into his pants and zipped up his trousers. 'Well, I'd better be going,' he said.

Amanda laughed softly under her breath. 'Now isn't that just like a man. They take advantage of a poor girl and then they can't wait to be off.'

Peter smiled. 'God help the Baines — I don't think they have the faintest idea of just what they're taking on board.' He kissed Amanda lightly on the lips. 'I'll phone you in the morning,' he said.

Amanda saw him to the front door and then made her way back to the lounge.

'Has Peter gone?' Sally enquired as she rejoined them.

Amanda nodded. 'He came, and then he went,' she confirmed, with a smile on her face.

Chapter Six

The grilled trout was excellent, particularly when washed down with two more bottles of wine from the well-stocked cellar. A large Irish coffee followed by two glasses of a vintage white port finished off the meal and gave Amanda a warm and comfortable inner glow which was almost as satisfying as a really spectacular shagging session.

Conversation during the meal had more or less skirted around the club's carnal activities in general, and Sally and Andrew's rather all-embracing sexual tastes in particular – so Amanda had a pretty shrewd idea that an invitation to join in a swinging threesome was fairly imminent. As it happened, her alcohol intake had suppressed what few inhibitions she still had, and Amanda had warmed immensely to Sally's open and friendly personality, so the prospect did not seem completely repugnant to her.

However, it was not to be. A brief ring at the doorbell and the chatter of voices from the foyer announced the arrival of paying customers and snapped Andrew into his genial mine host and businessman mode. He quickly scooped up the dinner plates from the table, throwing them into the open doors of a dumb waiter as he made his way to the bar and took up his position.

'So, no after-dinner frolics,' Amanda murmured,

in a slightly aggrieved tone. She was surprised with her own disappointment.

Sally's hand found Amanda's knee under the table. She squeezed it gently, allowing her fingers to stray just a few inches up the inside of Amanda's thigh.

'There's always you and me, dear,' she whispered.

Amanda felt a tiny and completely unfamiliar little shock of electricity ripple through her at the other woman's touch. She shivered briefly, before moving her knee so that Sally's hand fell away.

'Sorry, Sally — but I don't swing that way,' she said softly.

Sally shrugged. 'Don't knock it till you've tried it,' she said with a knowing smile. 'You're a girl who will enjoy all of life's pleasures, sooner or later. I can tell.'

Amanda smiled back. It was almost impossible to take offence with the chubby, ebullient woman. 'You may be right,' she said. 'I promise you that you'll be the first to know.'

The two women fell silent as three extremely well-dressed business types sauntered into the lounge and seated themselves on stools at the bar. The men all turned to face them, ogling Amanda's lush ripe body with undisguised appreciation.

'New girl, Sally?' called one of them, a large, bull-necked man in his middle forties.

Sally opened her mouth to explain, quickly, that they were insulting the club's new owner, but a sharply delivered kick on the shin cut her short. Amanda winked mischieviously at her over the table before turning to face the man who had spoken.

'That's right. You could be seeing a lot of me around here in future,' she shot back.

The man licked his fat lips in anticipation. 'Quite a lot of you to see, I should imagine,' he said, eyeing her well-formed breasts. He turned to nudge one of his companions suggestively. 'Things are looking up at the Paradise,' he said in a loud, boorish voice.

'But not tonight,' Sally interrupted. 'Amanda is here strictly on a look and see basis. I'm sure Angie and Carol will be in later, if you gentlemen want to play games.'

The three men fell to nudging each other and sniggering like schoolboys poring over their first nudie magazine. Sally shot Amanda a warning glance over the table. 'Come on, let's get out of here,' she whispered, starting to rise.

Amanda had received the warning message loud and clear. She got up and followed Sally out of the room without a word.

Only when they were well out of earshot did Sally stop, turning to face Amanda with a stern face. 'Believe me, it's best that you stay well clear of those three,' she said, seriously.

Amanda felt a little bit embarrassed. 'Sorry — I just thought I'd have a bit of fun with them,' she tried to explain.

Sally shook her head. 'Take my word for it — nothing is fun where that bunch is concerned,' she said. 'Don't let the expensive clothes and flashing bankrolls fool you . . . those three are animals. Their only kick is in humiliating women and generally giving everybody a hard time. We would have banned them long ago, but they're big spenders and there are a couple of girls who don't mind catering to their sick tastes for a big payoff.'

'And times are hard, right?' Amanda finished off for her, smiling.

Sally grinned back. 'Amanda – I really think I'm going to like you,' she said.

They continued walking down the corridor, passing a white-painted door which bore the sign 'Treatment Room'.

'What goes on in there?' Amanda asked.

Sally glanced upwards. Over the top of the door a small red bulb glowed faintly. Sally checked her watch. 'That'll be the Honourable Nigel getting his special therapy,' she said. She turned to Amanda with a devilish smile on her lips. 'Want a bit of a giggle?'

Amanda jumped at the chance. 'I'm always game for a laugh.'

Sally opened the door quietly and led the way into the clinical, white-painted interior. They were in a glass-fronted inspection and control booth, surrounded by banks of electrical and medical-looking equipment. Through the large glass panel, Amanda looked down on what appeared to be a small operating theatre. In the middle of the floor, laying on something which looked like a cross between a surgical operating table and a mediaeval torture rack, was a naked man. There were various traction devices strapped firmly to each limb, connected by a complicated series of wires, pulleys and gearing mechanisms to a central control panel, presided over by a gigantic female figure in a white uniform.

For a moment, Amanda took her for a regular nurse, with her tiny, starched white cap perched atop a mass of flaxen hair and the apparently clinical precision with which she was operating the controls.

Then she half-turned towards her patient, and Amanda could see that her white one-piece uniform was unbuttoned to the waist, allowing her two massive mammaries to swing free.

They were, without doubt, the biggest, whitest and most pendulous tits which Amanda had ever seen. The woman herself was built like an Amazon warrior, well over six feet tall and with a pair of shoulders which would put an American football player to shame even in full game-play gear.

'Who the hell is that?' Amanda breathed in awe.

'That,' said Sally, 'is the formidable Freda, our Swedish masseuse and therapist. Otherwise known as The Sprayer due to the spectacular over-production of her Bartholin's glands which enable her to squirt about half a pint of come when she orgasms. It's really quite a sight – better than the hot geysers in Yellowstone Park.'

'Can't wait to see it,' Amanda murmured without enthusiasm. 'And what is she doing to the poor bastard on the table. Is he kinky for torture or something?'

'No – Freda's giving him his special manipulation therapy. The Hon. Nigel Hampton-Wilde is one of our regulars. He comes twice a week for these sessions.'

'Is he sick?' Amanda asked.

Sally laughed. 'Only in the head, I guess. The Hon. Nigel is a man with a burning ambition in life.

Basically, he's an over-privileged rich twit who was born with a silver spoon in his mouth and a mass of grey jelly in his skull. In short, he's a total dick head who has been an abysmal failure at just about everything throughout his life.'

'So what's the great ambition?' Amanda wanted to know.

'Well the story as I understand it is that there was a boy in his dormitory at public school who could suck his own cock. This remarkable feat made the kid some sort of a school hero, it seems — and poor old Nigel has spent most of his adult years and a great deal of money trying to do the same. He's tried stretching his prick, and that didn't work — so this latest therapy is designed to make him supple enough to reach what he's got. Freda's got him to the stage when he can just about lick the tip of it with his tongue, but he's still several centimetres short of getting it in his own mouth.'

Freda adjusted a few settings on the manipulation table and turned back to the controls.

'Ah — Freda is about to crank him up for another attempt,' Sally observed. 'Want to go down and take a closer look?'

'Doesn't he mind?' Amanda asked, slightly bemused by it all.

Sally shook her head. 'He doesn't seem to. Sometimes I give him a blow job to ease his frustration when he can't make it himself. So he's quite used to an audience.' Sally pointed the way to a set of steps which led down into the treatment room. 'Come on — you said you wanted a bit of fun.'

Shrugging, Amanda followed Sally down into the

room. Freda looked up as they entered, a welcoming smile on her florid, slavonic features.

Sally waved at her. 'She doesn't speak much English,' she explained to Amanda. 'Most of Freda's communication is confined to grunts and hand gestures.'

Looking over the burly bulk of a woman, Amanda could believe it. It was easy to picture Freda wearing a horned helmet and belting out Wagnerian opera. She followed Sally's lead in giving a cheery wave, to which Freda responded with a nod and a grunt.

Amanda's eyes were totally mesmerised by the Swedish woman's gigantic boobs. They seemed to start from somewhere just below her neck and then spread in all directions to make up most of her upper torso. Each huge, soft and rubbery gland seemed to have a life independent of its sister, bouncing, quivering and wobbling furiously with every movement Freda made. Yet despite their enormous size, the massive mammaries were amazingly firm and well shaped — ballooning outwards like slightly elongated and uplifted medicine balls, each crowned with a dark brown aureole nearly two inches in diameter and stiff, protruding red nipples which looked like miniature pricks.

Finally, almost with reluctance, Amanda managed to tear her eyes away from the girl's formidable frontal development to look down at the man on the manipulation table.

Physically, the Hon. Nigel looked every inch the type which Sally had so adequately described in words. A typical chinless wonder, he had the weedy, awkward-looking physique of a young man produced after several generations of close interbreeding amongst the dwindling aristocracy of the country. His pale and watery blue eyes held little except a faint, sporadic flicker of residual intelligence, and a thin, mousey-looking moustache did absolutely nothing to lend his bland, sharp-nosed features any vestige of masculinity. He was, in short, a total wimp.

Amanda's eyes travelled down the lean, angular frame seeking the one place where nature might have made some concessions to manhood. She had not. Nigel's small soft prick lay curled on his lower abdomen like a newly hatched baby snake, morosely viewing the world through its single slitted eye. For a moment, Amanda thought that he only had one ball, but then realised that although there were actually a pair, they were extremely small and enclosed in a particularly tight and shrunken scrotal sac which gave that initial impression.

Nigel's blue eyes regarded Amanda dolefully, registering her disapproval. He squirmed uncomfortably on the table, but otherwise made no sign that her presence meant anything at all to him.

Freda finished making final adjustments to the various traction and stretching harnesses and turned a hand-operated cranking wheel a couple of times to take up the tension. As wires and straps gave up their slack and tightened, Nigel's body seemed to stiffen and stretch until he looked for all the world like a dead frog pinned down on a biology lab dissecting table.

Satisfied with the tension settings, Freda turned

her attention to the central control panel, pressing a small red electronic button. The table gave out a faint whirring sound and began to lift at each end, bending in the middle.

Nigel's prone body began to fold up like someone glued to a collapsing futon. Straps positioned just under the crooks of his knees took up the vertical strain, lifting his thighs and buttocks as the folding table gradually pushed his head nearer to his groin area.

Freda took her finger off the button. The table stopped with a faint sigh, holding Nigel in his uncomfortable contorted position. It was time for the next stage of the delicate operation.

Lifting her huge breasts with both hands, Freda moved closer to the table and bent over its pinioned prisoner. Easing herself down gently, she began to jiggle the pair of oversized blancmanges so that the jutting red nipples just touched and tickled Nigel's cock and balls.

Amanda couldn't resist moving in for a closer look, intrigued as to the effect such erotic stimulation might be having on the pathetic piece of equipment which passed for Nigel's pecker.

It was minimal. The Hon. Nigel's cock uncurled slightly, and grew noticeably thicker and longer — but there was no sign of any real stiffness.

The Swedish girl's face creased into a slight frown, and she grunted with exasperation. Abandoning the tit-tickling ploy, she ran a hot, wet tongue over her thick fleshy lips and smacked them together a few times, stimulating a generous flow of saliva. When her lips were thoroughly wet and shiny, and her generous mouth was almost drooling, Freda again bent over Nigel's prone body and applied the more direct approach.

Nigel's cock and balls disappeared completely into Freda's wet, sucking mouth. Slurping noisily, the girl lashed her tongue furiously against the soft meat inside her gently squeezing lips until saliva dribbled down on to Nigel's naked thighs. Freda's cheeks began to bulge as her oral ministrations had their desired effect. She pulled her head back slightly as the formerly flaccid tool began to stretch and stiffen in her mouth, stretching towards her throat. Slowly, gradually, Freda's wet lips slipped back, revealing more and more amazing inches of Nigel's glistening shaft.

Amanda stared, transfixed, at the incredible metamorphosis. It was like some baffling magical illusion, with a conjuror producing impossible objects from empty space. When, finally, Freda finished the trick by letting the swollen, pulsing head of Nigel's prick slip out from between her lips with a loud popping sound, it was obvious that the frog had turned into a prince.

The Hon. Nigel's cock was at last revealed in its full, throbbing glory, although Amanda could still not quite believe that something so small could turn into something so big. In full erection, Nigel's love poker was a good eight inches long, jerking stiffly upright like a flagpole in a strong gale.

Freda smiled proudly, more than satisfied with the results of her efforts. With a couple of expressive grunts, she pointed first to Amanda and then down to Nigel's ramrod, obviously handing out some sort of instructions.

Sally stepped in quickly to translate. 'She wants you to hold it in the right position while she flexes Nigel's spine,' she explained.

'Oh,' Amanda murmured, rather taken aback to be so abruptly dragged into the proceedings. Nevertheless, she did as instructed, moving towards the table and grasping the stiff prick firmly in her fist.

Freda nodded with satisfaction, gesturing for Amanda to bend the rigid rod slightly to the left as she reached under the table to make some adjustment to the now almost verticle rear section. With a slight hissing sound, the table made another slight bend, forcing Nigel's head and shoulders forward at a strange angle.

Nigel's blue eyes bulged, and his tongue protruded slackly from his mouth as the manipulation table pushed him into a near-foetal position. Amanda felt his stiff cock twitch in her hand.

'My God, is he all right?' she asked in some concern, as Nigel began to go noticeably red in the face and his prick pumped frantically in her grasp.

'Oh, he's OK . . . he's used to it,' Sally said carelessly, ignoring the fact that the patient was showing every physical sign of being choked to death. 'Just keep his prick straight and pointed at his mouth. Freda's about to go for gold.'

As Sally spoke, Freda had returned to the control panel and pressed the button once more. The table whirred into movement, continuing to fold its occupant up like a rag doll. Still holding Nigel's cock firmly, Amanda watched, fascinated, as his head was forced nearer and nearer to its bulbous, purplish helmet.

Inches shrank to mere centimetres as the folding table continued its inexorable course. Nigel's face was now the same blood-flushed colour as the head of his prick, but his popping eyes betrayed no sign of panic. Indeed, he seemed wildly excited, straining his tongue stiffly forward until it was almost touching the tip of his prick.

Caught up in the thrill of the bizarre human experiment, Amanda found herself trying to stretch his cock just to help him achieve his strange ambition. Gripping and squeezing it tightly as though to extend it like toothpaste out of a tube, she attempted to guide it into Nigel's slowly approaching mouth.

The tip of his questing tongue made contact. Nigel waggled it frantically, licking his own swollen glans. His lips were now less than two centimetres from the stiff, throbbing object of their desire.

Suddenly, with a shrill mechanical screech, the table ground to a halt, having reached the absolute limits of its traverse. Amanda tried giving Nigel's throbbing prick one last tug as though to stretch flesh where metal couldn't go, but it was useless.

Freda fingered the release catch on the control panel, and the folding table began to sink slowly back into its prone position. Nigel's body flopped and went limp, although his cock was still stiff and rigid in Amanda's hand.

She gave the still-twitching prick a little squeeze of consolation. So near and yet so far, Amanda thought, feeling an odd sense of pity for the hapless Nigel. To have such a pathetic ambition, and yet be unable to achieve even that, seemed the ultimate in punishment.

'Never mind, maybe you'll get there next time,' she said comfortingly, but Nigel's disappointed face told her that words of consolation were inadequate.

Sally moved up to stand beside her, noting that Amanda still held the erect tool firmly in her grip.

'Seems a bit of a waste, doesn't it?' she muttered, nodding down at it. 'Are you going to keep it all to yourself, or can someone else get a piece of the action?'

Amanda released her hold on the stiff cock, almost reluctantly. It was a strange and new sensation, having control of such an obviously excited male organ when its owner was more or less completely passive.

Nigel's rod continued to point at the ceiling, pulsating gently. Sally began to toy with it, flicking it back and forth with her fingers then pressing it down flat against Nigel's belly before allowing it to spring to attention again. She teased it and tickled it, inserting the tip of one sharp fingernail into the little slit at the top of the helmet and wiggling it from side to side so that Nigel's small balls danced in unison. Finally, tiring of treating it like a plaything, she slid her fingers around the long slender shaft and began to rub it up and down with slow, delicate strokes.

Freda had switched the mechanical bed off now and moved closer to join in with the fun. Pushing past Amanda, she barged Sally out of the way and stood over Nigel's prone form, regarding the delicious dick with obvious relish. She swilled saliva round in her mouth, then spat heavily on to the palm of one hand, smoothing it from there on to Nigel's cock so that it glistened smoothly. Then she too began to masturbate him, but there was no delicacy in her touch. Instead of slow, gentle strokes, she pumped it up and down furiously, the base of her hand slamming heavily down on Nigel's belly with each downstroke. Faster and faster she went, until her hand was almost a blur.

Amanda felt a little pushed out of things. She nudged Freda in the ribs with her elbow. 'I had it first,' she complained.

Freda obviously understood. She shrugged and moved aside, releasing the jerking organ to Amanda's manipulations, and yet another wanking technique. Grasping the cock firmly around its base in her left hand, Amanda used her right to jerk off just the top two or three inches, with short but fast strokes.

It seemed to have the greatest effect so far. Amanda felt the whole stiff shaft begin to throb more urgently, in almost perfect time with her strokes.

'He's about to shoot,' Sally cautioned from behind her. 'I think it might be a nice gesture to let Freda finish him off. After all, he is her patient.'

Sally had a point, Amanda conceded. She unloosed Nigel's quivering cock and stepped back. Freda needed no second bidding. Bending over, she wrapped her soft breasts around the fleshy flagstaff and squeezed them tightly together with her hands so that Nigel's prick was completely encased in a cocoon of warm, pliant flesh. Then, bouncing her tits up and down, she delivered her own Swedish speciality to the frantically jerking organ, occasionally flicking out her pink wet tongue to lick the glistening purple head.

Still strapped firmly to the bed, Nigel's body began to writhe against the restraining straps. His buttocks quivered and strained, attempting to pump upwards to plunge the head of his cock into Freda's close and inviting mouth.

But Freda was determined to tease him to the end. She moved her huge tits more urgently, kneading them in her hands so as to add a circular massaging motion to the straight up and down strokes which were already bringing Nigel close to the brink of orgasm. Tantalising, she pouted her thick, fleshy lips into a warm and inviting 'O' and let the tip of his prick just touch against them, while still denying him entry into her hot wet mouth.

It was more than any man could stand. With one final, convulsive heave of his buttocks, Nigel surrendered to the inevitable and let his cock spurt. Gobbets of glistening, pearly come spattered on to Freda's throat and chin as Nigel's tiny balls released their surprisingly full reservoir of seed and semen.

Freda released the spent prick from its fleshy prison and stepped back, wiping the come off her throat and chest with a corner of the table sheet. Still semi-erect, Nigel's cock gave a last couple of twitches and began to wilt, with a final pearl of almost clear fluid bubbling from its tiny slit.

Sally ran forward, lapping it up with her tongue and rolling it around her mouth, savouring the salty, soupy flavour. Then, turning towards Freda, she advanced with her tongue protruding once more, and began to lick at the girl's breasts where a few precious drops of the delicacy had dripped.

She looked up, briefly, at Amanda, rolling her eyes in a silent message.

Amanda understood immediately. Sally was sending her a clear enough communication. Stay if you want to join in – or leave us alone to our own pleasures.

Amanda considered for the briefest possible moment, finally deciding to leave them to it. She enjoyed sex in many of its pleasurable forms, and she was usually more than willing to add a new trick to her already extensive repertoire. But perhaps she wasn't quite ready to make that final jump into lesbianism. One day she might – as she had already intimated to Sally – but if that time ever came, Amanda felt that she would prefer it to be a personal, intimate thing rather than an orgiastic threesome.

'I think I'll just take an evening stroll around the grounds,' she announced diplomatically.

Nobody bothered to answer her. By this time, Sally was sucking enthusiastically on one of Freda's engorged red nipples, while the Swedish girl had her hand up Sally's skirt to manipulate her swelling clit with expert fingers.

Nigel, still hopelessly pinioned to his private torture rack, had no choice but to watch, which he was doing with slightly pop-eyed disbelief. Amanda strolled over to him on her way out.

'Just tell me one thing,' she said quietly. 'Why do you want to suck your own cock?'

Nigel rolled his eyes around the treatment room expressively, taking in the rapidly unfolding lesbian saga. He spoke for the very first time in the evening's bizarre proceedings.

'You meet a better class of person,' he said, in a cultured and somewhat haughty tone.

Chapter Seven

Peter Blake had been running over all his options on the drive back to London, and had managed to arrive at what he imagined would be the most lucrative decision.

Basically, he figured, he was now more or less back to square one, and it was now mainly a question of making some minor modifications to his original plans.

The sudden death of Norville Clements seemed to have turned out as a mixed blessing. Although it could have thrown a large spanner into the works if the financial state of affairs concerning his estate had come under close and expert scrutiny, Amanda's quick and unexpected appearance on the scene had saved the day. Whilst she was certainly nobody's fool, Peter was fairly sure that she was not too clued up on money matters and would accept most things at face value, without asking too many awkward questions.

And questions were one thing Peter needed to avoid like the plague − particularly when it came to the past and present running of the Paradise Country Club and his own personal plans for its future.

The simple truth of the matter was that Peter had been milking the old man's fund for the upkeep of the place for the past three years, ever since Norville had grown too feeble to visit the club for his former sexual sprees. Although it was only a few thousand pounds a year, the money had made a considerable difference to the running of Peter's expensive lifestyle, and an even greater difference to the maintenance of the club and grounds, which explained their present dilapidated state.

Peter's immediate short-term problem then was to cover his tracks on that front, while pushing ahead with his bigger master plan to cash in on the establishment's considerable capital value. To achieve one or both, he would definitely need Amanda's trust and cooperation for the next few weeks at least.

He felt his prick stir gently inside his trousers at the mere thought of Amanda, and smiled to himself. Yes, definitely mixed blessings he thought, remembering her hot mouth clamped around his cock.

He adjusted his trousers as he got out of the car, carefully tucking his stiffening prick behind the tight elastic of his underpants. It would not do to call upon one's virginal fiancée with an obvious hard-on.

The lady in question was yet another of those mixed blessings. Caroline Drummond was his fiancée in name only, since Peter had absolutely no intention of actually marrying her. Although she was attractive enough, and a useful and decorative social asset to be seen in public with, Peter was almost sure that she was sexually frigid, and that her constant promises of good and regular sex once their union had been blessed by clergy were meaningless. In Caroline's mind, he was sure, a good married sex life consisted of two minutes bonking in the missionary position, immediately followed by nine months of pregnancy and celibacy. It was not a prospect that Peter savoured.

However, on the plus side, she was the only daughter of Cedric Drummond, head of the Drummond Development Corporation, and she was, apparently, besotted with him. Peter had her eating out of his hand, if not out of his trousers.

The final factor in the complicated financial equation which would make Peter rich was of course Paradise. Drummond Development wanted the land for the site of an ambitious theme and fun park for the South of England, which would pose the region's first serious threat to Alton Towers and Euro Disney across the Channel. And they would pay a more than generous commission to anyone who could expedite their aquisition of the property. Peter had every intention of being that agent, whilst pocketing the remainder of the maintenance fund at the same time. With a little luck, and a lot of devious cunning, Peter hoped to make over a half a million pounds out of the deal.

Step one entailed making sure that the Paradise Country Club ceased to function as a viable commercial enterprise, one way or another. So if the place wasn't going to just run down of its own accord, it would have to be closed down — and Peter had already found a few allies on that score.

But a bit of extra help was always welcome — hence his unscheduled visit to see Caroline Drummond.

Satisfied that his erection had now subsided

enough to present a respectable front in more ways than one, Peter bounded up the front steps of the Drummond house and rang the front door bell.

Caroline herself answered the door, which was unusual. She smiled sweetly and demurely at him in greeting — the only way she knew how, thought Peter somewhat cynically.

She pecked him lightly on the lips. 'Hello, darling,' she breathed, in what was supposedly intended to be a husky whisper. 'Come in.'

Caroline escorted him through the palatial hallway into the main reception room. Peter lowered himself into the plush antique chesterfield, wondering where everyone was.

'Where's Mummy and Daddy?' he asked, unconsciously mimicking Caroline's almost reverential tones when she spoke of her parents.

'They had to go out to a charity ball,' Caroline informed him. 'So when you telephoned so unexpectedly, I gave the servants the night off as well. I thought we could have a nice evening alone. Would you like a drink, darling?'

Peter nodded. 'Umm, yes — scotch, please.' He relaxed in the chesterfield as Caroline crossed to the cocktail cabinet and poured him a niggardly measure of whisky.

'Well, isn't this nice?' Caroline asked, as they sat a foot or so apart, sipping their drinks.

'Lovely,' Peter agreed, without enthusiasm.

Caroline edged a few inches nearer to him. 'Just the two of us. Quiet and romantic.' She fluttered her eyelashes in what Peter assumed was supposed to be a flirtatious gesture.

It obviously demanded some sort of response. Peter leaned over towards her and gave her another, slightly more lingering, peck on the lips.

Caroline sighed contentedly and snuggled up against him. 'Have you come to talk about the wedding, darling?'

Peter wriggled uncomfortably. 'Well, no . . . not specifically,' he muttered. 'Actually, I was hoping to have a few words with Daddy, to tell you the truth.'

'Oh!' Caroline's ruby lips formed into a pout. 'And here I was thinking that you had come just to see me.'

'Oh . . . and to see you, of course,' Peter added hastily. 'You know I always want to see you, precious.'

Caroline flashed him another one of her demure smiles. 'Oh darling, you are sweet.' She relaxed again, leaning against him.

The smell of her discreet, but highly expensive perfume, was quite erotic. Peter glanced sideways at her, admitting to himself that she really was quite a desirable young woman. Caroline did, in fact, have the sort of face which turned men's heads in the street. Under a mop of short, bobbed golden hair, she had a pair of huge and expressive baby-blue eyes which could be either innocent or fiery, according to her mood. Her face was delicately structured, with high prominent cheekbones and a small, pert nose which lifted slightly at the tip, giving her a slightly aristocratic but not haughty look. And her full, generous mouth with its fleshy, soft lips definitely promised quite surprising depths of passion once she was aroused.

It was, in fact, a perfect plater's mouth, Peter found himself reflecting. Exactly cock-sized and soft and supple enough to play a perfect tune on a man's love-flute.

Peter shivered, shaking himself out of his erotic reverie. This was Caroline, his virgin fiancée, he was looking at. More than that, she was his ticket to half a million pounds and the pick of blow jobs from Brighton to Bangkok.

Caroline felt his eyes upon her, and some inner female sixth sense communicated that latent passion behind them. She quivered deep inside, imagining his virile and athletic body freed from the stuffy business clothes he always wore. Naked, muscular, drenched in the sweat of writhing passion, she thought of his hot flesh grinding against hers, the musky, animal smell of it in her nostrils and the salty taste of it on her lips . . . And his cock, hard and throbbing, dancing with the wild music of lust and the pulsing hot blood of passion. Rigid, unyielding, unthinking — a mere machine of stiff meat and muscle whose only function in life was to plunge into her virgin cunt and spurt its hot, sticky slime into the dry and burning emptiness of her womb.

If only he would read her mind, respond to her inner, hidden fantasies, Caroline thought. If he would just do what had to be done, break through the brittle protective crust of her conditioning, upbringing and inhibitions and penetrate to the hot, molten lava flow of the sexual volcano which seethed within.

But he was trapped, just as she was trapped, Caroline realised sadly. Though she had no doubt that Peter had the lusty sexual appetites of any man, he was basically a gentleman. He would attempt to seduce, cajole, arouse her to sexual passion and then give up when she would not, or could not, respond. She had no illusions about their relationship, and assumed that Peter thought she was frigid. If only he knew. If only there was some way she could let him know that she needed to have all control and all inhibitions taken away from her by brute force. That she wanted him to attack her like a crazed animal, ripping the clothes from her body and seize her tender flesh in his strong and powerful hands, squeezing her small, firm breasts until her small pink nipples bulged.

No foreplay. No gentle, thoughtful and loving kisses. No words of endearment or tender caresses. Just his great swollen prick driving like some mad living battering ram between the fleshy lips of her cunt and into its barren dryness. Forcing the chemical processes of her body to take over and transport her to places where her conscious mind was unable to go. Peter's cock, thrusting and pumping away inside her, making her juices prickle out from every pore of her cunt lining until it frothed and flowed like some wild tropical river.

The moment passed, wasted again. Peter finished his drink and stood up.

'Well, I suppose I'd better go. I need to make an early start in the morning.'

Caroline was also back to normal. It was business as usual.

'Where are you going?' she asked politely.

'Back to the country club, I'm afraid,' Peter said,

making it sound like a terrible but necessary chore, 'I've left the new owner there for the night and I think it would only be common politeness to go down first thing in the morning to see how she is.'

'She?' Caroline was instantly on the alert. Her feminine passions might be deeply buried in her psyche, but normal jealousy was right up there on the surface. 'How old is this new owner? Is she young?'

Peter saw the warning signs. 'Youngish,' he muttered vaguely.

'Pretty?'

Peter affected a careless shrug. 'Some men might think so, I suppose. A bit too tarty for my tastes. Rather common, I suppose you would say.'

Caroline digested this information carefully, studying Peter's eyes as he spoke. It was more than feminine intuition that told her he was lying — or at least not telling the complete truth. Emergency plans had already started to formulate in her head. Caroline did not trust sexually frustrated fiancés when it came to tarty, probably attractive women. Especially alone together in the remote setting of a country club.

However, she retained an aloof disinterest. 'I'll see you to the door, then,' she said calmly. She stood up, pursing her lips for another one of their chaste kisses.

When Peter had left, Caroline went straight to her bedroom. Throwing off her clothes, she stood naked in front of her full length mirror and appraised her own body critically.

It was not a bad body at all, Caroline told herself. Built for speed rather than comfort, but more than capable of giving enough pleasure to a man to make him want to come back for more.

She stroked her hands down the sides of her small but well-formed breasts, letting her fingers brush over the tiny pink buds of her nipples in a gentle caress. She toyed with them idly for a while, until the soft flesh hardened and changed in colour to a deeper shade of red. Fully erected, they stood out firmly and aggressively, giving her slightly pear-shaped breasts a much more jaunty and sexually provocative look.

Her fingers travelled down her body to her flat stomach, and then on to the soft insides of her thighs. She moved closer to the mirror, thrusting out her hips so that the fine, downy hair of her pubis was almost touching the glass. Caroline spread her legs slightly, exposing the fleshy pink lips of her cunt to the mirror's view.

She let herself fantasise again, trying to imagine what it would be like to have the swollen, throbbing head of a massive cock ramming its way through that impossibly small slit and into her inner recesses. Watching herself carefully in the mirror, Caroline dropped one hand to that virgin portal and began to rub her small and almost hidden clitoris with her fingers. She teased the small fleshy knob round in circles, then from side to side and finally in a gentle up and down motion.

With growing breathlessness, Carole felt her clit grow hot and hard, swelling with blood until it was the reflection of a tiny prick. Her finger movements became more urgent, vibrating against the now throbbing organ with faster, rougher strokes.

Slipping over the moistening knob, her fingers ran

up and down the soft lips of her slit, exploring the silky wrinkled flesh and the moist warmness inside. A tiny thrill rippled through her body as she felt the first bubbling secretions turning it into a wet, enticing tunnel, inviting her questing fingers to slide deeper and more adventurously inside.

In seconds, Caroline had two fingers fully inside her cunt, while her thumb took over the job of stimulating her hot and horny clit. Little grunts of pleasure rose in her throat as her passion mounted and her whole body quivered with a rising tide of sensual pleasure.

Finally, as her fingers rammed away inside her sopping pussy, the first tremor of orgasm shuddered out from somewhere deep inside and rippled over every inch of her body. She continued jerking her fingers furiously for a few more moments until she realised that a really big orgasm was not going to come and reluctantly slid them out, wet and glistening.

Caroline backed away from the mirror and flopped down on the bed until her passion had fully subsided and she was able to think clearly again. It was time to put her earlier plans into action.

She rose again and walked over to her vanity suite, sitting down and pulling open several drawers. First, she selected a padded, cross-shaping bra and clipped it on, reviewing the effects in the small circular mirror above the unit.

It definitely accentuated her modest bust, giving a much deeper cleavage and the illusion of more fullness below − but Caroline wasn't quite satisfied. She rummaged in the drawer again, finding two crescent-shaped padded cups which she slipped into position under her breasts inside the bra.

That did the trick. In an instant, she had turned herself from a real thirty-four into a more than passable fake thirty-six. Caroline set about the next stage of her metamorphosis.

From another drawer she selected a long black wig and a small white box. Opening the box, she took out a fine pair of tweezers and fished delicately for the two tinted contact lenses which it contained. Having gingerly fitted them into position, she slipped the black wig on to her head and adjusted it carefully. Then a touch of mascara and eyebrow pencil to her fair eyebrows and lashes and the illusion was complete.

Satisfied, Caroline got up and opened her spacious wardrobe, rummaging through racks of expensive clothes until she found exactly what she wanted. She took a rather daring, V-necked black frock from a hanger and slipped it on. Finally she returned to the full-length mirror to admire herself.

It was a complete and stunning change of identity. In a matter of a few minutes, a petite and demure blonde had been transformed into a raven-haired, green-eyed temptress. Caroline went back to the vanity unit to make the finishing touches to her new and more overtly sexual facial make-up and finally smiled with satisfaction.

She was sure that Peter would never recognise her, providing she kept him at a discreet distance. Now all that remained was to pack an overnight case and get down to the Paradise Country Club before he arrived.

She would just be another one of the paying guests, able to spy upon Peter and his mysterious woman without arousing any suspicion.

And, coincidentally, to find out just exactly what went on at this country club which both her father and fiancé seemed obsessed with.

Chapter Eight

After the earlier excitement and fun of the evening, Amanda was bored and more than a little frustrated. As soon as she had left Sally and Freda, she had retraced her earlier steps to the potting sheds, hoping to renew her acquaintance with Phillipe and his wonderful cock, but there was no sign of the young man. Amanda wondered where he actually lived on the estate, and made a mental note to ask Sally the way to the lad's bedroom at the earliest opportunity.

As dusk gathered, and the evening air grew slightly chilly, she made her way back to the mansion house and strolled into the lounge, hoping to find a bit of stimulation there.

The three men which Sally had warned her about earlier were still there, and they had now been joined by two buxom young wenches who Amanda assumed to be Angie and Carol. Both were reasonably attractive, with the plump figures and ruddy complexions of real country girls, but neither of them had the air of sophistication or sexual allure which Amanda felt were the prerequisites for a nightclub hostess.

It might be a rather good idea, Amanda thought, to phone around a few of the escort girls registered with her own agency to see if any of them fancied a working weekend in the country. Some of them would be sure to accept the offer as a welcome chance to earn a few extra quid, and it would most certainly give the Paradise a touch more class.

For the present, however, Angie and Carol appeared to be fulfilling their function as mere table decorations quite adequately for the basic needs of their companions. Judging from the number of empty glasses already on the table, the three men seemed primarily concerned with getting steaming drunk, with the girls being no more than two pairs of ears to listen to their lustful boasts and serve as occasional butts for a coarse joke.

No doubt Angie and Carol would be called upon to provide a more specific and personal service later in the evening – but by that time it would have ceased to matter if they looked like the back ends of a pair of sheep.

Or indeed if they were built any differently. None of the men looked as if they were particularly discerning, and once the dreaded Brewer's Droop had set in, Amanda doubted if any of them were capable of more than a few moments of stick it in, waggle it about, and spurt.

Amanda decided that they were best left to themselves and strolled over to the bar. She pulled up a stool and sat down, swivelling to review the lounge and its handful of other customers.

Andrew slid up the other side of the bar with smooth efficiency. 'Would you like a drink, Miss Redfern?'

Amanda turned back, smiling. 'Amanda, please,' she murmured. 'And yes, a vodka martini would be nice, Andrew.'

Andrew served her drink and leant on the bar with his elbows.

'Not exactly a promising lot, are they?' he observed, nodding out at the occupants of the lounge. 'But, as I told you, it gets much busier at weekends.'

Amanda had to agree with his assessment. She ran her eyes over the remainder of the clientele.

At a corner table, by the window, a middle-aged couple sat gazing lovingly into each other's eyes and holding hands beneath the table. Amanda pegged them at once as examples of the 'married man out with best friend's wife' syndrome. Or, possibly, a genuine married couple who had mistaken the establishment for a normal country pub. She confided both assessments to Andrew, who grinned.

'Actually, you're wrong on both counts,' he said. 'In fact, they are first cousins who have been living incestuously together for eighteen years and are out celebrating their anniversary.' He gestured to two other couples who seemed to be much more in keeping with the spirit of the place – a businessman with his pretty young secretary and fifty-year-old woman with the boy who came round to trim her hedges on Saturday afternoons.

'Both those youngsters will be getting a bit of a surprise later on tonight,' Andrew went on. 'She'll be taking something down all right – but it won't be shorthand, and he'll find himself clipping a very unusual bush with his teeth.'

Amanda giggled. 'You're a cynic with an extremely one-track mind,' she accused playfully.

Andrew laughed. 'Not at all, my dear. I'm just a realist with a sense of humour. And don't forget I've been here for many years. I know these people, they're all regulars. Want names?'

Amanda shook her head. 'Not for now. I always forget names anyway.'

Andrew picked up her almost empty glass and reached behind him to squirt in another vodka from the optic.

'That reminds me — I know a rather decent joke about names,' he said, handing the replenished glass back to her. 'Want to hear it?'

Amanda nodded. Andrew was cheering her up immensely.

'Well, there is this young Red Indian boy, you see,' Andrew began. 'And one day he corners the tribe's old medicine man in his tepee.

' "Tell me, O wise and ancient one," says the boy. "I believe that you have given names to all the people of our tribe."

"That is so, young one," says the medicine man. "But why do you ask?"

"Well, venerable and all-knowing one. What I want to know is how you manage to think up all those unique and wondrous names."

"Ah," says the medicine man. "It is a great and magical gift, bestowed upon me by The Great Father himself. Whenever a child is due to be born, I close my eyes and I meditate, chanting mystic mantras and concentrating upon the true soul of the universe. Then, at the very instant the child comes into the world, I open my eyes and give that child a name from the first thing I see. For instance, when your sister was born, I was sitting by a tranquil river in the moonlight. Therefore she is known as 'Moonbeam-

On-The-Water'. And when your brother came into the world, a hunting party of braves has just returned to the village with their latest kill, which was a fine elk. Even in death, the mighty beast looked proud . . . so I named your brother 'Proud Elk'. Now, young one, do you understand?''

"Oh yes, wise one," says the boy and starts to leave the tepee. Just as he is going out, the medicine man calls after him.

"But tell me, Two-Dogs-Fucking . . . why the sudden interest?" '

Andrew told the joke well, delivering the punchline with a perfectly straight face so that there was a split-second of reaction time before the point of the gag registered. Amanda laughed delightedly, clapping her hands in a gesture of appreciation.

'Not bad at all,' she conceded, wondering whether or not to respond with the tale of the terminally ill homosexual and the parrot and deciding against it. She wasn't really in the mood for getting into a heavy dirty joke session.

Instead, she nodded across the lounge at the only single customer. 'What about him?' she asked Andrew. 'What's the story there?'

Andrew glanced over at the young man who sat alone, supping at a half pint of bitter as though he intended to make it last all night.

'Ah – that's Giles Hadleigh, the young squire,' Andrew said. 'He owns most of the land which abuts on to our grounds. He also owns the riding stables which our guests use.'

Amanda took a longer and more penetrating look. The young man was dressed in the clothes of the country gentleman, but there was something a little run-down about his appearance, the faint but definite suggestion that all was not quite as it should be. His tweed hacking jacket had obviously seen better days, despite its elegant cut, and his twill trousers, immaculately pressed, were fraying very slightly at the turn-ups.

'I must admit he doesn't look like a rich country squire,' Amanda said doubtfully.

Andrew nodded, 'Squire in name only, I'm afraid. Actually he hasn't got the proverbial pot to piss in. Something rather sad about the impoverished gentry, don't you think?'

Amanda had to admit that the man did cut a somewhat pathetic figure. 'So what happened?' she asked.

'Death duties,' Andrew explained. 'His father died only last year, leaving poor Giles with a crippling bill. Even after selling off all the family silver and some of the traditional land, he's still in hock up to his eyeballs. At the moment, he just about gets by on an EEC grant for not growing things and what little he makes out of the stables. Damned nice chap, actually. You should meet him — only I have to warn you that he will probably try to touch you up and start talking about one of his balls.'

The prospect sounded intriguing. 'I'll go over and introduce myself,' Amanda said, pausing only long enough for Andrew to pour her another double vodka martini. She sauntered over to the table where Giles was sitting.

'May I join you,' she said politely.

Giles Hadleigh looked up, slightly startled at the

sudden and unexpected interruption. The initial pleasure at the sight of a young and very attractive woman which registered on his face was quickly replaced by a look of embarrassment.

'There's not much point,' he mumbled, sipping morosely at his beer.

Amanda didn't understand. 'Not much point in what?'

'Not much point in you joining me,' Giles confirmed. 'I'm afraid I have very little to offer a young lady of pleasure — even one as attractive as you.'

Amanda fell in. She smiled, both at the compliment and the misunderstanding. She had been called quite a few things in her life, but 'young lady of pleasure' was a definite improvement on many of them.

Amanda sat down at the table opposite him.

'Perhaps I'd better explain,' she said. 'My name is Amanda Redfern. I'm the new owner of the Paradise Country Club.'

Giles's face was a study in embarrassment and confusion. He spluttered into his beer, jumping to his feet.

'Oh, my dear lady . . . I'm so terribly sorry. Please forgive me . . .'

His voice tailed off as he stood awkwardly and tried to think of more profuse words of apology. Finally, he reached down, seized Amanda's hand and lifted it to his lips. He kissed it in a strangely old-fashioned gesture.

Amanda found it rather touching, and felt sorry for the young man's obvious discomfort. 'Please — sit down,' she urged him.

Giles sank back into his chair, still struggling to apologise.

'You see . . . I thought . . .'

Amanda cut him short with a gentle and reassuring pat on the arm. 'I know exactly what you thought . . . and in a place like this, that's perfectly understandable,' she told him, 'Now, can we start again?'

Amanda held out her hand, which Giles took and shook warmly. Amanda felt slightly disappointed, having expected another kiss.

'Giles Hadleigh. I'm pleased to make your acquaintance, my dear young lady.'

Amanda smiled inwardly. It was ironic — Giles had been right the first time, but 'dear young lady' did have a rather quaint ring to it.

'So — Andrew tells me you're our local squire,' she said.

Giles smiled apologetically. 'Not much of one, I'm afraid. What else has Andrew told you? That I'm as poor as a church mouse, I suppose.'

Amanda felt herself warming very quickly to Giles, with his old-fashioned gentlemanly courtesy and refreshing frankness. She looked at him more closely, liking what she saw.

Hard up he might be, but Giles had the mark of aristocratic breeding stamped firmly upon his features. It was quality bred in the bone, Amanda supposed — and with little imagination she could imagine his not-so-distant ancestors ruling the local peasantry with a rod of iron, lording it over the hoi polloi and no doubt exercising their *droit de seigneur* with the most attractive of the village virgins.

Amanda noted the finely chiselled face, the firm and almost cruel set to the lips, and the proud twinkle in the dark brown eyes. The overall effect was stunningly sexy.

'Did Andrew tell you I'm having a bit of trouble with my ball?', Giles said, suddenly.

The question rather threw Amanda, even though Andrew had warned her. She wasn't quite sure how a girl was supposed to respond.

'Oh, really?' she managed to enquire politely. 'Which one?'

'The really big one, I'm afraid,' said Giles, sounding extremely sad about it. As well he might, Amanda reflected.

'Yes − and when I say *big*, I really mean big,' Giles was continuing. 'Last year it was really massive. It really made quite a show. I had nearly three hundred people crowded into the Great Hall for the final unmasking at midnight.'

'Must have been quite a spectacle,' Amanda murmured, becoming more and more confused about the bizarre turn in the conversation.

'Oh, yes, it was,' Giles agreed enthusiastically. For a moment, his whole face brightened up with the memory of it. Then he became despondent again. 'But this year I'm afraid it is just going to be a giant flop. I just can't seem to find enough support. There's not the money about, you see.'

Amanda felt incredibly sad and sorry for him as the pathetic tale unfolded. To be burdened with all those financial worries was bad enough − but to have a dreadfully swollen ball and not be able to afford a jockstrap must be terrible.

'It must be awfully painful for you,' she sympath-ised.

Giles nodded miserably. 'Oh it is, believe me. I really don't know what I am going to do.'

Amanda felt a strong urge to help in whatever way she could. 'Have you thought about consulting a specialist? Someone who understands these things?'

'What, have someone else hold it for me, you mean?' said Giles.

'Well . . . yes, I suppose so.' Amanda had the strangest feeling that she was skipping off down a yellow brick road, like Dorothy in The Wizard of Oz.

Giles seemed to have taken her friendly suggestion as some sort of offer of personal help. His face brightened. He leaned across the table.

'I don't suppose you'd be willing to handle it for me,' he ventured. 'I mean, I'd raise what I could, but it might not be much.'

Amanda was beginning to trip out. She couldn't quite bring herself to believe she was actually having this weird conversation, yet her earlier encounter with the Hon. Nigel should have prepared her for anything. But somehow, Giles seemed too nice to be a weirdo. Nothing seemed to really fit. It was all very confusing.

'Now let me make sure I've got all this perfectly straight,' she said to Giles, trying to clarify the situation once and for all. 'You would like me to hold one of your balls for you, but you're not sure how much of a raise you can manage?'

'Not just one of my balls,' Giles corrected. '*The* ball. The big one.'

'Ah yes – the big one,' Amanda muttered. 'I

forgot. And would that happen to be the left or the right?'

Giles looked at her blankly. 'I'm not quite sure what you're talking about.'

Annoyance was beginning to creep in to Amanda's tone. Her confusion was fast turning to exasperation. 'Which ball, specifically, would you like me to hold for you?'

'Why, the Hunt Ball, of course,' Giles said. 'The big one . . . the social event of the local year.'

Amanda suddenly felt unutterably foolish. The strange sexual goings-on around her were definitely beginning to affect the workings of her brain, she thought.

'Ah, the Hunt Ball . . . of course,' she managed to croak weakly, hoping that Giles had not already written her off as some sort of congenital idiot.

'Yes – didn't Andrew explain,' Giles went on. 'When I inherited the land and title from my father, I also assumed his role as Master of Hounds for the local Hunt Committee. One of my responsibilities is to organise the annual Hunt Ball. In past years it has always been held in the family mansion, but, quite frankly, the old place no longer looks quite as grand as it once did. So it occurred to me that we could hold it here in the club, with your cooperation. You would have to lay on the food and entertainment, of course, but then all the takings over the bar would be yours. And the way most of the local gentry sling down the old G and Ts after a good hard ride, that could tot up to a considerable amount of the old mazuma.'

Giles obviously hadn't twigged to her earlier misapprehension Amanda realised with a growing sense of relief. Her hairs-breadth escape from acute embarrassment made her more than usually generous.

'Giles, I'd be more than happy to hold your ball here in the club,' she said. 'In fact, I'd probably be happy to hold your ball just about anywhere.'

Giles flashed her an odd look.

'And don't worry about the financial side of things,' Amanda went on. 'I'll treat it as a local PR exercise — the first gesture of the new management.'

Giles beamed at her, ecstatically happy. 'I say, that's magnificently decent of you, Amanda. If there's anything I can do to repay you . . .'

Amanda smiled at him warmly. Now that he was happy, his face seemed even more handsome. 'Well, there just might be something,' she murmured huskily.

A knowing smile spread across Giles' face. 'You mean there could be something else we could come together on?'

'Oh, I'm sure there are all sorts of joint ventures we could bring to a mutually satisfying climax,' Amanda said, and this time there was no possible mistaking the double entendre. Their eyes met over the table, flirting brazenly.

'Perhaps you would like to come down to the stable for a little evening ride,' Giles suggested, becoming more emboldened as he warmed to the new game.

Amanda grinned wickedly. 'And did you have a young stallion in mind which might be suitable for me?' she asked.

Giles appraised her with undisguised lust. 'Oh, I'm sure that I can arrange to mount you more than satisfactorily,' he promised.

Amanda didn't doubt it for a second. She rose to her feet. 'I can't wait,' she said. 'Shall we go?'

The interior of the stables was heady with a musky, animal smell which Amanda found erotically stimulating. She had never thought of horse dung as an aphrodisiac, but something was definitely getting through to her and causing that old familiar prickling between her thighs. The tingle spread out, rippling through her body in soft, delicious waves.

Giles led her over to a pile of fresh, sweet-smelling hay in one corner of the stable. 'Would you like to sit down while I saddle up a couple of horses,' he asked.

Amanda sank down on to the springy softness of the hay, feeling little wisps of it edge up under her skirt to tickle her buttocks and thighs. It was an extremely pleasant sensation. She let out a low murmur of appreciation.

'One of the great joys of the countryside, laying fresh hay,' Giles said, noting her reaction.

'I believe you,' Amanda said. She lay back, stretching luxuriantly. 'Aren't you going to join me?'

'In a tick,' Giles said. He crossed the stable and opened one of the stalls, beginning to lead out a huge, jet-black horse.

'Actually, Giles — I don't really fancy a ride right now,' Amanda called out. 'Well, not on a horse, anyway.'

Giles chuckled. 'I know, my dear. But Black Prince here does. I thought we could do with some background entertainment. We don't run to seductive music or blue movie shows out here in the sticks — but we can still lay on a bit of home-style sexual stimulation.'

Amanda didn't understand what was going on. Seeing her puzzled face, Giles explained.

'Black Prince has been working hard this week, so I think he deserves a bit of a treat.' He opened a second stall and drew out a beautiful chestnut mare. 'Amber is on heat at the moment,' he said, as if that explained everything.

Leaving the horses together, Giles returned to the hay pile and threw himself down beside Amanda. 'Now, we were going to discuss some mutually satisfying project, weren't we?' he said, grinning.

Amanda's attention was not fully on him as Giles began to nibble gently at her ear. Being basically a city girl, she had never really had the chance to study a horse's sexual equipment at close quarters before, and what she was seeing now was quite a surprise.

Black Prince may have had a tough week, but it certainly hadn't affected his stamina, Amanda soon discovered. She stared, fascinated, as the stallion frisked behind the mare, nudging her rump with his nose and playfully rearing behind her to show he meant business. Excited by her smell, his massive prong elevated itself into operating position.

Seeing a horse's hard-on for the first time was quite an awe-inspiring experience. Amanda's eyes were riveted by the sheer size and power of the monstrous equine phallus, and she found herself quite envying the mare who was in for such a treat.

Giles deftly removed her clothes, and began to nuzzle into the soft flesh of her breasts, licking and sucking the erect pink nipples. Across the stable,

Black Prince had finished his particular brand of foreplay, and reared up to mount the mare's chestnut rump. Amanda's eyes were still on the huge, steaming horse cock as it jerked into final stiffness for penetration.

Amanda felt herself stiffen involuntarily as the huge, rigid rod struck home. She let out a gasp of indrawn breath in sympathy as Amber gave a shrill whinny of excitement as the great cock slammed into her.

Giles, meanwhile, had begun to trace his fingers lightly around her pubis, following the fleshy line of her slit beneath the springy growth of hair. His tongue continued to play wetly over her excited nipples, and Amanda could feel his hot breath against her tender flesh.

She wriggled with mounting excitement and passion, sinking deeper into the welcoming softness of the hay. Giles slithered over on top of her, still nibbling teasingly at her throbbing nipples and beginning to slide his fingers past the hot bud of her stiff little clit and into her wet, juice-filled cunt. With his spare hand, he was deftly unclipping his belt and unzipping his fly to free his own stud equipment. Finally, he wriggled out of his trousers and took hold of Amanda's hand, pressing it down towards his excited cock.

'You might find this a little bit of a disappointment,' he said with a grin, noting that Amanda's eyes were still firmly fixed on the stallion's great tool as it thrust in and out of the mare's rump with increasing rapidity.

Amanda's hand closed around the thick stiffness

of Giles' twitching prick, and an involuntary spasm of surprise and pleasure made her shudder. She looked down at what she was fondling for the first time – and disappointment didn't enter into things.

In strict terms of inches in proportion to body size, Giles had Black Prince well beaten. His cock was at least nine inches long, and as thick as Amanda's wrist. As she held it tightly, Amanda could feel the bulging veins pumping rhythmically as his hot blood surged into the inflated tube of flesh.

'Jeez, Giles – have you ever thought of going in for the Derby?' Amanda gasped, only half-jokingly.

She began to pump the throbbing cock with a tight fist, jerking and squeezing it in a way that was both gentle and violent at the same time. Giles moaned, plunging three fingers deep into her soaking pussy and slopping them round in a circular motion which made her heave her buttocks up towards him with rising passion.

Amanda splayed her legs wide, easing the passage of his gyrating, probing fingers into her hot and horny wet hole as its hungry depths ached to be filled. She pulled on his huge organ insistently, urging Giles to move over her prone form and slip his welcome cock between her quivering, inviting thighs.

But Giles had other ideas. Pulling his fingers from her dripping fanny, he slid his hand around Amanda's smooth, rounded buttocks, his strong fingers digging into the soft flesh. Roughly, he pulled her over until she was laying face-down in the hay, smelling the musky sweetness of it in her nostrils and feeling wisps of it prickle against her soft lips.

'Now – bring your knees up,' he grated huskily,

as he pulled himself to his knees and straddled the back of her legs.

Amanda did as she was told, drawing her knees up until her round, white bottom reared up provocatively. Giles wriggled behind her, sinking his knees into the soft hay until Amanda could just feel the hard, hot knob of his throbbing cock tucked into the sensitive cleft of her buttocks.

Satisfied that he had adjusted their relative positions just about right, Giles inched in closer behind her and let the long shaft of his tool slide under her soft cheeks until the burning, pulsing thick tip of it was resting against the fleshly lips of her oozing slit. Giles slid it up and down against her dripping crack a couple of times, until her freely flowing juices had lubricated it thoroughly, then pulled back slightly, squatting down a little on his haunches until just the bulbous tip of his cock was again poised at the portal of Amanda's hungry hole.

Teasingly, he contracted his muscles so that his prick just jerked slightly against her fanny lips, then pulled back again as if deciding to call the whole thing off. Amanda squirmed in frustration, bucking her arse back against the retreating cock as though to suck it inside her.

With consummate timing, Giles chose that precise second to lunge forward again, burying his great prick deep inside her welcoming sheath. Amanda let out a gasp of pain and pleasure as the huge tool rammed home, writhing her buttocks against his belly frantically and feeling the swollen weight of his hairy balls against the soft cheeks of her behind.

Giles thrust into her repeatedly, his hands cupped

around her soft breasts to squeeze them roughly each time his shaft struck home. Amanda gasped, willing him to probe deeper into her, discover every last secret inch of her cunt, and belly, and womb with his mighty machine.

Above her own rasping breathing, and Giles' grunts of pleasure, Amanda could still hear the snorting of the black stallion and the excited whinnying of the mare as they too progressed their sexual conjunction towards its final conclusion.

To Amanda's eternal gratitude, Giles managed to outperform Black Prince by a good six minutes, continuing to ram hard and fast into her belly when the sated stallion had already retreated to his stall to tuck into another kind of oats.

They came together, Amanda's hot and slippery juices washing Giles' creamy sperm straight out on to the soft hay.

Exhausted, Giles flopped down, moving himself to where it was still dry and making room for Amanda to roll over and lay beside him. They relaxed for several moments, letting their passion seep away from them in ever-diminishing warm waves of satisfaction.

'That was fantastic,' Amanda murmured finally. 'Talk about the horse of the year show.'

Giles smiled. 'We must do it again some time,' he said.

Amanda snuggled against him. 'That,' she said emphatically, 'is a definite date.'

Chapter Nine

Giles dropped Amanda outside the club in his battered old Land Rover. He made no attempt to get out, and Amanda didn't see much point in inviting him in for a nightcap. A definitive performance needs no encore.

'Right — I'll be in touch with you about my ball,' Giles called as she sauntered up the front steps.

'I hope you'll be in touch about both of them,' Amanda shot back, and with a cheery wave, disappeared inside.

The lounge was now completely deserted, apart from Andrew behind the bar, casually wiping up the last few glasses. Amanda glanced at her watch. It was just after ten-fifteen. She seated herself at the bar and ordered a drink.

'Early closing tonight?' she asked.

Andrew smiled as he served her. 'We're well into the bonking hour now,' he explained. 'Perhaps the odd bottle of wine on room service, but that'll be about it for the night.' He paused, grinning. 'Enjoy your trip to the stables?'

Amanda looked at him in amazement. 'Do you know *everything* that goes on around here, Andrew?'

Andrew gave a little chuckle. 'No, not everything. But I do know hay when I see it.' He reached out and plucked several wispy pieces from Amanda's hair. 'I suppose he has talked you in to sponsoring his Hunt Ball?'

'Better yet,' Amanda said. 'We're going to hold it here, in the club. Should give the old bar takings a boost, eh?'

Andrew nodded thoughtfully. 'I'll need some help, though. Things have been run on a bloody shoestring around here for a long time now.'

'Yes, so I've noticed.' Amanda sipped at her drink and regarded Andrew closely, wondering just how far she could trust him. Although she had no doubts that he and Sally were into just about every kind of kinky sex trip there was going, she suspected that they were both perfectly straight when it came to business matters. And certainly, Andrew seemed to have his finger very firmly on the pulse of what was going on around the Paradise Club. She decided that there was no obvious harm in confiding in him.

'So what went wrong around here?' she asked bluntly. 'Even to a newcomer, it's pretty obvious that this place has seen better days. Was it just the recession — or something else?'

Now it was Amdrew's turn to have much the same thoughts and reservations about her. For a start, he wasn't sure about her exact relationship with old Norville and quite how she had acquired ownership of the club. And perhaps more to the point, what her future plans were. He and Sally had been happy at the Paradise. It suited their swinging lifestyle, and in past years had furnished them with a nice place to live and a decent income. Andrew suspected that they had both probably lost touch with the bigger world outside, and that life for a pair of middle-aged hedonists was no longer quite as simple as it had been back in the more free and easy 70s. Andrew had no illusions that they would both find it hard to adjust if they were pushed out of their fantasy land and back into the real world.

But that was a danger which had already been looming long before Amanda's arrival on the scene, and clearly had nothing to do with her. Therefore, it would seem to make very little difference whether he trusted her or not. On the other hand, she might be the one person who could be in a position to improve matters, if he had her on his side.

He regarded Amanda piercingly. 'You want some straight talking?'

Amanda nodded. 'That's exactly what I want.' She faced him, eye to eye.

Andrew made up his mind. 'OK,' he said. He moved to the row of optics behing him and unhooked an almost-full bottle of vodka. He set it down on the counter between them with two fresh glasses, filling both almost to the brim. 'You want to talk – then we'll talk. But first we get pissed. *In vino veritas*, as they say.'

Amanda lifted her old glass and drained it, picking up the new one. 'I'll drink to that,' she said, encouraged by Andrew's open and candid attitude.

'So tell me the background,' Andrew said eventually, when they had matched each other glass for glass a half dozen times or so. 'What was your relationship with old Norville, for instance?'

Amanda shrugged. 'A client – perhaps almost a friend. Nothing more.'

Andrew nodded thoughtfully. 'I liked old Norville,' he said. 'He used to spend a lot of time here in the old days. He knew how to have a good time, did Norville.'

He took a long, thoughtful swig at his drink. 'I'll tell you one thing,' he added, eventually, 'it would have broken his heart to see how run-down this place has become. Things used to get done around here when he still had control. We had a proper groundsman, more staff . . . and more customers. Something needed fixing, or replacing, and all I had to do was mention it to Norville and it would be sorted out.'

Andrew broke off with a deep sigh and drained his glass. He refilled it, topping up Amanda's drink at the same time. He waited for Amanda to move the conversation along.

'But he's only just died. And this place looks as though it has been falling to pieces for years,' she pointed out.

'Well, all I can say is that the rot started to set in when Norville stopped coming here regularly, and when he appointed the Blakes to run his financial affairs. The money for maintenance work dried up, and odd little things started to happen.'

Amanda seized on the last point. 'What sort of things?'

Andrew took another gulp of his vodka. 'Well for a start we began to get trouble with the local do-gooders and the Anti-Vice League. They had never troubled us before, but then suddenly there were protests and demonstrations and little visits from the police following anonymous tip-offs of illegal or immoral activities. It was more of an irritant than anything else . . . but it soon started to affect our local trade. People were afraid to come here in case they ended up in the middle of a police raid or a full-blown scandal.'

'And you think there is some kind of a connection?' Amanda asked, not sure quite what Andrew was getting at.

He shrugged. 'Who knows? I'm just giving you the background facts. You can juggle them around to make whatever conclusions you like.' He topped up his glass again, and almost drained it in one large gulp. 'Oh yes, there's one other rather strange little matter,' he added, as if on a pure afterthought. 'When Giles Hadleigh had to sell off land to pay some of his death duties, a company called Drummond Development suddenly showed up on the scene. But the odd thing was, they only wanted to buy selected parcels of land from him — every one of which had two things in common.'

Andrew broke off, gazing somewhat blankly down Amanda's cleavage.

'Do you know you've got the most incredible pair of tits?'

Amanda realised, suddenly, that Andrew was beginning to get quite sloshed. His eyes had developed a slightly glassy, moist look and he was starting to slur some of his words. She might not have much longer to get any sense out of him — and she was already intrigued by the odd web of coincidence which he had been weaving. Curiosity overcame any offence she might have taken at his personal comments. Instead, merely irritated by the interruption, she pressed him to continue.

'These two things . . .' she prompted.

Andrew tore his eyes away from her swelling breasts with some effort. 'Ah, yes indeed.' He slurped down some more vodka. 'As I was saying — all the parcels of land Drummond bought up had two things in common. Firstly, each one had some sort of farm building or permanent structure on it, so that it could not be classed as purely agricultural land . . . and perhaps more importantly, every piece of land they were interested in adjoined part of our grounds. Interesting, what?'

Amanda sipped at her own drink thoughtfully. 'Interesting, certainly,' she conceded. 'But I still don't quite see what you're getting at.'

'Ah.' Andrew waggled his finger drunkenly in the air. He was sinking into his cups rapidly now. 'You've missed the point. Give you three guesses as to the firm of London solicitors who handled the whole deal.'

Amanda's eyes widened. 'Blake, Blake & Watts,' she breathed.

'Eggshactly,' Andrew slurred, his eyes rolling wildly. 'Now the thing is, old girl . . . how well do you know Peter Blake?'

Normally perhaps, Amanda might have baulked at such an obviously personal and intimate question, but the vodka had loosened her tongue as well.

'I met him for the first time a couple of days ago. To be honest, I don't know what he is like as a solicitor — but as a man, I find him rather attractive.'

Andrew tried to nod in agreement, but his head

just sort of lolled around loosely as if his neck was turning to rubber. 'Sho does my wife,' he grumbled, but without apparent jealousy. 'Well I'm not sho shure I trust him . . . or his bloody firm, at leasht.'

Andrew's blurry eyes returned to Amanda's breasts. He leaned over the counter, swaying slightly from side to side, to stare more closely down her cleavage.

'Did you know you've got big brown hairs growing out of your tits?' he demanded.

Amanda glanced down, and picked out two or three stray wisps of hay, dropping them to the floor. 'Why don't you trust Peter Blake?' she prompted, becoming increasingly exasperated. The supposed 'straight talking' was rapidly degenerating into drunken ramblings.

'He'sh got a bigger cock than mine, for a shtart,' Andrew muttered, the corners of his mouth starting to tremble. His eyes filled with water, and Amanda realised that he was about to start crying.

'Look Andrew — I thought we were supposed to be talking seriously,' she reminded him, still hoping to steer the conversation back on to a normal course.

But it was too late. Andrew had already passed the point of simple inebriation and was now rapidly sinking into alcoholic melancholia. He began to blubber openly.

'Everyone sheems to have a bigger cock than me,' he sobbed bitterly. 'Ish snot fair.'

Amanda gave up any attempt to hold a serious conversation and tried to console him instead. She felt genuinely sorry for the pathetic figure in front of her, especially as he was normally such a bubbling and cheerful individual. She reached across the counter and patted his arm in a gesture of comfort.

'I'm sure that's not true, Andrew. I'm sure you have a perfectly nice prick,' she assured him.

But Andrew was beyond consolation. He continued to cry unashamedly, his whole body convulsed with heaving, racking sobs of abject misery. He lurched back from the counter suddenly, leaning drunkenly against the beer shelves while his fingers fumbled with his zipper. Finally managing to undo it, he flopped his prick out of his pants and tottered fowards again, slapping it down on the counter like a piece of meat on a butcher's slab.

'Now tell me the truth, old girl. Ishn't that the shmallest pecker you ever shaw?' Andrew demanded miserably.

Amanda wasn't at all sure what was expected of her. Confirmation of Andrew's worst nightmares would only make him worse, perhaps even suicidal, but she could hardly shower praise upon the wrinkled and wretched object in front of her with any real conviction. As Peter had observed earlier, even in full erection Andrew's cock was of modest length to say the least, and a peculiar tapered shape. Flaccid as it was now, it looked for all the world like a third ball with a small hole in it.

'Well I'm sure it looks a lot more impressive when you get excited, Andrew,' she muttered rather lamely. 'Anyway, it's what you do with it that counts.'

Andrew burst into a fresh flood of tears.

'Thash the bloody trouble,' he complained bitterly. 'Don't do much with it anymore. Lucky to get it up four or five times a day lately. Shno bloody use at all.'

Andrew banged his clenched fist down on his prick in a gesture of hopeless anger and frustration. Amanda winced, feeling the pain herself.

'Gonna kill the little bastard,' Andrew shouted suddenly. He upended his vodka glass, tipping its contents over his cock and balls. Before Amanda quite realised what he was doing, Andrew had produced a cigarette lighter from his pocket and was flicking it into life.

'My God, Andrew . . . what the hell are you doing?' Amanda screamed as Andrew touched the flame to his spirit-soaked cock. There was a faint sizzling sound as most of his pubic hairs dissolved into shrivelled and matted ashes. Pale blue-white flames licked up and down the prostrate pecker.

Amanda reacted instinctively, her hand moving in a blur as she reached out to douse the flames. Even the most pathetic of penises deserved better than public cremation.

Luckily there had not been all that much vodka left in the glass, and pure alcohol tends to burn off quickly. In a matter of seconds, Amanda had patted out the last little flicker of flame.

It was at this precise moment that Sally chose to breeze into the bar, accompanied by a slim and extremely attractive dark-haired young woman.

'Ah, Amanda — glad to find you here,' she said brightly. 'We have a late house guest. I found her in the reception hall, looking lost.'

Sally seemed to notice, a trifle late, that Amanda was busy patting her husband's cock on the bar counter top. 'Oh dear, sorry to butt in,' she added, apologeticlly.

Amanda removed her hand from Andrew's prick rather hurriedly. 'It's not what it appears,' she blurted out.

'Indeed it isn't,' Sally said disdainfully, noting the limp and shrivelled object which appeared to be laying in a small, wet puddle on the counter. Suddenly she wrinkled her nose in disgust. 'Good Heavens, what's that awful smell?'

'Burnt hair,' Amanda informed her. 'Andrew was trying to set fire to his prick.'

Sally screamed. 'Oh, my poor darling.' With surprising speed and agility for a plump woman, she vaulted over the counter and threw herself on her husband, bearing him to the floor. 'My poor, precious love. Are you hurt? Is little Horace in pain? Here my darling, let mummy kiss it better.'

Amanda moved away from the counter discreetly as the precise nature of Sally's emergency first-aid became apparent. Loud slurping and sucking noises emanated from the floor as she fastened her hot wet mouth around her husband's smarting prick to soothe away the pain of his penile pyrotechnics. Andrew's little whimpers gradually subsided, giving way to grunts of pleasure as little Horace rose, phoenix-like from the ashes.

Amanda turned to appraise the young beauty which Sally had brought in, and who was now standing red-faced with obvious embarrassment. She noted the expensive clothes, the deliberately provocative make-up and the Gucci weekend bag.

There was something not quite right about the

overall image, Amanda decided. The pieces didn't quite fit. At first glance, she would have said that the girl was a high-priced hostess, checking into the club for the forthcoming weekend in the hopes of picking up some good business. Yet there was also a definite suggestion of good breeding and upbringing, suggesting that the raven-haired beauty had been born to money and not found it lying on her back. The green eyes gave little away, but some feminine instinct told Amanda that a secret lurked behind them. The very same instinct told her that the sleek black hair was an expensive wig, and that the girl's prominent breasts owed at least some of their shape and size to artificial enhancement.

But it was her embarrassed look which really put Amanda on her guard. That, above all else was the one thing which really didn't match the outward image. Whoever the girl was, she deserved careful watching, Amanda told herself.

However, for now she was a customer, and from what Andrew had told her before he drank himself stupid, the Paradise could do with every customer it could get.

For her part, Caroline Drummond was having serious misgivings about her impetuous decision to descend on the Paradise at such short notice. Descent seemed to be the operative word, since she was already half-convinced that she had entered some kind of rural sanitarium for the sexually deranged. On her way up the drive, she had been sure that she had seen a young man sitting on the edge of the fountain in the moonlight, masturbating furiously. Even allowing for the tricks of dim light, and her extremely limited experience of the male genitalia, Caroline imagined that young man's penis had been monstrously oversized, perhaps even physically deformed. Now, it seemed that the staff of the place were apt to perform bizarre rites and sacrifices upon their sexual equipment which included self-immolation and cannibalism, judging from the way in which Sally was now feasting upon the barman's stiffened cock.

Caroline could only watch, with a mixture of shock, disbelief and prurient curiosity as Sally licked and sucked voraciously at the man's prick and balls, her head bobbing up and down like one of those disgusting kitch nodding-head dogs often seen in the back windows of Ford Cortinas.

Amanda caught the direction of her gaze, and the expression on her face.

'They are married,' she muttered, by way of explanation, but it didn't seem to make a lot of difference. 'Perhaps we'd better go and sit down at one of the tables,' she suggested, as an afterthought.

Caroline managed to tear her eyes away fron the scene on the bar floor, as Sally finished sucking the life back into Andrew's prick and prepared to straddle him to find out if the now throbbing Horace remained in full working order. She followed Amanda over to a nearby table and sat down.

'Now, what can I do for you?' Amanda asked, trying to get things back on to a straight business footing. 'I'm Amanda Redfern the owner.

Caroline regarded her warily, appraising the potential opposition to her nuptial plans for Peter Blake. She noted the lush, sensual lips, the mischievous twinkle in the blue eyes and the full, swelling breasts which obviously needed neither uplift or artificial padding, concluding that Amanda was perhaps more of a threat than her fiancé had been willing to admit. Putting all female jealousy aside, Caroline had to admit that the description 'tarty-looking' had probably been something of a cover-up on Peter's part. She had no illusions that the majority of men would find Amanda extremely sexy and desirable.

All in all, Caroline figured that she had best play things extremely cool, giving away as little information about herself as possible. She tried to ignore the grunts and squeals of carnal pleasure still coming from behind the bar, which at that very moment culminated in a shrill scream of sexual release as Sally climaxed and sprayed her hot juices all over her prostrate husband and the bar floor.

'Yes, my name is Fay Andrews,' Caroline lied. 'Some friends in London recommended this place as a nice retreat for a relaxing weekend. I'd like to check in, if you have a spare room.'

Amanda had no doubt that the girl was lying through her expensively capped white teeth. However, she had already decided to just play along and see what happened.

'Of course,' she said in a businesslike manner. 'If you'd like to come out to the reception desk, I'll get you a key.'

Amanda rose to lead the way, confident that she could sort out such a simple thing as allocating a room without bothering Sally, who was at that moment sucking avidly at Andrew's cock once again, eager to milk out the last few precious drops of sperm from the wilting weapon.

To be perfectly fair to the woman, she was distracted from her pleasures enough to try to call out a warning, but a mouth full of soft cock tends to have a muffling effect on the human voice, especially when coming from the floor behind a solid oak-built bar.

So all that Amanda actually heard was a sort of choked mumble, which could have been anything, and didn't sound terribly important. She had absoultely no idea that the message Sally was attempting to give her was in fact, 'Don't put her in room eight, for God's sake.'

The capricious hand of fate was very much in charge of events, however — choosing that very second in time when one tiny, apparently insignificant little oversight could change the future.

Much like a message intended for King Harold in the year 1066, when he failed to hear the shouted 'Keep your eye out for any stray arrows', the warning went unheeded.

And so began a chain of events which was to have a devastating effect on just about everything from Caroline's virginity to the future of the Paradise Country Club — sweeping Caroline, Amanda, Sally, Andrew, Freda, Phillipe, Peter Blake and several dozen helpless characters along with it.

But of course Amanda realised none of this as she walked behind the reception desk and unhooked the key to room eight from the pegboard on the wall.

Chapter Ten

Caroline glanced around the room as Amanda exited, closing the door behind her. It was not as bad as she had expected, seeming clean and functional enough, if a little sparse in terms of furnishings and fittings.

Basically, the room contained a king-sized bed, a fitted wardrobe, a vanity unit and a door which revealed the en suite facilities of a shower, toilet and bidet. There was one other door, which Caroline assumed to interconnect with the next-door room in case anyone should want to combine the two into a bigger suite.

And that was about it. There were none of the little extras which most modern hotels would have featured. Rooms at the Paradise, Caroline figured, were primarily designed for basic needs and functions – like undressing and hopping into bed. There really wasn't a great deal of call for such little things as teasmade machines and colour TV sets. However, Caroline found the condom machine in the toilet a trifle gratuitous.

She strolled over to the bed, prodding it experimentally. It wobbled violently under her touch, betraying the dubious sensual pleasures of a water mattress. Gingerly, Caroline sat down and tried to adjust to the new and somewhat nauseating experience of having the bed quiver like a living thing beneath her. With slight misgivings, she swung her feet up off the floor and lay full-length, holding her breath until the last wobbling wave had quietened down to a mere ripple.

Caroline decided that she was not at all impressed by the great claims made for waterbeds, and could only hope that she managed to fall asleep before she became seasick.

Laying there quietly, Caroline became aware of loud male voices penetrating the walls from the next room. Either the walls were particularly thin, or the men were particularly raucous, she concluded — eventually deciding upon the latter as she identified at least three separate masculine voices, all of which seemed to be thoroughly drunken and boisterous.

Between shouts, loud guffaws of amusement and yells of delight, Caroline was sure she could also identify a couple of female voices, although neither of them appeared to be sharing their male companions' high spirits. After her experience in the bar, Caroline could only make the wildest guesses as to what might be going on only a few feet away from her. Some kind of sexual orgy no doubt, she imagined — but whether it involved black mass, ritual sacrifice or the sodomising of live chickens she had no idea.

They were not thoughts that she wanted to dwell upon. What with the noise, and the bobbing of the waterbed, Caroline was not at all sure she was going to get much sleep, but she intended to try. It had been a tiring drive from London, it was getting late, and she wanted to look fresh for Peter Blake's arrival in the morning. Scrambling off the wildly sloshing bed, Caroline undressed quickly, throwing her clothes carelessly into a pile on the floor. She crossed to the vanity unit to remove her make-up.

Sitting down at it, Caroline was struck by the disproportionate size of the mirror which was mounted directly to the wall above the unit. It seemed particularly large, and was a rectangular shape as opposed to the more conventional round or oval mirrors she was used to. Beside the mirror was a small electrical switch, which Caroline assumed to control a concealed light fitting. She reached up and switched it on.

Instead of a light coming on, the rest of the lights in the room switched off, leaving Caroline in the gloom and staring at the almost magical disappearance of her own reflection.

For the mirror had suddenly turned into a window, and through it Caroline could clearly see into the room next door. Shocked and surprised, she flicked the switch again, and was once again looking at her own face in a mirror.

Although she had only read about such things, Caroline knew at once that what she had discovered was a two-way mirror device. She had no idea how it worked — although some dim memory of the principle of polarised light controlled by an electrical current surfaced from the depths of her memory.

But work it undoubtedly did. Like a child fascinated with a new toy, she switched it on again and stared as if mesmerised at the scene in the next room.

There were indeed three men and two girls, as she

had guessed from the overheard conversations. All were naked and engaged in a sexual romp which was only slightly less bizarre than the ones she had imagined.

One of the men had just seated himself on a high-backed chair, with his legs splayed open wide and his stiff, hairy prick pointed at the ceiling. He called over to one of his companions, who had obviously just finished fucking one of the girls and was now wiping the end of his sticky cock with a piece of tissue.

'Come on Joe, don't be a greedy bugger,' the man on the chair complained. 'Send those two slags over here so I can have some fun.'

Joe laughed drunkenly, gesturing to the girl nearest to him with the sperm-soaked tissue. 'You heard what George said, Angie. Now you get over there and give him a good seeing-to.' He turned his attention to the second girl, who was lying submissively on the bed as the third man toyed irritably with his semi-flaccid tool, trying to coax it into erection. 'You too, Carol — maybe Henry will get a hard-on watching you and Angie do your best double act.'

Meekly, both girls made their way over to the seated George, to do whatever it was that he expected of them.

George had very definite ideas about his pleasure. Grabbing Angie roughly by the arm as she came near, he pulled her to his side and pointed down at his rigid shaft with one stubby finger.

'Now you just climb up on that and stick yourself like a pig on a roasting spit,' he commanded gruffly. 'And fuck me nice and slow, to make it last, or I'll ram it up your tight little arse.'

Carol obviously had past experience of George's sexual preferences, because she was already getting down on her hands and knees on the carpet.

George chuckled. 'That's right, baby. You get down there and suck my balls while Angie is riding my prick. And get 'em right in your mouth, and use your tongue.'

Caroline's finger was straying to the control switch of the trick mirror to turn off the depraved scene before her eyes, but some deep, dark urge welled up from inside her to stay her hand. Instead, she continued to watch as the sexual saga unfolded, feeling a strange tightness in her throat as the girls did as they were told and moved into position.

Angie straddled the seated man, wiggling her hips as she lowered herself gently until the tip of George's cock nuzzled against her soft and swollen cunt lips. She moved her buttocks in a slow, circular motion, allowing the dripping juices from her hot fanny to lubricate the head of George's prick and ease its entry into her tight sheath.

Carol, meanwhile, had knelt on the floor like a dog, and waited with her mouth hanging slackly open and her tongue hanging out until her friend had impaled herself upon George's glistening shaft.

Angie lowered herself slowly on to George's quivering cock, wriggling her arse furiously as the stiff meat filled her hungry hole. Carol crawled forward, and with head pressed up against her companion's undulating buttocks, she probed with her outstretched tongue to find George's huge, swollen balls. Finding them, she sucked first one and then the other hairy globe into her mouth and began to slosh them around with wet, slurping sounds.

Caroline continued to watch, horrified and yet fascinated at the same time as the two girls deployed themselves for George's pleasure.

Or was it really pleasure, she found herself wondering. There was something mechanical, even inhuman about the performance which suggested that the participants were not really interested in the undoubted joys of sex. It was as if they were all merely acting out some sexual spectacle as though it was expected of them. They were like players on a stage, dumbly enacting their roles as outlined in some fixed and humourless script.

Caroline's eyes strayed to the other two men. The one called Joe seemed to have lost all interest having slaked his lust once. Crossing to the bedside cabinet, he picked up a bottle of scotch and lifted it to his fat lips, slurping greedily.

The third man, who still lay passively on the bed, just toyed irritably with his own semi-flaccid weapon. Nothing really registered upon his face, not even boredom. Although his dull, glassy eyes took in what was happening around him, Caroline wondered just how much of it was actually registering in his drink-sodden brain.

And the girls, Angie and Carol. They were completely passive, taking no obvious enjoyment from their sexual ministrations to the seated George. They were just doing what they were told, and lending their bodies in the most intimate ways possible without any emotion whatsoever.

There was no pleasure there, Caroline told herself

— and although there was no question of force involved, and they were clearly performing quite voluntarily — Caroline could only wonder about their motivations. Purely mercenary, she supposed, as both girls were quite obviously whores and thoroughly resigned to their roles.

Even George, who was on the receiving end of the sexual attentions of two attractive girls, showed no sign of pleasure. His face was contorted into a fixed and sickening leer as though displaying to the world: 'Look — I'm a big, virile man and this is how I treat women.'

He was obviously becoming bored, even as Angie rocked herself on his stiff cock, lifting herself up until it almost popped out of her wet hole and then dropping down again to bury its pulsing length in her hot, slick sheath.

He reached up to take Angie's bobbing white breasts in his hands, squeezing the soft flesh roughly and manipulating the erect brown nipples with his thumbs. Stretching out one leg, he rubbed his foot under Carol's bushy pubis, trying to get his toe into her wet slit as she continued to suck and nibble at his balls.

Finally, deciding that he needed some extra stimulation, he called over to his companion on the bed.

'Hey, Henry — stop playing with your prick and come and use it like you're supposed to.'

A stupid grin spread across Henry's face. With something of an effort, he raised himself from the bed and ambled over, still fondling his large but half-hard cock. Reaching the fornicating trio, he stood uncertainly for a few moments, eyeing both girls and trying to make up his mind what to do.

But, once again, it was George who took control of the situation and handed out the orders. He took his hands from Angie's breasts, and gripping her head, turned it sideways.

'Let's see you suck some life back into that,' he said, nodding at Henry's flaccid prick.

Obediently, the girl lowered her head, while continuing to bob up and down on George's cock. Henry grinned stupidly, and edged closer so that she could reach his prick with her mouth.

Watching it all from the other side of the two-way mirror, Caroline felt a warm and moist trickle down her naked thigh as the submissive girl sucked the thick soft cock into her mouth and began to gobble hungrily. Caroline's fingers strayed, unbidden, to the mouth of her virgin cunt, feeling the juicy secretions which were starting to bubble from inside to make her delicious little clit button hot and wet. She began to tweak the stiffening little organ between her finger and thumb, her eyes now totally hynotised by the scene of mounting lust in the next room.

Angie had to draw back her head slightly now, as Henry's cock swelled in her mouth and began to assume its full, erected size. The huge organ pushed her lips apart, and saliva dribbled from the corners of her mouth as she opened it wider to accommodate the throbbing thickness of it.

Henry began to thrust his hips towards her, driving his now massive cock in and out of her slavering mouth. Angie's jaw was hanging open slackly, and Caroline could see her tongue slurping and swirling around the thick shaft as Henry forced it deeper and deeper into her throat.

Caroline felt tiny shivers of pleasure ripple across her throbbing little clit. Her own mouth fell open as she gasped for breath and plunged three bunched fingers into her oozing slit to fill the aching void behind it.

Suddenly, she realised that she actually envied the little whore who was now totally filled with hot, throbbing cock. No doubts, no hang-ups, no feelings of shame or self-recrimination. Just two massive male organs pumping away inside her, filling her cunt and mouth with hot and horny flesh.

Caroline felt hot and shivery all over now, and her fingers pumped in and out of her soaking hole with increasing rapidity. Somehow, she knew that she was on the verge of exploding into the most powerful orgasm of her life.

So intense was the sensation that all other thoughts had been driven from Caroline's mind. The entire universe was just cock and cunt and the shuddering pleasures of the flesh. Watching one girl being fucked, one man being sucked and frigging herself with her fingers, Caroline was a part of the whole orgy and not merely a voyeuristic observer.

She was so totally caught up and obsessed with her own approaching climax that she failed to hear a faint warning rattle from the handle on the interconnecting door. In the next room, out of the limited field of vision afforded by the two-way mirror, the drunken Joe was attempting to get into what he thought was the bathroom. Too late, Caroline awoke to the danger and remembered that she had not checked if it was locked or not. Then, suddenly, the door was open and a drunk, naked man was staggering into her room.

Caroline opened her mouth to scream, but nothing came out. She rose from the vanity unit, backing away as Joe lurched towards her, a leer of surprise and delight on his face.

Joe called out to his companions. 'Hey, guess what? I've found another one in here, and she's a real cracker.'

Caroline, still backing away, felt the edge of the bed connect with the back of her knees and then she was falling on to the wildly slopping surface of the water mattress, bouncing up and down so that her firm, pear-shaped breasts jiggled enticingly and her sopping cunt with its tiny pink-budded clit and surrounding aura of springy blonde curls presented a perfect target to the excited Joe.

And he had the perfect weapon to plunge into it, score the perfect bullseye. In a flash, his cock had jerked into erection as he took in the full potential of this delicious young beauty which a kindly fate had been fit to throw in his path.

Grasping his heavy balls in the palm of his hand, he lifted them as though making an offering as he moved purposefully towards the bed. The action served to make his thick prick even more rampant and aggressive.

To Caroline, laying at a lower level on the bed and looking up at the monstrous cock, it was like some weird fantasy in which she was being stalked by some fabulous mythical beast, half-man, half-animal. She could only stare, wide-eyed at the organ itself, as

though afraid to face the reality of the man or
creature behind it. Be he satyr, centaur or minotaur,
it seemed of only trifling importance. There was only
that huge phallus, thick and long and pulsing with
knobbled veins and surmounted by a bulging
purplish helmet.

Fear, and her ignorance of the male organ at close
quarters, made it seem even more huge and
threatening. And the now certain knowledge that it
was to be rammed into her, forced into that tiny
passage which had known only her own slender
fingers, made her feel weak and faint.

And yet, behind the fear, underneath the horror,
another and less easily understandable emotion was
beginning to surface in her mind. It was a kind of
exultation, even gratitude for the blind and unfeeling
logic of the situation.

There was something quite relieving about the
inevitable. It removed choice, and thus doubt. In
some strange way, it made the unthinkable
acceptable. Caroline knew that her virginity was
about to be taken, perhaps savagely, away from
her . . . and she was almost glad.

After all, a voice deep in her subconscious argued,
wasn't this exactly what she had always wanted,
fantasised about? To be taken, violated, without
emotion or any room for guilt?

With this realisation, Caroline's sense of fear
evaporated, to be replaced only with a strange kind
of yearning. She wanted it to be done, and over with.
She wanted that huge swollen prick to slam into her
cunt, plunge up her slippery and oh-so-hungry canal
and smash through that delicate yet armoured

doorway into true womanhood.

As if reading her thoughts, Joe threw himself on to the bed, covering her body with his own. Caroline gasped as she felt his body weight forcing her down against the bouyancy of the waterbed. His cock was stiff and hard against her belly, and she could feel the burning heat of it against her soft flesh. Joe's slobbering mouth closed over hers, with his thick tongue thrusting roughly against her soft lips, prising them open. Then a gush of foul, whisky-soaked breath filled her throat, and his tongue was probing the inside of her mouth.

Strangely, surprisingly, Caroline found herself responding, meeting his questing tongue with her own, playing, flirting with its slimy hardness. She pressed her head back into the resilient water mattress, drawing back enough to purse her lips around his curled tongue, sucking at it as though it was a juicy cock.

Joe gave a little guttural grunt of pleasure, registering the erotic significance of the gesture even through his booze-induced stupor. He lifted his face from hers, grinning down at her.

'So that's it baby. You want my cock in your mouth. You want some good stiff meat between those pretty little lips of yours.'

Joe pushed himself up into a squatting position, resting back on his haunches still straddling Caroline's thighs. His rigid rod quivered just inches above her belly, its accompanying pair of swollen balls resting softly in the nest of springy hair around her fanny.

'There you go, girl . . . help yourself,' Joe said, generously.

Caroline forced her head up from the bed, confronting the one-eyed monster which now pointed directly at her face. She reached out, tentatively, to grasp it in her hand, marvelling at the way its thick, hot hardness seemed to swell in her grip, filling her clenched palm. Stroking her hand up and down its throbbing length, Caroline could feel it pulsing and quivering beneath her fingers like a mighty pump engine just ticking over quietly, not yet quite primed to spurt up its reservoir of hot, thick, slimy spunk.

A shiver of hunger and deep, yearning need rose from somewhere in her belly and rippled out past her tingling clitoris and down her trembling thighs. She gripped the hard cock even tighter, feeling herself push at it, as if to force Joe to move backwards. Caroline spoke for the first time, her voice hoarse and throaty with repressed desire.

'No,' she grated out from between clenched teeth. 'I want your big thick cock in my cunt. I want to feel it thrusting deep into my belly, growing and swelling and throbbing away inside me until I feel as though I am being split in two. I want you to fuck me like a crazed animal, use me like a slut, a cheap and willing sex machine. I want your prick to ram into me with brute, blind force until I am screaming and pleading with you to stop. I want you to push, and thrust, and heave and ream and pump and spurt into the deepest parts of my body.'

A wicked grin creased Joe's brutish face. 'You got it baby,' he grunted. Lifting his knees, he positioned himself inside her thighs and pushed her legs roughly apart. Caroline could feel the hot juices running freely from her hot pussy as the swollen lips parted ready to receive the blunt, bulbous head of the fat fucking machine.

She held her breath as Joe grasped his cock in one hand and guided it into position. He rubbed the head against her slimy entrance a couple of times to make it shiny and smooth and then slipped the first two inches into her, poising himself to make the single deep thrust which would bury his long cock up to its hilt in her scalding, juice-filled canal.

'Oh, you're tight, baby. You're really tight and hot,' Joe muttered appreciatively. Even in his drunken state, he sensed instinctively that Caroline was not one of the well-used whores he was used to. That, and a dim but growing realisation that he might be about to enjoy a very special kind of treat, made him act more gently than he would normally have done.

He controlled his entry with slow deliberation, sliding into the hot wet tunnel that was Caroline's cunt and grunting with unexpected pleasure as it seemed to wrap itself around his stiff length like a warm and comfortable soft glove, contracting gently and rhythmically against his own pulsing blood.

Joe's consideration was not what Caroline wanted or needed right now. The aching hunger inside her screamed out for total and immediate satisfaction, and the last niggling little tendrils of guilt in her mind seemed to remind her that there should be a sacrifice, an offering, a penance of pain. Caroline reached up abruptly to grasp Joe's buttocks in both hands, her long fingernails digging into the soft flesh like the talons of some mighty bird of prey. Clawing at his arse, Caroline pulled him savagely down to her, simultaneously thrusting her hips up to meet him in one convulsive, heaving motion.

The entire eight, bone-hard inches of Joe's impressive prick thrust, piston-like, into the smooth sleeving of Caroline's well-oiled shaft. There was a momentary resistance as the plunging head of the intruding cock met the intact hymen, and then the delicate membrane was ripped aside for ever.

Caroline gritted her teeth against the expected pain, but it was only fleeting, washed away completely in the flood of pleasure and sensual gratification as her body exulted in the knowledge of true womanhood.

Caroline groaned softly with all consuming and delicious satisfaction of it all. She rolled her arse around, feeling the spongy resilience of the waterbed take up the movement and mirror it, feeding it back into her body in rippling waves of sensuality. She rolled her hips, rising to meet every deep thrust Joe made as he caught her infectious enthusiasm for the simple yet splendid pleasure of the sexual act.

Joe dropped his face to her breasts, his hot mouth slavering, sucking and kissing the valley between the two firm, pear-shaped delights. He flicked out his tongue, curling it under the soft roundness of each in turn, licking off the delicate and slightly sweet taste of her expensive bath oil.

'Oh baby, you taste really nice, like a woman ought to be,' he murmured, and Caroline thrilled to his appreciation of her body.

Now that the great barrier had been broken, she felt herself able to relax and fully enjoy all the finer nuances of lovemaking. Now it was no longer just blind fucking, but the thrill of one body responding to another body, the magical chemistry of man and woman, cunt and cock, balls and womb. Caroline was not naive or self-deluding enough to even pretend that what she was feeling had anything to do with love, or emotion — but there was an underlying and quite moving power at work as their two bodies writhed and pumped together.

Caroline thrust upwards against Joe's heaving thighs more forcefully, some buried feminine instinct telling her how to control and relax inner muscles and flex her pelvis so that he plunged more deeply into her with every thrust. She was sure that she could actually feel the blunt head of his cock thudding against her cervix each time he slid deep inside her, and the sensation caused a contracting spasm which shuddered along her spine to every part of her body.

Joe's breath was coming in deep, irregular gasps now. His mouth and teeth worried and nibbled at her small, stiff nipples and Caroline could feel the spattering of his hot, wet saliva as each panting breath sprayed it from his drooling mouth. He was man, he was animal — and most importantly to Caroline at that moment, he was hers. Her first man, first fuck, first taste of true freedom — and for that alone she felt a strange sense of tenderness towards him.

She needed to hold him to her, possess his body as he was possessing her. Caroline raised her legs, wrapping them up around the small of his heaving back and gripping him in a tight, vice-like embrace. Her cunt was a hungry hole, sucking at his prick, massaging and milking at it to draw out every hot drop of his boiling sperm.

Joe moaned with even greater pleasure. 'Oh, lady — you're really something. You really are the hottest-assed piece of cunt I've ever had,' he panted, redoubling his efforts to plunge even more deeply inside her with every stroke.

Caroline's grateful cunt took everything he had to offer, and still demanded more. She squeezed him savagely with her legs, as though she could pull his whole body inside hers, consume him completely.

And, suddenly, before she had even suspected its approach, her orgasm was upon her, bubbling up from somewhere deep in her mind to take posession of her body. Caroline let out an involuntary scream as wave after wave of the most powerful sensation she had ever known rolled and heaved and surged and crashed through every part of her being. With each delicious tremor, she could feel the hot wet gushes of love-juice pumping out from her glands into her already soaking cunt.

To Joe, it felt as though his prick were suddenly engulfed by a boiling, bubbling geyser which had erupted without warning. His cock jerked, momentarily as though trying to recoil from the hot liquid assault and then surrendered, totally overcome by the sheer intensity and passion of Caroline's climax. With one last weak thrust, he plunged his prick back deep inside her and felt the pumping release of his own ejaculation as it spurted out into her belly.

He collapsed with a deep, shuddering gasp and rolled off her, flopping back on to the eddying surface of the waterbed.

'Jesus Christ, lady . . . that was bloody beautiful,' he muttered.

Caroline lay silent, content to luxuriate in the gently pulsing afterglow of her orgasm. She felt complete, a woman at last, and how she should be.

And she knew, once and forever, that her life had changed and would never now be quite as she had previously imagined it might be. She knew now exactly what sort of woman she truly was, and with that knowledge came the certain realisation that marriage, and Peter Blake, and the safe and respectable facade of domesticity and motherhood was not for her. Or at least, not for a while, anyway.

She glanced sideways at Joe, seeing him clearly again for the drunken, boorish slob that he was, but it didn't matter. For those few minutes, he had been her handsome hero, her valiant knight, her ardent lover. And she would always be grateful to him for doing what had needed to be done in releasing her from the terrible prison of her own upbringing and conditioning. She felt an odd compulsion to kiss him tenderly upon the cheek, but resisted it.

Joe, looking into Caroline's eyes, only dimly realised part of the special thing which had gone between them. He propped himself up on the bed, his gaze travelling down towards his diminishing prick, glistening with a frothy slime of semen and love-juice, slightly tinged with blood. His mouth fell open, slackly, with surprise. Belatedly, realisation dawned.

'Hey, you were a virgin,' he muttered, slightly taken aback.

Caroline smiled dreamily. 'But no longer, thanks to you.'

A few more moments of peaceful silence passed between them, finally broken abruptly by coarse voices from the doorway into the next room. Caroline looked up, suddenly alarmed to see George and Henry leaning drunkenly against the jamb of the door, staring at her lecherously.

'Well see here. Old Joe has got a nice piece of cunt all to himself,' George said, pointedly.

Henry licked his lips, taking his cue from his mate. 'Wouldn't be surprised if the useless bugger hasn't left her still hot for a real cock inside her,' he said.

Joe swung his legs off the bed with surprising speed and agility. He strode straight to the doorway, pushing both men roughly back into their own room.

'The lady,' he said, with special emphasis on the word, 'is perfectly satisfied and wants to go to sleep.'

He followed them through the door without another word or a backward glance at Caroline, but she understood. Seconds later, she heard the positive click of the latch in the door as Joe locked it, as if sealing some secret and unspoken pact which had been made between them.

Caroline lay reviewing what had actually happened to her and musing on the future for several minutes. Finally, she fell into a deep and dreamless sleep.

Chapter Eleven

Caroline awoke early, slightly disorientated by the fact that the morning sunlight seemed to be streaming into her bedroom from the opposite side to normal. Still a little groggy with sleep, she sat up in bed.

The wild rolling of the waterbed snapped her back to reality, and the memories of the previous night flooded in to her conscious mind in a rush. As if to check that it hadn't all been one of her vivid erotic dreams, she threw back the thin duvet and looked down at the bed between her thighs. The small, brownish patch of dried blood and the semen which stained the virgin sheet quickly confirmed that it had all been very real indeed.

Fully awake now, Caroline leaned back against the headboard of the king-sized bed and tried to analyse her thoughts.

Mentally, she had steeled herself against a wave of self-loathing, and she was surprised when it didn't come. Even conjuring up a mental picture of the drunken, slovenly Joe failed to evoke any sense of disgust. Indeed, his actual face refused to come into clear focus, and it was only the image of his stiff and angry-looking red prick which formed a clear image. And the memory of that brought only a somewhat self-satisfied glow of pleasure.

Emotionally, then, she was unscarred. Caroline

tentatively flexed her thighs, testing for the physical effects of her deflowering. Apart from a slight dull pain in her belly, and some smarting around the lips of her fanny, she felt absolutely fine.

She swung herself off the bed and crossed the room to her overnight case, rummaging about until she found a jar of cold cream. Scooping some on to her fingertips, she sat back down on the bed, opened her thighs and began to apply it to her sore cunt.

The cool, slippery cream brought immediate relief to the delicate flesh – but the touch of her fingers brought something else. With a delicious shiver of surprise mixed with pleasure, Caroline realised that she was horny. Her initiation into the delights of carnal lust had tripped the 'on' switch of some inner sexual dynamo – and now it seemed that the motor was running permanently.

Delicately, she probed past the bruised and swollen lips of her labia, her fingers seeking the soft, moist folds of her vaginal passage. Past the sensitive area, Caroline thrust two fingers deep inside herself, opening and closing them like a pair of scissors and beginning a slow and sensuous rotating motion against the itching walls of her cunt.

It was not enough. What minor pleasure she had gained from masturbation in the past now seemed like the taste of fish paste compared to caviar. Two fingers, however skilfully manipulated, were just no substitute for a good, stiff cock. Caroline thrust more deeply into herself, hoping that the additional penetration would ease the aching hunger, but it was no good.

Fuming with frustration, Caroline looked around

the bedroom for a suitable object which could be pressed into service. In quick succession she considered and rejected the handle of her hairbrush, a roll-on deodorant and the bedside lamp.

Still furiously pumping her fingers in and out of her hot slit, Caroline tried a bit of lateral thinking to her problem. Short of getting dressed and going to find a handy male at 8.30 in the morning, there had to be another way of gaining some sexual satisfaction. She had already considered the possibility of knocking on the interconnecting door and inviting Joe in for a rematch. The room next door had been completely silent ever since she had awoken, and Caroline assumed that the three men had sneaked off back home to their wives once the previous night's frolics were over.

She considered the nature of the Paradise Country Club. The waterbed, the two-way mirror and the next-door orgy left little doubt that the entire establishment was more or less devoted to the pursuit of sexual gratification. That being so, perhaps the management had seen fit to provide a few extra frills and thrills for their paying customers. Caroline managed to hobble somewhat ungraciously to the vanity unit, it being difficult to walk in a ladylike manner with two fingers jammed up one's cunt. With her free hand, she began to rummage through the drawers.

In the second drawer down, she found what she was looking for. Next to a thoughtful and varied collection of pornographic magazines and fancy ribbed condoms, lay an impressive-looking nine-inch battery-operated dildo.

With the minor thrill of someone who has discovered buried treasure, Caroline lifted the masturbatory marvel from the drawer and looked at it. The rubberised substitute prick was obviously based on an Eastern design, taking the form of a rather deformed and shrivelled mandarin, with a rounded head and sloping shoulders. Luckily, thought Caroline, the manufacturers had chosen an unusually tall old mandarin for their model, and equipped him with a neat little electric motor which enabled him to jump up and down on the spot at the rate of about ten hops per second. Personally, she found the lighting-up green eyes a trifle over the top, but then it was no time to be fussy about matters of good taste. Gratefully, she carried the welcome little wank machine back to the bed and lay down, drawing up her knees and opening her thighs.

The moulded, helmet-shaped head of the old mandarin slipped easily between the eager hot lips of her fanny. Caroline eased the whole thing in, inch by inch, feeling the love-juice begin to prickle out inside her hot shaft as her body reacted to its thick stiffness. With the dildo half-way into her hungry hole, she thumbed the small button on its base and the little old mandarin jumped into life like a demented jack-in-the-box.

The vibrating movement brought an immediate electric-like tingle of excitement and pleasure, which rippled down her hot shaft in tiny waves of tingling sensation until it reached her belly. Caroline let out a deep, shuddering moan of pleasure as she thrust the dildo in as far as it would go.

Its thick and ribbed stiffness was more than enough to make her feel totally filled. Caroline missed the actual body-heat of Joe's pulsing prick, but other than that it was a pretty fair substitute. She pulled it out slowly, pressing the sides of it against her throbbing little clitoris and allowing the vibrations to stimulate the little bud into full erection. Breathing heavily, Caroline eased the throbbing maching back again, burying it until the little old mandarin's sandalled feet had almost disappeared inside her.

Out again — then in once more, a little faster. Caroline's cunt was hot and slippery now as the love-juices flowed freely. Her thrusts speeded up in tempo, burying the dildo up to its base time and time again with increasing excitement as the first pre-orgasmic ripples began to shudder through her body. Caroline's hand was moving in a blur now, the waterbed rocking wildly beneath her as she wiggled her arse and tried to spread the delicious sensations of the vibrating dildo to every part of her vaginal passage.

Little grunts of pleasure were torn form her throat, to quiver over her slack lips as her mouth opened to let out the scream of orgasmic release which she knew was now well on its way.

It came, not as the single, violent spurt of release which she was expecting, but as a series of pulsing shocks which racked her whole body as each trembling spasm ran into the next. There was no scream — only a succession of groaning sobs which bubbled in her saliva-filled mouth and sprayed out in little flecks of spittle across her hot lips.

The incredible orgasm went on and on, as though it would never stop. Caroline seemed to sense that the waves of exquisite pleasure were only limited by the physical stamina of her wrist, which was already beginning to ache with tiredness.

Reluctantly, Caroline called it a day, plunging the dildo as deep into herself as she could with one last thrust and clamping her vaginal muscles tightly against it to milk the final quivers of sensation from its vibrating length. Her body seemed to melt into the sloshing movements of the waterbed as the violent shocks of orgasm subsided gradually until they were no more than faint, throbbing pulses of delicious pleasure.

Only when the tremors had faded through ripples into a final continuous quiver of warm satisfaction did she switch off the vibrator and pull the lifeless dildo from her wet, oozing cunt. She lifted it slowly to eye level, regarding the glistening manikin with a smug and self-satisfied smile.

'Do you know something?' she told the wizened old mandarin. 'I've never fucked a Chinaman before. Thanks'

Finally exhausted, Caroline let her arm flop on to the bed and relaxed to enjoy the warm tingling of fulfilment.

Half an hour later, Caroline decided that it was her stomach's time to get something satisfying inside it. Time for breakfast. She rose, crossing the bedroom to the en suite bathroom to take a shower.

She had never actually been tempted to sing in the

shower before, but this morning was different. The absolutely perfect and only way to start a new day, Caroline decided. She broke into a spirited rendering of 'I've got you under my skin' as the hot water sprayed against her naked flesh.

Massaging shower gel against her skin, Caroline found yet another new pleasure in the appreciation of her own body. She creamed a soapy lather against the soft fullness of her breasts, marvelling at their firm ripeness and their jaunty, provocative shape. She let her slippery fingers glide over the firm proturberance of the stiff little nipples, playing and teasing with each one in turn. Moving her hands down over her flat, smooth stomach, she stroked the insides of her thighs and worked the hairy bush of her pubis into a creamy froth. Her fingers began to stray towards her slit once again, and with a mental effort, she pulled them away. She was going to have to learn new disciplines, she reminded herself. Having awoken the sleeping beast of her own sexuality, she now had to learn how to tame it, keep it under control. She had broken free of frigidity, and had no desire to immediately become a slave to nymphomania in its place. Enough was enough — for the time being at least. She rinsed off the last of the lather and stepped out of the shower to dry herself with a clean, thick towel.

Dressed, made up and feeling better about herself than she had in her entire life, Caroline sauntered in search of the breakfast room.

Apart from Amanda, who was just finishing off her last slice of toast, it was deserted. Caroline figured, correctly, that most overnight guests at the

Paradise didn't usually want to be too public first thing in the morning and the breakfast was not high on their list of priorities.

It seemed rather pointless and impolite to sit down at an empty table on her own. Caroline crossed the room to Amanda's table.

'Mind if I join you?'

'No, of course not.' Amanda welcomed her with a cheery smile. 'Have a good night,' she enquired innocently, as Caroline sat down opposite her.

Caroline wondered, briefly, if Amanda was taking the mickey. Perhaps the rooms were all bugged for sound and video as well as having two-way mirrors, she thought in a moment of panic. The thought that there could be a home movie of herself being bonked by a large and drunken country bumpkin was rather alarming. Fears of blackmail rushed, irrationally, into her head, quickly followed by a mental picture of Daddy's face as he watched the incriminating tape.

'Are you all right?' Amanda enquired solicitously. 'You've suddenly gone as white as a sheet. Are you feeling ill?'

Caroline pulled herself together with a mental jolt, scanning Amanda's concerned face for any trace of threat or double meaning. She relaxed, finally convinced that the other woman was quite genuine.

'No, I'm fine . . . really,' she said, managing a weak smile.

'Oh, good,' Amanda said, taking a sip at her tea. 'Fay, isn't it?'

Caroline looked bemused. 'Fay?' she muttered

blankly, having completely forgotten the false name she had registered under.

'Fay . . . your name. That's right, isn't it?'

The penny dropped. 'Oh, yes of course. Silly me — I don't think I've quite woken up yet,' Caroline blurted out, trying to cover herself.

The bluster did not go unnoticed, confirming Amanda's suspicions from the previous evening that woman was not quite what she appeared to be. However, any further conversation was pre-empted at this point by the arrival of Sally coming in from the kitchen, alerted by the unexpected sound of voices.

She stood over Caroline, looking slightly embarrassed.

'Look, I'm awfully sorry, but we're not really geared up for full breakfasts at the moment,' she muttered apologetically. Sally didn't bother to expand though the mere fact of seeing someone seated at a breakfast table had thrown her completely.

Caroline shrugged benignly, glad for the interruption. 'That's OK,' she said graciously. 'How about some toast and a pot of coffee?'

'Sure.' Sally was equally relieved. She returned to the kitchen, thankful that she didn't have to start the day dealing with an awkward customer.

'So, planning to stay long?' Amanda asked, returning to the conversation.

'The weekend, at least. It much depends on what there is to do around here.'

Amanda regarded her piercingly. 'What sort of

things did you have in mind?'

'Oh — just to generally relax. Charge up the old city batteries. Get a bit of the country air.' Caroline let her guard down for a moment. 'And of course, if there are any eligible men around . . .'

She let the end of the sentence hang in the air, from where Amanda snatched it like a hawk scooping up a sparrow.

'Eligible for what, exactly? This isn't what you might call ideal husband-hunting country.

Caroline couldn't stop a smile forming on her lips, thinking of the recent reassessment she had made about her life, and attitude to the male species in general.

'Men are only good for one thing . . . and that one thing is pretty good.'

Amanda couldn't argue with that. She smiled, picking up her cup of tea and brandishing it like a toast glass. 'I'll drink to that,' she said, taking a sip.

The moment of the humour seemed to break the mutual guard between them. Suddenly they were just two young women, who shared a similar outlook on a common subject. They both relaxed visibly.

Amanda thought, suddenly, of Peter Blake's impending visit, realising that the sudden appearance of Caroline might be turned to her advantage. She really wanted some time on her own to suss the Paradise Club out, without Peter looking over her shoulder. Whatever else he was, he was a gentleman on the surface at least, and would be perfectly chivalrous if pressed into it. And Fay — or whatever her real name was — was a very attractive young woman, who could well distract him for long enough to give her the free time she wanted.

'Look – I tell you what,' Amanda said generously. 'I have a friend, a young solicitor, coming down here later this morning. The truth is, I really have a lot to do and I can't afford to spend much time with him. Perhaps he could show you around the place or something, while I'm busy.'

Caroline forced herself not to react. The last thing she wanted was for Peter Blake to get too close to her, in case her disguise was not quite good enough. On the other hand, she did need to gain Amanda's confidence and to find out exactly what went on within the confines of the Paradise Country Club.

Caroline decided to play it by ear for the time being. She feigned a look of interest. 'Oh really? What's his name?'

'Peter Blake. He's really quite a nice chap. I'm sure you'll like him.'

'Oh, I'm sure I shall,' Caroline said, without a trace of sarcasm showing in her voice. 'What time is he arriving, by the way?'

Sally returned with the toast and coffee at this point, and set it down on the table. Caroline poured herself a cup of coffee and spread butter on her toast, nibbling at it. Just as Sally was turning to leave, Amanda called her back.

'Oh, Sally – did Peter phone to say what time he would be coming?'

Sally nodded. 'Oh yes, I forgot to tell you. He called about an hour and a half ago to say he was on his way. He should be here any minute, I should think.'

Caroline nearly choked on her mouthful of toast,

drawing a concerned look from Amanda and a quick slap on the back from Sally.

'Are you all right?' Sally asked, worried.

Caroline nodded, spluttering out the last few crumbs of buttered toast. 'I'm just not as hungry as I thought I was,' she managed to blurt out between coughs. She cast a sudden eye at her watch. 'Goodness me, is it that late already? The morning's wasting away.'

She slurped down a few gulps of coffee in a most unladylike manner and stood up hurriedly. 'I think I'll go and have a nice massage,' she announced, it being the first excuse which sprang to mind. 'I suppose you do have a massage parlour?'

Amanda missed the sudden warning look which Sally tried to flash at her, answering immediately. 'Yes, of course. If you turn left from the reception area, it's about three doors down on your right.'

'Super.' Caroline began to back away from the table, anxious to get out of public view as quickly as possible.

Sally managed a rather neat little side step, cutting off her retreat temporarily. 'Are you sure you wouldn't rather take a nice stroll around the grounds? The azaleas are rather pretty at this time of year.'

Now it was Amanda's turn to become worried. The thought of a young, attractive woman encountering Phillipe before she did was highly unwelcome. 'Perhaps you'd rather take a morning ride. We do have an excellent stable of well-trained horses.' Amanda had no qualms about sharing Giles, but Phillipe was most definitely her exclusive property until she had managed to get herself wrapped around that beautiful prick.

Caroline was starting to get a bit panicky, as both women seemed intent on preventing her escape. Casting a furtive eye over her shoulder towards the door, she sidestepped past Sally and managed a polite, if somewhat nervous smile for Amanda.

'No — I think a massage is just what I need,' she assured them both, and turning on one pretty ankle, made good her escape.

Sally watched her disappear with a dubious look on her face. 'I'm not so sure that was a very good idea,' she confided to Amanda.

'Why not?' Amanda asked innocently. She didn't quite follow Sally's line of reasoning.

'Well . . . you know, Freda,' Sally explained awkwardly.

Amanda took the point. There was no need for Sally to explain further. She gave the woman a secretive smile.

'Something tells me that young woman is more than capable of looking after herself,' she said emphatically.

'Even Freda?'

Amanda nodded, grinning. 'Even Freda.'

Chapter Twelve

At that precise moment, Peter Blake was just turning up the drive. He slowed the car to a crawl, partly to save the suspension from the many potholes and partly to give his plans for the day a final run-through in his head.

Just ten minutes previously, it had all remained basically simple, much as he had worked out the previous night. With no immediate hurry, he would let Amanda get a feel of the place, realise just how run-down and seedy it all was and then hopefully come to the only logical decision to get out of it with whatever cash she could. That way, he would have had weeks to get the best of both worlds — continuing to cream off Norville's maintenance fund and cream into the delectable Amanda.

The call on his car phone from Caroline's father had rather abruptly interfered with his planned timing. It was no longer a leisurely matter. Cedric Drummond had informed him, rather forcefully, that he wanted the whole deal sewn up within the month. A large amount of development money was shortly coming on the market at particularly attractive interest rates, and Drummond Development needed full control of the property to capitalise on the offer. Failure to achieve this ideal state of affairs would make a severe dent in Peter's planned half a million profit — and in simple terms, fifty thousand bucks was better than fifty thousand fucks.

So his new objective was to persuade Amanda to close the place down and sell out as quickly as possible. If that failed, he would have no choice but to resort to Plan B, which was more complicated and might, possibly, have repercussions which would not please the American company willing to put up the front money. This in turn would displease Cedric Drummond, who would then no doubt pass on his displeasure to a certain young solicitor whose outstanding creditors were becoming increasingly pressing. All in all, Plan B was a highly dicey scenario, and had to be treated as an absolute last resort. Unaware that Andrew had already planted seeds of doubt in Amanda's mind, Peter was counting on his charm to swing her round to his way of thinking in a matter of days rather than weeks.

He slowed the Volvo to a halt outside the main entrance and climbed out, striding towards the front door in a determined manner. It was time to get to work on Amanda. For the moment, he put his secondary problems, like getting shot of Caroline once he had his hands on her father's money, right out of his head.

Caroline was having much the same thoughts as she scurried down the passageway towards the massage room. In a matter of less than twenty-four hours, Peter Blake had changed from a fiancé to an unwanted problem. Although she still fancied screwing him, she had no desire to make it a legal or a permanent arrangement. However, explaining away the sudden and miraculous loss of both her maidenhead and her inhibitions could present difficulties, and the plain truth might well deter him from boldly going where a man had gone before, to paraphrase from *Star Trek*.

And if Peter suddenly shied away from her, then Daddy might start asking awkward questions. Caroline was well aware that the two men were quite close, and that Peter met with full parental approval as a potential husband. She suspected that there was also something else going on between them, but as she never really concerned herself with her father's business dealings, she had never pursued the matter.

For the present, Caroline would prefer that her father did not find out that his daughter had rather abruptly changed from a demure little socialite to a man-hungry sex-pot. Quite apart from anything else, it might affect the size of his allowance, which was currently rather generous.

With these thoughts in mind, Caroline reached the door of the massage room and stepped in, totally unaware that she was about to encounter a large Swede with bisexual tendencies and the orgasmic capacity of a female elephant. Had she known this, she would probably have gone in anyway, such was her new spirit of sexual adventure.

Amanda finished her third cup of tea and waited for Peter's arrival. She too had been doing some deep thinking, in which he played a prominent part. Andrew's words of warning the previous night had tipped her off to the strong possibility that there was something underhand going on, and that Peter Blake probably knew as much, or more about it than anyone else.

The trouble was, that a little snippet of secondhand information was not enough to base any conclusions or judgement upon. And to press Peter in any way might well forewarn him that she knew more than he suspected in the first place, thus making him clam up completely.

It was a bit like the old conundrum about the two guards on the gate to Hell — one of whom was committed to telling the truth whilst the other was bound to lie. The only answer was applied logic, playing one off against the other and then making a lateral conclusion based on each one's reaction to the other. It was all a bit 'Does he know that I know that he knows', Amanda mused.

The immediate course of action seemed to be to make Peter feel secure in his own position while she obtained some further information. And the next person in line who might be able to throw some light on the matter would appear to be Giles. So Amanda needed to pacify Peter, probe him very discreetly for clues as to what questions to ask, and then keep him busy while she went off to put those questions to Giles.

That was where Caroline would come in useful. Her sudden appearance on the scene was quite fortuitous, Amanda thought, completely missing the other point that it was also highly coincidental.

But then Amanda wasn't normally a devious person, and all this thought of intrigue and double-dealing already had her head spinning. A modern-day Mata Hari she most certainly was not. Wisely, aware of her own limitations, Amanda decided to take it one simple step at a time.

Freda sat on the edge of the exercise table, idly amusing herself with the rounded end of a weight-training barbell and reflecting, miserably, upon the quality of her life.

Everything had been so full of promise back home in Sweden, especially when her father had found the money to send her to that exclusive school of physiotherapy in Stockholm. The future had looked rosy — a high-class clinic in London, rich clients and the chance to use her skills and quasi-medical ambitions to turn the obese, the scrawny and the underdeveloped into glowing, healthy, perfect specimens of man and womanhood.

Instead, she was reduced to giving relief massage to randy old men and almost constantly washing come-stains out of her nice white uniforms. Just for once, Freda daydreamed, it would be so good to have a trim, firm young body under the touch of her manipulative fingers, feel the warm vibrancy of healthy flesh instead of the cold, lard-like consistency of flab.

So the sudden appearance of a slim, raven-haired beauty through the massage room door was like the answer to a prayer. Dropping the barbell to the floor with a clatter, Freda rose to her feet and appraised Caroline with something akin to hero-worship.

'Massage?' Caroline enquired tentatively, somewhat overawed by the sight of the Swedish girl's massive Amazonian physique.

'Massage, yaas,' Freda responded throatily, nodding her head with wild enthusiasm. 'I massage damn goot, you see.' It was probably the longest sentence she had strung together in several months, her sheer excitement miraculously lending her the gift of tongues.

She gestured to the exercise table and then to a row of clothes hooks on the wall. As Caroline got the message and walked towards the wall to undress, Freda took advantage of her turned back to deftly unpick the last three buttons of her crisp white top so that her massive breasts were fully exposed.

The sudden appearance of two huge, creamy-fleshed mammaries was not something which could really go unnoticed. However, Caroline pretended to ignore the obvious fact that she had placed herself in the hands of a female flasher. Trying very hard not to stare at Freda's prominent red nipples, she padded back, completely naked, across the room and lay face-down on the table.

Freda stood over her, taking the chance to relish the slim, smooth lines of the girl's back, the provocative flare of her hips and the rounded, firm perfection of her small but beautifully shaped bottom. As Caroline's head was turned away from her, she also took the opportunity to drop her hand, reach up under her skirt and rub it against the mouth of her gaping, oozing cunt until it was wet. Freda had learned by experience that this was far handier than having to unscrew the lid off the pot of massage cream, and did the job just as efficiently.

Licking her lips in anticipation, Freda bent over the recumbent Caroline and placed her large hands on the girl's smooth, rounded shoulders. She began a firm, but surprisingly light, circular massaging action with her strong fingers, gliding her thumbs under and around the contours of hidden muscles.

Caroline gave a delicious little shiver of pleasure. 'Oooh, that feels good,' she murmured appreciatively.

Freda nodded her head in agreement. 'Yaas, it feel damn goot,' she muttered under her breath, moving her hands slowly down the curve of Caroline's back.

Bending over slightly further, Freda turned her attention to Caroline's pert bottom, kneading the firm flesh of each rounded cheek like mounds of dough. As she worked, her dangling breasts swung up and down like a pair of soft, fleshy pendulums, the two erect nipples just grazing the small of Caroline's back with a featherlight touch.

For someone who had yet to learn the full significance of erogenous zones, the effect was electrifying. Caroline stiffened and jerked on the exercise table like a galvanised frog on a dissecting slab. A tingling sensation which seemed like both fire and ice at the same time shot up and down her spine. She felt her fanny constrict and tighten, as though clicked on like the shutter of a camera. There was a sudden rush of blood to her face and lips, and even pressed firmly down against the mattress of the exercise table, Caroline was sure that she felt her own breasts suddenly swell and stiffen.

It was, in short, an instant and total turn-on. Caroline groaned, under her breath as this latest revelation struck home. 'Oh my god — it's women, too,' she thought, in a moment of near-panic. Visions of explosive and convulsive orgasms every time she went to the beauty salon or had her hair washed swam before her eyes. And being measured for a new dress would present all sorts of embarrassing problems.

Then Freda slapped her buttocks lightly and prodded her under the tummy, urging her to turn over onto her back. Caroline obeyed, feeling as weak and as easily dominated as a plate of jelly – and immediately came face to face with two soft white breasts that cried out to be nuzzled into, and two tempting stiff nipples which looked as sweet and enticing as two ripe cherries.

Caroline shuddered with pleasure and a total sense of helplessness.

'Oh, what the hell?' she muttered under her breath, and lifting her head took the nearest tempting fruit between her hot lips and began to suck greedily.

Amanda was still in the breakfast room as Peter walked in. She greeted him cheerfully.

'Good morning, Peter. Have a pleasant journey down?'

Peter nodded, sitting down. 'God, this place looks even more depressing in the cold light of morning,' he said, wanting to get the conversation off on the right tack.

He'd been expecting agreement, but didn't get it. Amanda smiled sweetly.

'Oh, really. I'm getting quite fond of the place myself.'

They were not words that Peter wanted to hear. They sounded potentially very expensive. His general buzz rating for the day dropped several points. There was worse to come.

'Actually, I've already made quite a few plans to brighten things up around here,' Amanda went on. 'We're going to hold a Hunt Ball next weekend, and I've called quite a few girls from the escort agency and invited them down. Could start to get quite lively again – perhaps even tempt back some of the old regulars who haven't been coming so much recently.'

'Hunt Ball?' Peter was immediately suspicious. It had to be someone else's idea – but whose?

'Super idea, don't you think,' Amanda enquired brightly. 'I was talking to young Giles Hadleigh, our local squire, last night. He gave me the idea. He owns the estate which adjoins us, so it would be a nice neighbourly thing to do, I thought.'

'Yes, very,' Peter muttered without enthusiasm. 'But where's the money going to come from to hire staff, buy in supplies and all that sort of thing?'

'Oh, I'm sure we'll manage.' Amanda was far too confident, Peter thought. Her next statement was even more worrying. 'By the way, talking of money. Andrew sort of suggested that old Norville had some sort of a contingency fund for the general upkeep of the place. Do you know anything about it?'

Peter felt a cold shiver travel up his spine. 'God, she knows something,' whispered a tiny warning voice in his head. Nevertheless, he forced himself to keep calm. 'No, I can't say I do,' he lied.

'Oh well, never mind.' Amanda seemed to accept it at face value. 'Anyway, getting back to Giles Hadleigh. He was telling me that some development

177

company has been buying up parcels of his land which butt on to ours. Drummond Development, or something. Ever heard of them?'

The cold shiver became an icy avalanche. Peter hoped tht he wasn't trembling as much on the inside as he was internally.

'Never heard the name before,' he managed to croak out. The coldness had started to give way to hot flushes. Peter was feeling quite feverish.

'You don't look at all well,' Amanda observed. 'Perhaps a nice stroll outside in the fresh air would do you good.'

Peter nodded. Anything to get out of this breakfast-table witness box. 'Yes, perhaps we could have a game of tennis or something.'

Amanda looked surprised. 'Oh, not me, silly. I'm going to be far too busy. No, we've got a rather attractive young female guest staying for the weekend. Fay something or other. I was hoping you'd be a perfect gentleman and escort her around for an hour or so.'

'Ah.' Peter was temporarily at a loss for words. 'Actually, I was rather hoping that you and I could . . . you know,' he managed to get out eventually.

'Sorry, no chance of that, I'm afraid.' Amanda dismissed the suggestion with a wave of her pretty blonde head. 'No, it will have to be Fay. Actually, she went down for a massage about twenty minutes or so ago. She should be through any minute. If you stroll down there now you should just catch her as she comes out. I've already mentioned your name to her, and said that you would probably offer to show her around.'

Peter grunted non-committally, hiding his annoyance and frustration. He liked to be in a position of control, and resented other people making plans for him. Besides which, he had far more important things to do than act as escort to some empty-headed bimbo.

But it was not to be. Amanda finished the last dregs of tea in her cup and stood up, preparing to leave.

'Well, can't hang around. Lots of things to do,' she said brightly, granting Peter the favour of a brief peck on the cheek. 'Perhaps I'll bump into you later.' With that, she was off, leaving Peter feeling much like the spare prick at the proverbial wedding. He reviewed his immediate and somewhat limited choice of options.

Basically, there were only two. He either wandered around pointlessly with this Fay Something or Other person, or he wandered around pointlessly on his own. Peter came to the only sensible decision and set off in the direction of the massage room. He would take a look at the mysterious Fay from the privacy of the observation room before committing himself. If he liked what he saw, he could take things from there. Peter was well aware that many women found a massage was a sexual turn-on, and became quite randy.

In which case, the morning need not turn out to be a total washout.

* * *

For Freda, it was rapidly turning out to be the best morning since she had been gang-banged by the local village Tug-o-War team. She squealed with pleasure and excitement as Caroline's hot wet mouth sucked greedily on her burning teats, plating them like little pricks. She groaned as Caroline's hands lifted and squeezed her huge breasts, her sharp fingernails digging into the soft flesh and leaving tiny, crescent-shaped red weals against their milky whiteness. She shivered with sensual pleasure as Caroline's perfectly capped teeth nibbled upon each erect and quivering nipple in turn.

Shrugging off her uniform, Freda exposed her Junoesque body in all its glowing glory. It was a fine, athletic body of which she was inordinately proud. Finely honed muscles rippled beneath the taut flesh of her abdomen and thighs. And beneath her tight, flat stomach, sheltering in a springy bushy of curly blonde hairs, lay the muscular lips of a cunt which could crack walnuts.

The sight of Freda's body in all its nakedness seemed to inflame Caroline even more. She writhed on the exercise table, twisting herself on to one side so that she could reach out and stroke one hand down the rippling, muscular belly towards the Swedish girl's hairy honeypot.

Freda's big blonde head nodded enthusiastically at the feel of Caroline's cool fingers on her hot skin. She shifted her feet, spreading her legs wider to expose the sleek, Scandinavian slit which was already dripping with juice. She began to rock gently, from one foot to the other as Caroline's fingers reached her pubis and entwined themselves in the mass of curly hairs. Twisting her neck, she leaned forwards over the table and lowered her mouth towards Caroline's own blonde bush.

That the soft, downy fair hairs did not match either the tint or texture of Caroline's jet black wig hardly seemed of any relevance as Freda nuzzled into the pubic mound, her tongue snaking out to taste the treasure beneath.

At first, she licked gently, running her tongue up and down the soft fleshy crevice formed by Caroline's swollen cunt lips. The Swedish girl grunted appreciatively as the sexy, slightly musky odour of Caroline's bubbling juices filled her nostrils. Then, reaching to spread the soft folds of flesh apart between finger and thumb, she went to work with more vigour, tonguing the stiff pink bud she had exposed with fast, lapping strokes which took up the woman's flowing love-juice like a cat takes up cream.

Caroline's fingers had now found their way into her own succulent cunt, and Freda rocked and pumped herself against them, fucking herself on Caroline's hand. With her free hand, Freda stroked her partner's firm, taut breasts with undisguised appreciation, thrilling to the feel of the small but deliciously shaped mounds with their small and delicate hard nipples.

Both women were now in an advanced state of sexual frenzy, and so engrossed in the exploration and discovery of each other's bodies that they failed to notice Peter slipping into the room and making his way to the observation booth.

Reaching the security of the glass cubicle, Peter

watched the two women's lusty liaison with detached curiosity, appraising each participant in turn.

He found the massive, Amazonian physique of the Swedish girl a little daunting, but strangely exciting. Idly, he speculated upon ramming into her from behind, wrapping his arms around that broad back to fondle and play with those gigantic soft breasts. With little imagination, Peter could almost feel the clamping power of the girl's vaginal muscles on his stiff prick, and the mere thought of it made his balls twinge.

He turned his attention to the other girl, who looked like a delicate piece of Dresden pottery against the huge and muscular body of her companion. But once again, she was not lacking in raw sexual appeal. Peter mentally fucked her in the missionary position, slamming deep into her tight little cunt as she wrapped her slim and shapely legs around the small of his back and squeezed him tightly, drawing him in ever deeper into her encasing sheath.

He focused in on the girl's face, flushed with the hot blood of advanced sexual arousal. Her soft, mobile red lips fluttered and pouted with passion as she sucked and licked at the impossibly huge breasts. Her eyes were moist and bright with passion, rolling wildly in ecstacy as Freda's darting tongue played on her clitoris and lapped into her molten slit. It was the face of a totally sensuous woman, one who was capable of throwing off all inhibition and allowing herself to be completely devoured by lust.

For a second, Peter thought that he could see another face behind that face; those lips pulled into a haughty and disapproving pout; those eyes cold and impassionate.

But it was an illusion, of course. Peter was sure that he had never set eyes on the girl before, for she had the sort of face and figure that he would have remembered.

Absently, his fingers dropped to his fly to shift the position of his throbbing and rapidly stiffening prick as it bulged uncomfortably inside his tight trousers. Straightening his cock, Peter was aware that it was almost up to his waistband, the twitching head of it painfully constricted by his belt. He loosened his belt quickly, dropping his fingers inside the waistband of his trousers to gently pinch the helmet of his cock between his finger and thumb before lifting it to a more comfortable position. Relieved, he rubbed his hand gently over the throbbing bulge, aware that he now had one of the most fierce and painful erections that he could remember.

The sheer intensity of his arousal made him consider a course of action which he would normally have dismissed as preposterous. Yet everything he had seen and heard about the Paradise Club was totally preposterous, his fevered brain rationalised. His experience with Andrew and Sally, Amanda sucking him off in the passageway, the stories he had heard about the sexual capacities of the massive Swedish masseuse. From what he had heard, she would certainly have no objection to him simply strolling down to take part in the most inventive and abandoned sexual threesome. He was less sure about the girl – but then any woman who could let herself go with such total and unbridled passion would surely not draw the line at a little straight heterosexual fucking.

Peter's brain gave up the fight to think clearly as his cock took over total control. Regardless of anything, it wanted to bury itself up to the hilt in the beautiful dark-haired girl's pussy, to ream away in her silky, slimy sheath until it could release its awful pressure in a spurting, pumping ejaculation of release inside her.

Hardly conscious of his own actions, Peter unzipped his fly, pulled out his rigid prick and let it point like a marker arrow towards the object of its desire. Handling it gently and lovingly, much like a dowser with his divining rod, Peter began to follow its faint twitching towards the juice-filled well of Caroline's cunt.

Lying slightly on her side and contorted into a twisted position to reach Freda's tits, Caroline saw him approaching, prick in hand. An icy-cold wave of horror washed over her at the thought of being recognised in her current situation. With invention born of sheer desperation, Caroline pulled her fingers out of Freda's sopping cunt with a loud and liquid slurp. Reaching down over the side of the massage table, she thumbed the height control button. Then, as the bed whirred into life and began to sink slowly towards ground level, Caroline grasped the electric flex which connected it to the power supply and gave a mighty yank.

There was a spitting, crackling flash as the power socket was ripped out of the nearby wall and the main fuse blew. Entirely lit by fluorescent light, and with only a tiny transom window for outside ventilation, the massage room was immediately plunged into gloom, and the bed stopped about two feet from the floor.

Freda grunted with frustration as the juicy cunt she was so avidly sucking at suddenly sank away from her hungry mouth. Alerted that something was amiss, she looked round a split second before the lights blew to see a large, stiff prick advancing in her direction. The momentary confusion on her face was immediately replaced with a look of joyous wonder. The morning was magical, turning up treats beyond her wildest dreams. With the uncanny precision of a predatory owl, she reached out in the dark for the advancing cock and seized hold of it, guiding its owner into the suddenly nocturnal shenanigans.

Peter felt the welcoming squeeze on his throbbing member and took it as an open invitation. In the gloom, he could just make out the vague outline of the girl on the bed – now laying at the perfect height. Wordlessly, he shook himself free of Freda's grip and moved into position at the foot of the bed. Grasping the dark-haired girl's slim ankles, he pulled her down the bed and threw her shapely legs up over his shoulders. His eagerly twitching prick found its own way to the dripping mouth of Caroline's hot honeypot, and with one heave of his hips, Peter buried himself deep inside her.

A violent shiver of pure bliss rippled up from his loins as Peter's cock slid effortlessly into the warm and welcoming shaft of Caroline's cunt. It was, just as he had imagined, the perfect pussy, tight and deep and trembling with tiny fluttering muscles which seemed to massage every inch of his thick rod with an electrical caress. It was as if this cunt had been precision built for this very cock, designed by a master craftsman to accommodate this particular flesh piston with zero tolerance all round. Even as he slid in, until his balls were hard up against the girl's smooth and rounded arse, Peter knew that this was going to be the fuck of his life, and something deep inside him thrilled to the incredible perfection of it all.

Caroline let out a scream of unbelievable joy at the cock which she had dreamed about for so long finally shafted into her. It seemed to fill her completely and utterly, fucking both her body and her mind at the same time. It was, she was sure, the absolute epitome of what a cock should be. Long and thick and stiff with unleashed power, thrusting into her like a steam hammer.

The ministrations of Freda's tongue on her clitoris had raised Caroline to a fever pitch of sexual excitement. And now this wonderful tool had taken up the job of satisfying those deep inner parts which only a cock could reach. More than ever, Caroline was convinced that she had been born to fuck, and that all the previous years of her adult life had been merely a prelude to this moment.

In the darkness, Freda grinned with satisfaction as she heard the unmistakable sounds of a good stiff prick ramming into a well-oiled cunt; Peter's heavy breathing as he thrusted like a demon and Caroline's little groans of pleasure each time the meaty tool slammed up against the mouth of her cervix. In the faint shaft of light from the transom window, she could see Caroline's head rolling wildly from side to

side, her mouth hanging slackly open and her red
tongue lolling out over her soft, hot lips. Adroitly,
Freda threw one leg over the table until she was
straddling Caroline's breasts, facing her. Gently,
Freda lowered herself down on to the soft cushions
of Caroline's tits and inched forward until her gaping
slit was pressed up against the girl's chin.

Caroline saw what was expected of her and
responded eagerly, lifting her head until her mouth
was pressed tightly against the soft and fleshy lips
of Freda's labia. Shaking her head like a terrier,
she nuzzled into the oozing flesh with her lips and
tongue, rubbing the Swedish girl's huge and erect
clitoris with her nose. The tangy taste of Freda's
copious juices filled her mouth and throat, and
Caroline gulped them down like the ambrosia of
the gods. Freda grunted with pleasure, pressing
herself even more tightly against Caroline's hungry,
sucking mouth and feeling the first delicate shivers of
pre-orgasm begin to ripple through her massive
frame.

Peter was quick to see the possibilities of this new
positioning. Reaching forward, he wrapped his arms
around the Swedish girl's broad back and felt for her
huge breasts, bouncing them up and down like soft
and wonderful toys. A new wave of sensation hit him
with a shock of indescribable pleasure. Fucking the
perfect cunt and fondling the most glorious tits in the
world at the same time was a totally mind-blowing
experience. Revelling in it, Peter fingered Freda's
massive stiff nipples and felt a warm glow of
satisfaction as the big girl shivered with added
pleasure.

It was all too sensual and perfect to last for long. Caroline, with a mouth full of cunt and a cunt full of cock, was already starting to jerk spasmodically as the tremors of orgasm racked her body. Her pleasure waves were transmitted through the encasing walls of her hot hole directly to Peter's throbbing prick and conveyed along its thick shaft to his primed and loaded balls. Freda, being sucked and fondled by two different sexual partners at the same time, was well on her own route to release. The juices were spurting, not trickling, from her voluminous fanny now, gushing out over Caroline's face as she vainly tried to suck down the increasing flow.

As if on some unheard signal, the whole room was suddenly charged with an incredible burst of sexual energy, and the wildly copulating trio climaxed almost simultaneously.

Freda let out a deep and throaty roar as her orgasm exploded like a volcano. Caroline screamed and spluttered as a veritable geyser flow of hot juices sprayed out over her face and neck. Peter groaned as his balls seemed to jump, firing their full charge along the rigid barrel of his weapon only to be immediately repulsed by the liquid onslaught of Caroline's own spectacular climax. The heady, tangy odours of sperm and love-juice suddenly filled the room as each one of the trio shuddered into the final exhaustion of sexual release.

Weakly, Caroline saw fit to voice what they were all feeling. 'Jeezus — that was some fuck,' she murmured, to no one in particular.

The sound of her voice was like a flash of *déjà vu* to Peter. He strained his eyes in the dark, trying to make out the girl's face more clearly.

'Don't I know you?' he enquired tentatively.

Caroline felt a momentary twinge of alarm. She lowered the timbre of her voice, distorting it to a husky growl.

'You bloody well do now,' she said.

As if this was a trigger to release the sexual tension in the room, all three of them suddenly collapsed into helpless laughter.

Chapter Thirteen

The Hadleigh Manor estate looked to be in about the same generally run-down condition as the Paradise Country Club grounds, Amanda reflected as she walked up the long and weed-festooned drive to the house. She noted Giles' scruffy old Land Rover parked outside the main door, and whilst it didn't exactly improve the image, it at least meant that he was probably at home and her journey hadn't been wasted.

Amanda walked up the stone steps and pulled the old-fashioned bell handle. Deep inside the cavernous old building, she heard a faint metallic rattle.

After a few moments, a woman in her mid-thirties opened the door and regarded Amanda suspiciously. With something of a jolt, it occurred to Amanda that she had not asked Giles if he was married, and that the unscheduled visit could prove embarrassing for all concerned. Then the woman spoke, putting her mind at ease.

'I'm Miss Waites, Mr Hadleigh's housekeeper,' she said. 'What can I do for you?'

'I'd like to see Giles, please,' Amanda said.

'And who shall I say is calling?' Miss Waites seemed to look down at Amanda over the bridge of her long, thin nose with something akin to distaste. Something told Amanda that she did not take kindly to attractive young blondes calling on her lord and master, and Amanda wondered if she harboured some forlorn hopes in his direction.

'Just tell him that it's Amanda – from the Paradise,' she said brightly.

Miss Waites' disapproving look became openly hostile. A slight shiver trembled through her angular frame. 'Ugh, that disgusting place,' she muttered. 'And what makes you think young Mr Hadleigh will want to talk to you?'

'Just try him,' Amanda snapped back. Miss Waites' haughty manner was beginning to annoy her.

Miss Waites gave a disdainful toss of her head and flounced off into the recesses of the house. Moments later, Giles appeared, smiling apologetically.

'Sorry, perhaps I should have warned you about Miss Waites. Bit of a dragon, but she does her job efficiently enough. And she's cheap.' His eyes twinkled mischievously. 'Well, it is nice to see you, Amanda. Come for a rematch of our little roll in the hay?'

Amanda grinned. 'Later perhaps. Right now I'd like to ask your advice on something.'

'Of course.' Giles smiled ruefully. 'Just as long as it's not on financial management. I don't seem to be very good at that, I'm afraid. Anyway, do come in.'

He turned into the house, gesturing for Amanda to follow him. Walking through the hallway, she noticed several bare patches on the walls where it was clear that paintings had once hung. Progressing through the house, it was also obvious that most of the furniture had been removed.

Giles noticed the direction of her gaze. 'Yes, just

about everything moveable has already gone, I'm afraid. All except me and the bills.' He turned into a large panelled library which still had an antique chesterfield and a few chairs in it. 'We might as well go in here. It's about the only room left in the house where you can sit down comfortably. It's either that or the master bedroom.'

'Bedroom later,' Amanda reminded him. 'I never did talk sensibly when I'm flat on my back.'

'So, what can I do for you?' Giles asked after they had ensconced themselves on the chesterfield.

Amanda thought for a few seconds, planning out her questions and general line of enquiry. She was still on uncertain ground here, after all. She knew nothing about Giles Hadleigh except that he was a damned good fuck, and she wasn't sure how far to trust him. On the surface, he seemed affable enough, if a little bit vague when it came to financial matters – but that could of course be merely a front. On balance, she decided, there was little to lose by confiding in him completely.

'I wanted to ask you about your dealings with the Drummond Development,' Amanda opened, getting straight to the heart of things. 'I understand they recently bought up several parcels of your land.'

Giles nodded. 'Mmm, probably,' he said vaguely.

'Probably?' Amanda couldn't make up her mind if he was hedging or just being completely thick. 'Don't you know?'

'Well, I did sell some land,' Giles confirmed. 'But to whom, exactly, I couldn't tell you. You know how these operations work . . . parent companies, holding companies, subsidiaries, affiliated companies . . . they're all just names on bits of paper.'

Amanda was not clued up in the ways of corporate managment, but she conceded the point. 'OK, then how about the firm of solicitors who handled the deal? Did you ever have dealings with a Peter Blake?'

Again, Giles looked a trifle blank. He shook his head vaguely. 'Can't say the name rings any bells. Anyway, why are you so interested? Thinking of selling up yourself?'

Amanda hadn't prepared herself to have the interrogation turned round quite so completely. 'No, but why do you ask?' she countered, aware even as she put the question that the whole conversation was getting rather silly.

Giles shrugged carelessly. 'Oh, I just thought that if you were thinking of selling up, I might get a better price for the rest of my land, that's all. It would make sense for a development company to want a single large area rather than lots of bits and pieces, wouldn't it?'

Amanda nodded thoughtfully. 'Yes it would,' she agreed. Gradually, the puzzle was all starting to make a bit of sense, even though Giles wasn't being too helpful. However, she still needed some hard information, and some names.

'So who *did* you actually deal with?' she asked.

'Oh, I didn't actually deal with anybody,' Giles said. 'Miss Waites handled everything. I just signed a few papers, that's all.'

Amanda was both relieved and deflated at the same time. The final piece of information explained why Giles was so vague, and probably cleared him of any suspicion of involvement in any possible plot. On the other hand, it meant that she was not going to get much further in pursuing this particular line of questioning.

'So Miss Waites handles all your personal business,' Amanda queried, changing her tack.

Giles nodded. 'Mmm, more or less.'

'And what else does she handle around here, I wonder,' Amanda murmured suggestively.

Giles was a bit slow catching on. When he did, he laughed dismissively. 'Oh, Good God no. Miss Waites isn't into that sort of thing at all. She's secretary of the local Anti-Vice League, for a start. Thinks your place is a total den of iniquity — like Sodom and Gomorrah rolled into one.'

Amanda laughed. 'Sodom all, I say. You're here today and gone Gomorrah. Might as well have a bit of fun while you can.'

'Admirable sentiments,' Giles agreed enthusiastically. 'And talking about a bit of fun, fancy a trip to the stables?'

Amanda considered the matter. It was quite obvious that she wasn't going to learn much more of any importance. She already had a few more clues to work with, and some new avenues to explore. Miss Waites and her connection with the Anti-Vice League was interesting, for a start. Andrew had mentioned problems with them, beginning soon after Peter Blake had become involved in the management of the Paradise estate. It was definitely something which merited further investigation.

But it could wait. Amanda glanced down at the front of Giles' trousers, already displaying a healthy bulge as he recalled their previous romp. She reached down and stroked her hand over his stiffening cock.

'Why bother with the stables?' she murmured sexily. 'I reckon we can get all the oats we need right here.'

Giles didn't argue. He merely made himself a bit more comfortable in the chesterfield and opened his legs slightly as Amanda's fingers reached the catch on his fly zipper. Amanda licked her lips suggestively. 'Anyway, there was one little thing I didn't quite get around to last night . . . and I wouldn't want to get a bit of straw stuck in my throat.'

She began to inch the zipper down, sliding off the chesterfield at the same time so that she was kneeling in front of him. Glancing up, she flashed him a lascivious leer. 'It's not only a horse which can be a plater, you know.'

Giles let out a slow sigh of anticipation, settling back further into the comfortable upholstery. His eyes were firmly fixed on Amanda's lush, soft lips as his throbbing prick popped out of his trousers.

Outside the room, Miss Waites turned away from the keyhole in disgust. Eavesdropper and busybody she might be, but she was certainly no Peeping Tom. Besides, she had to go and report what she had just heard to that nice respectable Mr Blake.

She missed the slurping, liquid sound of Amanda's hot wet mouth clamping over her employer's rigid love shaft as she began to work on it with her lips and tongue.

It was not a sound she would have recognised anyway, in the manner that Amanda identified the

196

faint noise of soft footsteps creeping away from the door.

She smiled inwardly, the size of the stiff cock in her mouth preventing her lips from curling into the required shape for an outward one. She had had dealings with many Miss Waiteses in the past, and had formed one conclusion. What they all needed was what she had right now — only rammed up their tight and dried up little pussies instead of between their lips.

With that dismissive thought, Amanda wiped Miss Waites from her mind for the time being and concentrated her attention upon Giles' magnificent tool. It was a prick that she could definitely become quite fond of, Amanda thought, as its pulsing length slid into her throat. She crouched lower, tilting her head up so that she could give Giles the full benefit of her deep throat technique. Taking in a deep breath through her nose, she gulped its entire length in and held it there, constricting the muscles of her throat and gullet. She sucked on it until she was choking for more air.

Giles groaned softly as Amanda pulled her head back slowly, allowing the underside of his cock to slide over her waggling tongue. She kissed and licked the swollen purple head for a few seconds, before drawing another deep breath and swallowing it again until her lips were pressed into the wiry bush of his pubic hairs. Giles groaned again, and Amanda felt his prick throb in her throat as he fought with himself to avoid coming there and then.

Amanda guessed that Giles wasn't used to such skilled fellatio, and that he probably couldn't hold out for much longer. Somewhat reluctantly, she let the beautiful tool slide out of her mouth again, planting wet kisses upon its shiny helmet while she struggled out of her clothes.

Finally naked, she stood up and reached out for his hand.

'Now, what were you saying about the master bedroom?' she murmured, pulling him to his feet.

Chapter Fourteen

Phillipe watched Miss Waites scurrying up the club driveway and his heart leapt with love. Miss Waites always affected him like this, whenever he saw her — but it was a deep and all-consuming love, born from mental yearning rather than bodily lust.

For Miss Waites reminded Phillipe of his mother, sadly dead these past ten long years following the tragic accident with his father and the meat cleaver.

Though only nine years old at the time, he remembered his mother with warm affection. Comforting, cosseting images sprang to mind of warm, soft breasts in which she would cradle his head when he was hurt, or confused, or upset by the taunts of the other boys in the village who did not understand his childish simplicity.

She had always been overflowing with love, had his mother. Phillipe recalled how she would stroke and kiss him when she undressed him for bed, invariably bestowing particular affection upon his 'pretty plaything' as she called it. With deep, maternal feeling, she would stroke it until it grew stiff, than cover it with warm kisses, cooing and making strange little gulping noises in her throat as she did so.

She had always told him what a very special plaything it was, and how he must take very great care of it and not let any of those naughty girls in the village try to take it away from him. It was a message which Phillipe had taken very much to heart, growing to physical if not mental adulthood with the knowledge that he had something very precious and wonderful between his legs.

In his childlike, innocent mind, Phillipe would always equate love with the image of his wonderful mother, who had possessed such an overflowing abundance of it. Enough even to bestow on all those French sailors who used to come into the house at nights when his father was working the late shift at the local pig-slaughtering factory.

She had been very protective towards their pretty playthings as well, Phillipe remembered, judging from the exciting things he had seen them doing together in the bedroom as he wandered past on his way to the toilet. Whatever it was that they had been actually doing, it had obviously given his mother much pleasure, if her giggles and little screams of joy were anything to go by. Perhaps one day he could do the same for the wonderful Miss Waites, Phillipe thought. Perhaps the nice young blonde lady he had met the other day would be kind enough to teach him what to do.

Thoughts of his beloved mother had started the familiar sensation of tightness in his trousers. Phillipe unzipped himself and took out his stiffening cock and began to stroke it just as she had done all those years ago. Of course, it was much bigger now, for some unaccountable reason, but playing with it still brought the same warm and wonderful sense of pleasure.

It was a great pity his mother had not lived to see how his pretty plaything had grown. Phillipe was sure that she would have been proud of it, just as he was. If only his father had not had the terrible accident with the meat cleaver on the night he came home from work early. Phillipe was sure that he had not meant to bury it in the top of his mother's head, any more than he had meant to chop off the sailor's pretty plaything. He had never been fully able to understand why the policemen had taken his father away, or why he had come to England to stay with his Uncle Norville.

Miss Waites was halfway up the drive now, on her way to the house. Phillipe could contain his bounding love no longer. Jumping out from behind his azalea bush, cock in hand, he waved to her, smiling warmly. For some strange reason, Miss Waites let out a scream, and began to run wildly towards the house. Puzzled, Phillipe crept back behind his bush and started to daydream about his mother once again.

Miss Waites was about to run up the front steps when Peter Blake emerged through the front door, looking around agitatedly.

'Ah, Miss Waites,' he said, recognising her. 'I suppose you haven't seen a very attractive dark-haired girl around here, have you?'

Peter was slightly confused. One minute he had been laying in post-coital stupor with the most exciting woman he had ever met in his life, and the next she had snatched up her clothes and made a run for it.

Miss Waites collapsed on the steps at his feet, clutching his trouser legs and babbling incoherently.

'Mr Blake . . . save me, I beg of you. I'm being chased by some horribly deformed pervert.'

Cursing under his breath at the untimely and unwanted distraction, Peter bent down and helped the distraught woman to her feet. She had obviously seen the Phantom Wanker, he realised. He cast one last hopeful glance around the grounds for a glimpse of Caroline before giving her his undivided attention.

'You'd better come into the house,' he said, supporting her up the last few steps and ushering her in through the doorway. The passion of his life would have to wait. Meanwhile, it wouldn't do any harm at all to ingratiate himself a bit more with Miss Waites and her Anti-Vice cronies. The way things were looking with Amanda, he was going to need their help. And soon!

Caroline peered over the top of the bar in the evening lounge as Peter Blake escorted the strange woman through the reception hall. Satisfied that they weren't coming in, she ducked down again and hastily finished dressing. It was now utterly imperative that she avoided him for the rest of the day. She could only hope that he would not be staying the night, for Caroline was rather looking forward to sampling some other delights of the Paradise Club over the coming weekend — and it would make things awkward if she was hiding out from Peter all the time.

She had just finished adjusting her clothing when Andrew appeared up out of the cellar. Caroline recognised him at once as the lunatic who indulged in penile pyrotechnics and groaned softly under her breath. Out of the fat into the fire, she thought, quite unaware of the unintentional pun.

Just at that minute, she didn't want to be too close to any man, let alone one who took his pecker out in public and then tried to barbecue it on pub counters. Caroline had a lot to think about − most of it to do with the male species and whether she was doomed to spend the rest of her life getting shafted at five minute intervals. So, rather than hang around to find out her own reaction to an almost inevitable proposition, she decided to make a break for it. The delighted smile on Andrew's face faded quickly as she gave him a brief wave and headed for the door.

He watched her disappear with great disappointment. He had been hoping to show her the latest results of his unique brand of amateur photography, having just developed and printed a fresh batch of prints in the cellar. He waved the still wet print in his hand after her departing back, but it was too late. Sadly, Andrew lay the print flat on the counter and appraised it. It was not a bad picture at all, he thought, considering the difficult circumstances under which it had been taken.

Not even Sally knew that Andrew had put in a whole series of peep-holes in key rooms around the club through which he practised his own version of candid camera. It was his secret hobby, which he had managed to keep from her for over five years, recording the many and varied sexual exploits of the guests and developing them in his carefully hidden darkroom in the building's cavernous cellars.

Of all his little vantage points, Andrew regarded the spyhole into the massage room as his favourite. Over the years, he had built up a portfolio of photographs which would have brought tears to the eyes of any serious porno collector. Equally, it was a collection which would have brought his instant death and dismemberment had the formidable Freda ever laid eyes on it.

However, Freda did not star in this latest shot, which he had taken only that morning. Due to the odd angle of the spy-hole, the pictures had just caught the naked Caroline laid out on the bed whilst in the background, Peter Blake advanced towards her with a stiff prick sticking out of the front of his trousers. Again due to the strange angle of the shot, the photograph made it look as though Caroline was somehow strapped down on the bed like a sacrificial victim, with Peter as her evil sexual torturer.

There would have been other photographs, since the camera was set on automatic exposure, but for some strange reason the lighting had suddenly failed. However, Andrew was more than pleased with his single print, since it showed off Caroline's excellent little body to perfection.

Which was why he had thought she might appreciate an enlargement as a souvenir of her visit.

'Andrew − are you in the bar?' Sally's voice called out from the reception area.

Hastily, Andrew snatched up the photograph and slid it under the till seconds before his wife came in to give him his orders for the rest of the morning.

Outside in the grounds, Caroline figured that she

needed to get as far away as possible from the house
for at least a couple of hours. Then, hopefully, Peter
would have concluded whatever business he had
planned and returned to London. The trouble was,
what was she going to do to fill in the time? Suddenly
she remembered someone mentioning a riding
stables. A brisk canter around the countryside
seemed an excellent solution to the problem, she
thought, and set off in the general direction of the
Hadleigh estate.

Half-way down the drive, Caroline spotted
Phillipe peering out from behind his azalea bush just
as he first laid eyes on her. Remembering from her
arrival the previous day that her present route would
take her right by what appeared to be his favourite
lurking place, Caroline hesitated in her stride. She
wasn't sure what to do for the best. Certainly, in the
light of everything which had happened in the last
few hours, Phillipe didn't seem to represent quite the
same threat — but Caroline wasn't quite convinced
that her new-found sexual expertise and experience
qualified her to cope with dim-witted flashers with
monstrously oversized pricks.

She looked around for potential avenues of escape,
and saw Amanda cutting across the grass from the
Hadleigh Manor grounds, on a path which would
intercept hers if she deviated from her present course
down the driveway.

Caroline tried to think, quickly, about the
consequences of bumping into Amanda. Having
been so eager to team her up with Peter, it was likely
that Amanda would again suggest that they could get
together, and might even insist on accompanying her

into the house to make the necessary introductions, unaware that they had already met each other under the most intimate circumstances imaginable. And that could be a problem!

On the other hand, she could head in Phillipe's direction and hope that Amanda would assume a tryst and discreetly leave them alone. On balance, that seemed the best option. Caroline resumed her original course, striding out a little more quickly.

Phillipe watched the approaching woman with great interest, trying to fit this newcomer into the general scheme of things. She didn't look remotely like Miss Waites or his departed mother, and so would probably have no interest in his pretty plaything. On the other hand, she could turn out to be like the naughty village girls his dear mother had warned him about all those years ago.

So he too looked around for a means of escape — and spotted Amanda coming across the grass in his general direction. Phillipe was suddenly very confused. He wasn't used to conflicting desires, his life usually being utterly simple and basic. Yet now he had a complex problem to work out and a choice of decisions to make. He really wanted to meet the nice blonde-haired lady again so that she could teach him all the nice things to do to Miss Waites with his pretty plaything. But the dark haired village girl could get to him first, and make him do things which would upset his mother and Miss Waites. Of course, he could always run away from both of them and seek sanctuary in the privacy of the potting sheds — but then he might never learn the secret of all those jumping and thrusting and wrestling things which had given so much pleasure to his mother. It was all far too complicated for his childlike mind to cope with.

Amanda had already changed her direction slightly when she recognised Caroline's long dark tresses. Having found out little from Giles, other than confirmation that he was one of the sexiest men she had ever known, there remained the slight mystery of this attractive stranger who was apparently using a false name and didn't seem to fit into the normal run of Paradise customers. So, having failed to solve one puzzle, she might at least get a chance to shed further light on another. She waved, cheerily in Caroline's direction and speeded up her pace of approach.

Caroline, in turn, hurried up her own footsteps towards the azalea bush, as Phillipe cowered behind it, frozen with indecision. The option of making a run for it was becoming more and more attractive. He rose from his crouching position, assuming the stance of an Olympic sprinter on the starting blocks.

Amanda saw his head pop up from behind the azalea bush and noted Caroline's purposeful stride in his direction. A sudden panic seized her at the dreaded thought that Caroline could get to that wonderful cock before she did. She broke into a loping trot in Phillipe's direction.

It was the straw which broke the camel's back for the totally confused young man. Phillipe took off like a startled rabbit, heading for his safe bolt-hole in the potting sheds. Caroline, caught in the awkward position of obviously hurrying in his direction, had little choice but to scurry after him. Amanda, now convinced that this raven-haired interloper was intent on plundering her personal treasure hoard, broke into full pelt in pursuit of them both.

'And so I can only assure you, Miss Waites, that I fully agree with you about the disgusting things which go on around here,' Peter Blake said, as he showed Miss Waites out of the front door. 'And, as you say, it is high time that someone did something about it. You can count on my full support for any measures you think fit to get this terrible place closed down as soon as possible.'

Miss Waites smiled with inner satisfaction. She had been right to bring her information to the pleasant Mr Blake, and she was convinced that she now had his full moral support in her fight against this den of vice and licentiousness. He had left her in no doubts that he too was doing everything in his power to bring about its immediate closure.

'The main thing is that we protect the young squire from being caught up in any scandal,' she reminded Peter as she prepared to depart. 'Heaven knows how dear Giles allowed himself to be talked into this Hunt Ball idea, but it must not be allowed to happen. I dread to think what sort of disgusting orgy it would turn into.'

'Oh, indeed, indeed,' Peter agreed, pursing his lips into a faked look of disapproval. He was equally pleased with the results of their discussions. With the help of Miss Waites, and the full backing of her formidable Anti-Vice League colleagues, killing off the Paradise Country Club should now be a cinch, despite any plans which Amanda might come up with.

Peter's total hypocrisy didn't bother him at all. This was business, and personal feelings didn't enter into it.

He shook Miss Waites' hand firmly, escorting her over the threshold to the top of the steps. The morning's business concluded, Miss Waites turned to walk down the steps — just in time to see a young man with his huge penis hanging out of his trousers race across her field of vision, avidly pursued by two wildly excited women.

It was too much. Miss Waites felt her legs go weak underneath her. A fuzzy red haze swam in front of her eyes. A hot flush spread over her whole body as everything seemed to go blank.

Peter caught her rather neatly as she swooned, scooping her up in his arms. He wondered, dimly, why Amanda and his newly found beloved were chasing the Phantom Wanker across the grass.

Amanda, glancing towards the house as she ran at that precise moment, wondered why Peter Blake was cuddling Miss Waites on the front steps.

However, for the moment, that was unimportant. She switched her full attention back to the chase.

Chapter Fifteen

For Cedric Drummond, managing director of the Drummond Development Corporation, it has been a thoroughly lousy morning.

It had started badly with a transatlantic phone call at 5.00 am, informing him that his potential US backers on the theme park project wanted to suddenly advance their schedule by several weeks. It had got worse following his own phone call to Peter Blake, when he had learned that the full acquisition of the Paradise Country Club was not going quite so smoothly as planned. And it had become a positive nightmare after the second transatlantic phone call telling him that a top American executive was now flying in to talk some hard business on the afternoon Concorde.

Cedric was fuming. If there was one thing he hated more than working on Saturday mornings, it was American business executives. He hated them for their brashness, their constant hurry, their insistence that all problems were only minor and temporary ones, and their infuriating habit of making phone calls without checking what the time zone was at the receiving end.

However, he did not dislike their money – which was why he had agreed to pick up one Randy Brandich III at Heathrow airport and drive him

211

down to the club for a first-hand appraisal of the site.

Committed, he summoned his housekeeper to make the necessary arrangements.

'Ah, Mrs Beddowes. Can you tell the chauffeur to get the Rolls ready for two o'clock. We'll be driving down to Heathrow to pick up a passenger and then on down to Hampshire. Oh, and can you ask my daughter to come and see me?'

Mrs Beddowes coughed nervously. She knew from experience when he was in a bad mood, and what she had to tell him would not improve it any.

'I'm sorry, Mr Drummond, but Miss Caroline is not in her room. As far as I can see, she hasn't been home since the other night when you and Mrs Drummond went to the fund-raising party.'

Cedric scowled. 'What do you mean, she hasn't been home? Just where the hell is she?' he demanded.

Mrs Beddowes smiled apologetically. 'I'm sorry, but I have no idea.' She began to back out of the room. 'I'll go and give the chauffeur your message.'

Cedric paced up and down the room a few times, his general bad temper getting worse by the second. The fact that his daughter had stayed out was not in itself particularly annoying. She was an adult, after all. What was really infuriating was the fact that she wasn't available when he needed her. He had been planning to take Caroline with him, hoping that her feminine charms could take some of the heat off. Assuming that Randy Brandich III was the virile, manly and thoroughly all round nice-guy type of American rather than the limp-wristed arty variety, Caroline might have been able to give him a topic of conversation other than business on the drive down to Hampshire. Equally, she would have come in useful as a means of getting Peter Blake safely out of the way if need be once they got there.

He wondered, momentarily, where she actually was and what she was doing. Had he known, Cedric's mood would not have been improved in the slightest.

Phillipe reached the imagined safety of the potting sheds with a few yards to spare. Scurrying inside, he dived for the darkest corner and crouched in the shadows, hoping that his pursuers would leave him alone once they realised that he had gone to earth.

He hoped in vain. Caroline charged in, with Amanda close on her heels. The impetus of Caroline's high speed entry into the confined space of the shed took her almost its full length before she stopped dead, suddenly aware that there was nowhere else to run. Amanda, rushing in behind her, was also ill equipped to make an emergency stop. The two women collided heavily, the force of their impact taking them both the last few feet into the corner where Phillipe lay, shivering. They collapsed together, virtually on top of him.

Several moments passed before either girl got her breath back. Sheepishly, they both reviewed their rather ridiculous situation.

Caroline managed to speak first. 'Why were you chasing me?' she asked Amanda.

The question rather threw Amanda for a moment. Thinking about it, there really wasn't an adequate answer which sprang readily to mind. Instead, she went on the defensive, posing a question of her own. 'Why were you chasing Phillipe?' she demanded.

Caroline looked blank. 'I wasn't chasing anybody.'

'So why were you running?'

'Because you were chasing me. Why were you chasing me?'

'Because you were running. Why were you chasing after Phillipe?'

'Because you started to chase me. And what has Phillipe got to do with it, anyway?'

Amanda started to get the oddest feeling that reality had suddenly turned out to be nothing more than a tape recording which for some reason had got stuck and was now repeating itself endlessly. 'Do you think we ought to start again?'

'Good idea,' Caroline said. 'So — why were you chasing me?'

Amanda groaned, trying another approach. 'What's going on between you and Phillipe?'

'Nothing, I've never even met the guy,' Caroline said honestly.

'Then why were you chasing him?' Amanda asked, realising even as she spoke that she had managed to put them both straight back on to the endless loop.

Both women fell silent for several moments. In the silence, they both became aware of Phillipe making strange whimpering noises underneath them. Caroline realised that she was sitting on his stomach. Amanda realised that she was sprawled with one leg across his throat and, apart from being half choked to death, the poor lad was utterly terrified.

They both moved hurriedly, allowing Phillipe to struggle up to a half-sitting position in the corner, where he grasped his erect phallus defensively and began to croon a soft French lullaby to it.

'So what's your interest in Phillipe?' Caroline asked at length. 'And who is he anyway?'

'Phillipe is our gardener,' Amanda said, answering the second part of the question first. 'And as for my interest, take a wild guess.'

Caroline followed Amanda's rather pointed stare down to its focal point, suddenly falling in. 'Ah, I see what you mean,' she murmured. 'Private territory, is it?'

'Too private,' Amanda confirmed. 'As far as I've been able to establish, it's totally virgin territory.'

Suddenly, Caroline understood completely. She began to grin knowingly. 'And you thought I was trying to get there before you?'

Amanda nodded. 'That's why I chased after you. I've had my eye on that beautiful cock for the last three days. Damned if I was going to let someone else beat me to it.'

Caroline glanced back at Phillipe, who had now grasped his huge prick between both hands and was rubbing it up and down with long, slow strokes. She turned back to Amanda. 'If you don't take your chance while you can, it looks like Phillipe is going to beat you to it himself.'

Amanda flashed the other girl a warning look. 'Don't even think of sharing.'

Caroline shook her head with a smile. 'Amanda, believe me. I've already had more than my share this

215

morning. I'm quite happy to sit this one out, thank you. Only I'll just rest here and watch for a moment, if that's all right with you.'

Amanda thought about it. 'Just look — not touch?' she questioned.

Caroline crossed two fingers. 'Word of honour. I'd leave you both in peace, but I'm trying to hide away from Peter Blake.'

The thought did occur to Amanda to ask why she should be hiding from someone she had supposedly never met, but there were more pressing matters to attend to. The first important thing was to pacify the obviously disturbed Phillipe and get his confidence again.

She nudged Caroline in the ribs, indicating for her to move away to allow a bit of manoeuvring space. As Caroline shifted herself a few feet to the left, Amanda sidled up alongside Phillipe and put her arm gently around his shoulder in a sisterly embrace. Hugging him to her, she began to talk softly and comfortingly to him, even though she wasn't sure if he could understand her words.

'It's me, Phillipe . . . remember? I was showing you all the nice things a boy can do with a girl.'

Amanda felt the lad's tension ebb away from his tightly bunched muscles as he visibly relaxed in her embrace. Phillipe looked up at her, and the fear in his eyes seeped away as he did remember. Everything was all right again, he realised. The nice blonde lady wasn't angry with him, and her dark-haired friend was harmless. And more importantly, he was going to learn how to make Miss Waites laugh, and giggle, and make all those funny pleasure noises in her throat when he played his mother's favourite games with her.

A warm and delicious feeling crept through his whole body as he also remembered the moist heat of the blonde lady's body underneath her skirt. His fingers itched to feel that secret place again, to probe that wonderful soft and slidy and liquid entrance which sucked, and squeezed, and melted under his touch with such exquisite gentleness.

Phillipe remembered it all, and a gush of love and gratitude surged within him as he realised that the nice blonde lady was offering him a second chance. Slowly, he let one hand drop from his pretty plaything on to her lap, his fingertips thrilling to the shiny feel of the thin material of her skirt, and the warmth of the body heat beneath it.

Amanda smiled inwardly at the gentle touch of the boy's hand. She remained still, continuing to hug him. It was up to Phillipe to make the moves now, she realised. She had to let him choose his own pace, discover his own adult sexuality for himself. There was very little wrong with Phillipe, she was sure. Perhaps he wasn't an Albert Einstein, but then he wasn't some helpless mental retard either. He was just a lonely young man who had crossed the line between adolescence and adulthood without a guide, and had been languishing in a strange and foreign place without any sense of direction. Something bad had happened to him, Amanda sensed. Something which had made him feel desperately shy and alone, and vulnerable. People had just dismissed him as an idiot, when all he really needed was love, and understanding, and tenderness.

Phillipe felt a growing sense of pride and power within himself. The pretty blonde lady was not going to laugh at him, or run away from him. The feel of her arm around his shoulder gave him a strange sense of comfort and reassurance, which although an unfamiliar sensation, seemed at the same time oddly right — like something which should always have been so.

There were other, even stranger ideas crowding within him. Phillipe found images forming inside his mind — images which at first made no sense at all and then all the sense in the world. He was crawling out of a long, dark tunnel towards light — and although he had never realised that he was in a tunnel before, somehow he had always known about the light.

He pressed himself against Amanda's body, seeking to merge with her warmth, melt into her flesh. He felt his hand move across her soft thigh as though of its own volition as his fingers led the way along a path they already knew.

Amanda felt the new sense of purpose in his touch, and sensed the dramatic changes which were taking place. She dropped her hand on to his, squeezing it gently, to show him that she understood.

Phillipe's fingers curled upwards to intertwine with hers for a moment, returning the gesture of understanding. Then his hand pulled away from hers, alive with a new strength and knowledge.

Amanda felt a shiver of anticipation ripple through her body at the new urgency of Phillipe's touch. The hand gently stroking her thigh was the hand of a man responding to the feel of a woman.

She spread her legs as Phillipe's fingers slid down her skirt, curling under the hem of the material to find the warm flesh beneath.

Phillipe leaned over towards her, and Amanda turned her face to meet his. Their eyes shared a very special moment of tenderness and understanding as, clumsily but gently, his lips pressed upon hers. Amanda let the crude attempt at a kiss linger for a while before responding. Then, parting her lips slightly, she edged out the very tip of her warm, wet tongue and let it slide between Phillipe's tightly pursed lips, prising them apart.

Phillipe caught on with surprising speed. His own tongue snaked out, gliding smoothly into her mouth to lick the underside of her soft lips before probing between her teeth and thrusting deep into her mouth. Their tongues met and clashed, winding around each other like a pair of copulating vipers.

Emboldened by his success with the kiss, and aware of the surge of strange passion rising within him, Phillipe plunged his hand under Amanda's skirt and pulled it up to her belly. His fingers returned to the search for that magical soft place, sliding around the warm softness of her thigh and into the hot valley of her crotch.

Amanda sighed deeply, opening her thighs even wider as she felt Phillipe's fingers encounter her springy bush and begin to stroke the mass of curly blonde hairs. She felt the prickling, bubbling sensations of her own vaginal secretions as her hot cunt sent urgent messages to her glands, urging them to lubricate every inch of her yawning shaft with the welcoming juices of love.

Phillipe's questing fingers found the shallow cleft of her labia and travelled down it, over the hillock of her clitoris and towards the mouth of the deep valley beyond.

Amanda groaned as his fingers thrust into her, sliding wetly into her inner depths. She rolled her buttocks in a gentle, grinding motion, spreading her hot juices over his stiff fingers and feeling the hardness of his palm pressed against her throbbing clit. She was gushing like a hot geyser now, her juices spurting past the obstruction of his two fingers and trickling wetly down her thighs.

Satisfied that Phillipe was doing a more than adequate job in preparing her cunt, Amanda turned her attention to the massive and beautiful cock which was to fill it. Phillipe's hand dropped away from the thick, pulsing shaft as Amanda's hand dropped lightly on to his lap and her fingers began to creep around the line of his trouser waistband, tugging gently but insistently. He snapped open the top fastening and unbuckled his belt to help her, remembering that the French sailors had always had their trousers down around their ankles. He wriggled helpfully as Amanda inched his trousers over his hips and then pulled his underpants down to join them.

Phillipe was surging with excitement. It was all looking so good, feeling so absolutely right. For a moment he felt terribly guilty about his secret – that all this learning and experience was really for Miss Waites – but then he took comfort from Amanda's continued hugging and realised that she was giving her help willingly and demanding nothing more from him than his cooperation. Eager to do everything just right, he kicked his legs until his trousers lay in a crumpled heap at his feet.

Amanda's hand dropped to the left of his thighs, cupping gently around the soft, leathery sac of his bulging scrotum. She tickled the underside of his huge balls, lifting each one in turn with her fingertips as though weighing them, assessing their ripeness. Then her hand moved upwards, stroking across their swelling roundness to grasp the thick base of his pretty plaything.

Amanda shuddered with pleasure as her fingers wrapped themselves around the warm and gently pulsing column of Phillipe's magnificent prick. She marvelled at its size and stiffness, acutely aware that she had never before in her life handled a cock which her fingers could not completely encompass. The mighty rod of flesh quivered under her touch as she slid her hand slowly up and down its incredible length, her fingers tracing out the throbbing, knobbly and snakelike veins which pulsed beneath the skin. Even as she stroked it, the wonderful weapon seemed to stretch and stiffen even more, the warm skin becoming tauter and more smooth as it was stretched tight against the rocklike shaft.

The faintest note of worry sounded inside her brain. Would she be able to get such a monstrous cock inside her without her belly splitting open? How would Phillipe react once his latent sexuality was fully released? Amanda was suddenly aware that she might be taking on more than she had bargained for.

As if confirming her thoughts, she heard Caroline's voice murmur softly from a few feet away.

'That really is one hell of a prick, Amanda. Are you sure you can handle it on your own?' she said, with the faintest hint of envy.

'You promised — look but not touch,' Amanda reminded her, hissing out of the corner of her mouth.

'All right, I won't say another word.' Caroline lapsed into a sullen silence.

Amanda returned her full attention to Phillipe's mighty member, sliding her hand to the very top of the rigid and quivering shaft and cupping the hot and shiny smooth head in her fist like a rubber ball. She squeezed it gently, noting the pearly bubble of seminal fluid which oozed out of the tight little slit. Using the tip of one finger, Amanda smeared its slimy stickiness around the circumference of the bulging helmet until it glistened dully in the shadowy light.

She detached her arm from Phillipe's shoulder and scrambled to her knees, straddling his bare legs. Phillipe's fingers popped out of her sopping cunt, letting a small gush of hot juice spurt out to run down her creamy thighs. Edging forward, Amanda rubbed the mouth of the dripping organ against the base of Phillipe's proud ramrod, rising on her knees to smear her slimy secretions up its formidable length.

It was show time. Amanda rose to a crouch, grasping the stiff love machine and guiding it towards the open and hungry mouth of her hairy slit. Settling the bulbous head into the hot cleft between her thick and blood-engorged labial lips, she lowered herself gently until she could feel the pressure of the blunt shaft against the vaginal muscles.

Another moment of near-panic swept over her as she realised the the bull-like cock was not going to slip easily into her tight orifice. It was like trying to fit an oversized cork into a bottle neck, she thought, as she thrust down harder and felt increasing resistance.

Then, magically, the throbbing head popped between her wet lips and was easing its way into her well-lubricated shaft. Amanda spread her knees wider, thrusting her pelvis forward to stretch her cunt as widely open as possible. Gingerly, she began to lower herself on to the flesh spike, feeling a delicious shudder of excitement as it slid into her inch by wonderful inch.

Still several inches short of full penetration, Amanda felt the great knob pressing against the restriction of her cervix, and felt like sobbing with frustration. To have found such a magnificent cock, only to be cheated of enjoying its full majesty, seemed a particularly cruel trick of fate. She tried flexing her knees again, sliding up from the thickest part of the fleshy column to its slightly more tapered tip.

She held her position for a few seconds, savouring the sensation of the thick plug filling the very mouth of her hole and throbbing erratically against the stiff button of her clitoris. Then, with a recklessness born of her earlier frustration, Amanda collapsed upon the full and frightening length of Phillipe's giant cock, impaling herself like a sacrificial virgin. As the mighty muscle tore into her, Amanda was beyond any thoughts of pain or even internal damage. All she knew was that she had to consume this god-like tool in its entirety, swallow it whole into the aching chasm of her own body.

The pulsing rod slammed into her, filling her very belly until she thought she would burst. Then Phillipe's cock was part of her, and she was part of it. Two individuals had melted and merged into a fused mass of flesh with no real consciousness but a single, totally driving purpose.

Amanda grunted as the fat, wet lips of her cunt slapped against Phillipe's belly with a liquid smacking sound. She felt him buck beneath her like an unbroken stallion, fighting not so much to unseat its rider as to demonstrate its superior animal strength and power. She opened her mouth to scream as Phillipe thrust upward, but only guttural, animal-like gasps passed across her lips. As if bent on some wild and self-destructive urge, she matched each one of his pelvic thrusts with a violent lunge of her own, trying to surrender what was left of her body to the violent and raging beast which was devouring her.

She rode the pulsating pole like a demented monkey on a stick, sliding up and down on its gleaming length on a virtual torrent of hot juice. Again and again she felt it plunge into her very womb and beyond until she felt she had nothing else inside her. No gut, no intestines, no kidneys or liver or lungs or heart. She was just a bag of flesh which was completely and utterly filled with hot, steaming cock.

There were no early warning signs of orgasm. No plateaus, no shuddering waves of sensation, no mounting ripples of pleasure. Amanda didn't come, she erupted. Like a star bursting into supernova, she exploded over Phillipe's prick in a single, all-powerful burst of pure energy which seemed to spring, fully charged and all-consuming, from somewhere deep inside her.

Her cunt poured juice like a burst watermelon. Her very blood seemed to boil in her veins and evaporate out through the pores of her flesh. The very life which sustained her most basic bodily functions seemed to be sucked up and swallowed by the incredible burst of energy and washed away, leaving her drained and empty.

Amanda collapsed on top of Phillipe, fearing that she no longer had the power to draw breath, or that her heart was too weak to pump her vital and life-giving blood through her veins ever again.

Phillipe felt the boiling torrent of her love-juice on his sensitive organ, still rock-hard and rigid inside her. The thrilling shock of it seemed to blast the last cobwebs of fuzzy thought from his mind, and suddenly he remembered clearly what he had seen on those nights he had spent outside his mother's bedroom door, aching for love.

And, in a flash of deep and penetrating insight, he realised that his mother too had ached for love in her own way . . . and how she had found it.

A vivid mental picture of his mother writhing beneath the heaving buttocks of the sailors flashed into his mind like a photograph. Reaching up to Amanda, he lifted her by the hips and rolled her on to her back, crawling on top of her. His cock was still wedged firmly in her tight and fluttering vaginal passage. With love and tenderness welling in him, Phillipe began to fuck her with surprising gentleness, sliding his huge cock in and out of her oozing cunt with long, slow strokes as he buried his mouth in the small of her throat and kissed her neck repeatedly.

Amanda groaned with pure pleasure as the hot shaft filled her again, seeming to pump back some of the energy and life force which the violence of her orgasm had drained away. She felt the gentle power of a complete man surging inside her, and thrilled to the knowledge of what she had achieved. Gazing deeply into Phillipe's gently smiling eyes, she saw the new light of understanding which danced in them, and she knew that for him, there would never be any going back.

Phillipe's heart fluttered with joy as he saw and felt Amanda's pleasure. He was learning fast now, noting how her body quivered with excitement when he speeded up his thrusts and how she trembled with anticipation when he slowed down. His hips began to pump in a regular, thrusting cadence and he adjusted himself to her rhythm and needs. He kissed her hot mouth between pants for breath, blew gently into her hair when she looked feverish, and wiped the perspiration from her forehead with a gentle, featherlight touch of his fingertips.

He felt her body writhe beneath him as she squirmed her hips upwards from the floor, eager to swallow his whole length again. Phillipe lifted himself on his elbows, and, speeding up his tempo, began to thrust into her with short, rapid, teasing strokes. Amanda whimpered, grinding her pelvis up against his and reaching up to dig her sharp fingernails into the soft cheeks of his arse.

'Come on you beautiful bugger,' she hissed out between gasps for breath. 'Give me all of it. Pump that lovely cock of yours in as deep as it will go.'

Even though he didn't understand all the words, Phillipe got the message. Drawing his cock out until only the knobbly head was still inside her, he paused momentarily before plunging back in like a steam piston, burying his thick shaft up to his balls.

Amanda shrieked with pleasure. 'Yes, that's it,' she cried happily. 'Again.'

Philippe let himself go, pumping and thrusting into her cunt like an out-of-control machine. Each shuddering stroke evinced a wet, slurping squelch from Amanda's foaming crack and a low moan from her hot lips. Her breathing was becoming more erratic now, and Phillipe could feel her fingernails raking his buttocks as she clawed at him in feverish excitement. The old familiar tingle of pleasure was now rippling through his own body, although it seemed more urgent and intense than when he played with himself.

Caroline had watched it all with mounting excitement, feeling her cunt become hot, then moist and finally a soaking, steaming tropical valley. So far, she had been as good as her word to stay out of things completely, but now she could take no more.

'Look but not touch, eh?' she muttered to herself. 'Well, I guess that only meant Phillipe's cock. I didn't say anything about his mouth.'

Jumping to her feet, she tore at the fastening of her skirt and slipped it to the ground, pulling off her damp panties. With a couple of eager, bounding steps, she was standing over Amanda's head, facing Phillipe. She thrust out her hips provocatively, fingering her wet slit. 'You look hot,' she murmured to Phillipe. 'Fancy some refreshment?'

Another flash of memory surfaced in Phillipe's feverish mind. Another mental picture of his mother spreadeagled on the bed with her white, fleshy thighs open and the curly black head of a kneeling sailor bobbing up and down between them. He rose on to his hands and knees like a dog, lifting his head until Caroline's dripping honeypot was inches from his face.

Caroline grinned with satisfaction. She edged forwards, dropping both hands to her cunt to pull the fleshy lips apart, exposing the pink, stiff bud of her twitching clit.

Still pumping furiously away into Amanda's hungry hole, Phillipe buried his mouth into another succulent cunt, licking and sucking at the tangy juices of Caroline's lush young body. Again, instinct quickly took over from lack of experience. At first, Phillipe sucked the whole of Caroline's cunt into his hot mouth like some juicy peach, nibbling and sucking at the ripe flesh like a starving man. Then, he pulled his head back slightly, extending a firm, stiff tongue to lap up and down the oozing crack.

Caroline gurgled with delight, rocking herself backwards and forwards so that Phillipe's tongue could probe deeper inside her. The young man caught on fast, curling his tongue into a stiff tube and waggling it about from side to side as Caroline thrust herself on to it.

Caroline's love-juice began to flow copiously as Phillipe's tongue reamed her, dripping down on to Amanda's face and open, gasping mouth. Amanda was past caring. She merely sucked in and swallowed as the pungent liquid filled her mouth, accepting it as a simple by-product of the incredible fucking she was receiving from Phillipe. His beautiful cock inside her was the only thing that really mattered. She had that, and Caroline was more than welcome to any minor pleasure that was left over.

Phillipe was delirious with joy. He seemed to have learned more in the past fifteen minutes than he had in his entire life. And with not just one, but two beautiful teachers. The fact that he was also discovering the most amazingly exciting physical pleasure was something of a bonus. Miss Waites was going to be very, very pleased indeed!

He continued fucking and sucking with the zeal of a university graduate swotting up for final exams. And as far as Amanda and Caroline were concerned, well on target for graduation with honours.

Amanda's second orgasm was fast approaching as his mighty, meaty fucking machine plunged in and out of her pulsating pussy. She rode the first shuddering spasms like a rollercoaster, her heart pounding with excitement as she mounted each rising wave then thundering into adrenaline-boosted acceleration as her body hovered on the plateau of sensation before diving into a new trough of stomach-churning sensation.

Caroline could hear the sloshing of his huge organ as it churned in Amanda's wet cunt, and the sound alone was nearly enough to bring her to her own peak. With Phillipe's tongue and lips working on her own hot crack, she was more than satisfied with the bodily pleasure she was receiving. Despite her appreciation of Phillipe's admirable weapon, she did not begrudge her companion getting its full benefit — or not for the present, anyway. She had already made up her mind that she would receive her share of that particular cock in the very near future, when Amanda was not around.

Phillipe felt Amanda's body shudder beneath him as the second wave of orgasm racked through her. Her cunt tightened on his cock like a clamp, squeezing it with little pulsing spasms as if to milk out its precious juices. He felt his balls quiver with anticipation at the sensation, urging their leader to give way, allow them to fire off their overcharged load.

The milking sensation ceased abruptly as Amanda's cunt gushed another hot spurt of come and then went flaccid and receptive once again. Phillipe found a last burst of energy and pumped into her with renewed vigour, slamming his cock in so hard and deep that his heavy balls slapped against the base of her fanny, wet and sticky with the slimy fluids that were spurting from it. A tremor ran through his loins, his cock burned as though it was on fire, and his head began to pound to the beat of a thousand jungle drums. He pressed his head forward, burying his tongue deep into Caroline's cunt and nuzzling the soft, hot lips with his lips as the tremor turned into an earthquake, rocking his whole body from the tips of his toes to his hair follicles. With a mighty roar, he plunged into Amanda one last time and let go.

Amanda felt the force of his discharge deep inside her belly and thrust against it, just as her own secondary orgasm broke within her. In a liquid flood, sperm and love-juice clashed like two surging waves, melting and mingling into one another. Her own triumphant scream was like a descant to his bass, with Caroline's fluttering soprano of satisfaction an incidental accompaniment to the orgasmic concerto.

Chapter Sixteen

'So why were you trying to hide from Peter Blake?'
Amanda asked as she and Caroline walked away
from the potting sheds. It seemed as good a time as
any to get at least one of the current mysteries sorted
out.

Caroline looked a little sheepish. She felt
embarrassed for all the subterfuge and disguise, but
there really didn't seem to be any further point in
keeping up pretences as far as Amanda was
concerned. Having just shared such an intimate
experience, they were now virtually sisters under the
skin – and Caroline felt drawn to Amanda's openess
and total lack of inhibition. It was an attitude to life
that she wished she could have had a lot earlier.

'I suppose I'd better tell you everything,' Caroline
said finally.

'What a good idea,' Amanda agreed, with the
faintest hint of sarcasm in her voice. She fell silent,
waiting for Caroline's revelations.

'Well, my name's not Fay, for a start,' Caroline
said, letting her defences down completely. 'It's
Caroline . . . Caroline Drummond. And Peter Blake
is – or was my fiancé.'

Amanda stopped dead in her tracks. 'Drummond?
Any connection with the Drummond Development,
by any chance?'

Caroline nodded. 'That's my father's company. Peter sometimes works for him. And I think they both have some sort of interest in this place, although I'm not sure what. That's why I came down here in disguise − to find out what's going on, and to find out what was going on between you and Peter.'

Amanda digested the information carefully. It still left a lot of loose ends but at least she finally had the proof that Peter Blake was up to something, and it was probably something underhand. She probed for a little more hard information.

'You don't seem terribly clear about the state of the engagment between you and Peter. Is it on, is it off . . . what?'

Caroline shrugged. 'Who knows? Technically, I suppose, we're still engaged − although I'm not sure I want to be. As a matter of fact, physically we sort of consummated things this morning, only Peter doesn't know that. And in the light of everything which has happened in the last thirty-six hours or so, I'm not sure if Peter would still want to be engaged to me either.'

Amanda was getting slightly confused. 'Perhaps you'd better tell me exactly what *has* gone on in the last thirty-six hours,' she suggested.

Caroline took a deep breath and launched into the saga of her sexual awakening, sparing few details.

'So what about you and Peter?' she asked when she had finished.

Amanda shrugged. 'We screwed a few times. Purely physical, nothing personal. And I think he screwed Sally too, but that's nothing. Everybody screws Sally, as far as I can tell.' Amanda paused for a moment. 'Come to think of it, Peter Blake seems to be screwing us all, one way or the other — and not necessarily with his prick.'

'So what are you planning to do?' Caroline wanted to know.

'Get the bastard before he gets me, I suppose. Once I find out exactly what he's up to.'

'I could help you,' Caroline suggested helpfully.

Amanda regarded her quizzically. 'Why should you want to help? You've got nothing against him.'

'Oh yes I have,' Caroline declared vehemently. 'The swine was unfaithful to me. I shall be revenged.'

There was a minor flaw in this line of reasoning, which Amanda felt duty bound to point out.

'You haven't exactly been a nun yourself,' she ventured.

'Ah — but he was unfaithful to me before I was unfaithful to him,' Caroline reasoned. 'And besides — he screwed me this morning without knowing I was me. I could have been anybody, for all he cared.'

Amanda shook her head. It was not a line of logic that she cared to pursue. She decided to accept the offer of help at face value. 'So what are we going to do to the bastard?'

'How about locking him up in the massage room with Freda for a couple of hours?' Caroline suggested brightly. 'After that, he might be willing to talk.'

Amanda considered the idea, finally rejecting it. 'No, the bastard would probably enjoy it.'

'True,' Caroline conceded. 'I suppose we could take a tip from your head steward and set fire to his prick.'

Amanda shuddered. 'Too drastic. No man deserves that – not even a snake like Peter Blake. No, it needs to be something subtle, yet persuasive. I shall have to think about it for a while.'

'The point is – what are we going to do in the meantime?' Caroline wanted to know. 'If he sees me and recognises me, there are going to be all sorts of awkward questions to answer, and if he sees us together he'll figure out that we're on to him. We can't hide out in potting sheds with young French studs all day.'

Amanda's eyes glinted at the reminder. 'Now that's not a bad idea at all,' she said with a grin. She shook the idea out of her head with an effort, becoming serious again. 'Where were you going before we bumped into each other?'

'To the stables. I fancied a ride. On a horse, that is,' she added quickly, just to clarify things.

Amanda thought for a few seconds. 'Not a bad idea,' she muttered, on reflection. 'Giles could take us round the estate to look at all the parcels of land your father has bought up. Maybe that will give us some clue as to what his plans are. And it will keep us both out of the way for an hour or so.'

'Perfect.' Caroline endorsed the suggestion with enthusiasm. 'Peter will never come looking for us, that's for sure. He hates horses, and anything to do with them. In fact, he's scared stiff of the things. You know how some people have a phobia about spiders or snakes . . . well Peter's like that with horses.'

'Is he now?' Amanda digested this information

with great interest. 'Now that could become very useful indeed.'

With the germ of a fiendish and Machiavellian plot in mind, Amanda led the way towards the stables.

Miss Waites was coming round at last. Her eyelids fluttered open weakly as consciousness returned and she started to take in her surroundings. She glanced around fearfully, checking that there were no men with exposed penises in the immediate vicinity.

It seemed to be all right. Miss Waites opened her eyes fully, to take in Peter Blake hovering over her solicitously.

'Where am I? What happened?' Miss Waites croaked faintly.

Peter helped her to sit up on the sofa in which he had unceremoniously dumped her after carrying her in to the evening lounge.

'You passed out on the steps — so I brought you in here,' he informed her. 'You'll be fine now.'

Peter crossed to the bar as Miss Waites pulled herself together. He squirted a double measure of brandy into a tumbler and carried it back to her.

'Here, drink this down. It will make you feel better.'

Miss Waites lifted the glass to her lips without thinking, shivering as the heady fumes filtered up her nose and made her eyes water. She thrust the glass away at arms length as though it were hemlock instead of Hennessy.

'I never touch the demon alcohol,' she protested vigorously.

'Nonsense. Medicinal purposes only,' Peter assured her, gently guiding the rim of the glass back to her mouth. 'Doctors recommend it for people who've just had a nasty shock.'

Miss Waites was not totally convinced, but the nice Mr Blake seemed to know what he was talking about. Obediently, she drained the fiery liquid in one gulp. He was right — it did make her feel better.

'I'll get you another,' Peter said, taking the glass from her hand.

Three purely medicinal double brandies later, Miss Waites was on fighting form again.

'Mr Blake — we have to do something, and do it right away,' she said, with alcohol-inspired conviction. 'Two sex-crazed women chasing half-naked men all over the grounds is really the last straw. It is time for action.'

Peter nodded miserably. If Miss Waites had not passed out, he would probably be chasing one of these sex-crazed women across the grass himself right now — with great enthusiasm. However, it was pointless to cry over spilt milk for the moment. He might as well turn the disappointment to his advantage.

'What do you suggest?' he asked.

Miss Waites bounded to her feet with unaccustomed agility, making a mental note to acquire a bottle of brandy for the medicine cabinet at the first available opportunity. 'We shall contact the members of my committee at once,' she declared. 'Lead me to the nearest telephone.'

She took a step forward, lurching slightly. Miss Waites supposed that it was something to do with blood rushing to the head after a faint. She leaned against Peter for support and let him prop her up as they made their way towards the phone cubicle in reception.

'Back so soon?' asked Giles, as Amanda and Caroline turned up on his doorstep. He gave Amanda an affectionate squeeze. 'You could become a very enjoyable habit, do you know that?'

Amanda felt a warm glow at Giles' obvious interest. He was, most definitely, a habit she wanted to cultivate. Sex games with Phillipe were one thing for a quick thrill, but it took a man with the maturity and experience of Giles to give a woman sustained pleasure.

'This is Caroline,' she said, introducing her companion. 'We thought we'd like to take a ride around the grounds.'

'Great — I'll just go in and change into my jodphurs.' Giles pecked Amanda on the cheek and bounded into the house.

The show of affection had not been lost on Caroline. 'You seem to have the entire male population of this place pretty well sewn up,' she observed.

Amanda whirled on her, suddenly protective. 'And this one is definitely not even look, let alone touch,' she warned.

Caroline laughed girlishly. 'No chance, my dear Amanda. He didn't even glance at me — didn't you notice? I'd have no chance there, I can assure you.'

Amanda hadn't really thought about it, but now that Caroline had pointed it out, she had to admit that it was true. Giles hadn't shown a flicker of interest in the other girl, attractive as she was.

'Well, what are you waiting for?' Caroline asked. 'You have a man who is hot for you in there taking his trousers off. So why are you wasting time standing here talking to me?'

Amanda had to admit that she did have a point. 'And what are you going to be doing?'

Caroline shrugged. 'Don't you worry about me. I'll go and choose a horse. I'll be picking my ride while you're getting yours.'

Amanda didn't need any more encouragement. 'I'll see you in the stables, then,' she said, and ran into the house in pursuit of Giles.

She ran straight into his open arms, just inside the door. There was an expectant, almost arrogant grin on his face. 'What took you so long?' he joked.

Amanda's eyes flashed briefly. 'You big-headed bastard. You were sure that I'd come running in here after you, weren't you?'

Giles nodded. 'And I was right, wasn't I?' He pressed her against his body so that she could feel the hardness of his ready-erected cock.

Amanda felt her legs go a little weak, but still felt that his presumptuousness demanded some token resistance. 'And you really think that I am going to chase after you with my knickers down any time you want?' she demanded.

Giles nuzzled her ear with his lips. 'It's what we both want, isn't it?' he countered. His mouth moved to hers, covering it and crushing her soft lips, preventing her enthusiastic and affirmative answer.

Amanda dropped her hands to his waist,

unbuckling and unzipping his trousers with practised and nimble fingers. His trousers slid to the floor, quickly followed by his underpants. His stiff prick reared up, lifting the material of her skirt.

Giles seized her by the waist. 'Turn around,' he hissed breathlessly. 'I want to give it to you from behind.'

Obediently, Amanda turned to face the wall, lifting her hands to brace herself against it. She spread her feet, sticking her bottom out provocatively.

Giles lifted her skirt over her smooth, rounded bottom, hooking his thumbs into the thin material of her panties and pulling them free. He pressed himself against her trembling buttocks, letting his rigid tool rest under the crease between her soft cheeks. Amanda thrilled with pleasure at the feel of the hot rod against her cool skin.

'Ooh, put it in, Giles, please,' she murmured, trembling with anticipation. She wiggled her arse against his stiff part, feeling it roll and slide between her legs.

Giles kissed the back of her neck, sliding his finger around her thighs to probe for the entrance to her wet slit. 'Easy does it,' he whispered into her ear. 'This may be a quickie — but that doesn't mean we have to rush it.'

He began to move his hips gently back and forth in a simulated and sensuous fucking motion. Amanda squirmed with pleasure as the thick shaft throbbed between her thighs, and Giles' fingers gently kneaded the soft folds of her labia like warm, moist dough.

'Spread your feet a bit wider. Stick your arse out a

bit more,' he whispered into her ear. Amanda responded at once, arching her back to raise her bottom to a more jaunty angle. Now, as he moved in and out of her thighs, Amanda could feel the thick head of his prick glide along the dripping cleft of her cunt between his fingers.

'Please, Giles, no more teasing,' she whimpered, aching for the stiff cock to plunge into her.

Giles chuckled. 'All right — but only because you asked nicely.' He pulled back, taking his throbbing part in his hand and guiding it towards her hungry and expectant hole. Amanda braced herself against his plunging entry, gasping as Giles pumped into her with one push, until his belly was pressed right up against her buttocks. He began to move slowly, with short, jerking strokes which took the head of his cock slamming against her cervix like a pile driver.

'Faster, Giles, do it faster,' Amanda pleaded, gyrating her pelvis against each deep, slow thrust.

Giles let out a throaty chuckle in her ear. 'I'll tell you one thing — you're not a filly I'd want to ride in a dressage event. I've only just started to trot, and you want to break into a full gallop. However, anything you say.'

With that, he began to ram into her hard and fast, gripping her thighs in vice-like fingers and pulling her on to each stroke of his plunging cock. Amanda squealed with delight, her pleasure heightened by the slow build-up and the consummate skill of a practiced cocksman. His furious plunging brought her to a frenzy of excitement in a matter of seconds. Amanda felt her knees buckle beneath her as she climaxed in a long, shuddering gush of liquid heat.

Giles rammed into her flooded canyon a dozen or so more times until he too jerked, stiffened, and sent his own ejaculation spurting into the maelstrom.

Amanda collapsed against the wall with Giles pressed against her back. They both stayed there for several minutes, getting their breath back. Finally, Giles slipped his wet and wilting cock out of Amanda's well-satisfied pussy and picked up his trousers from the floor.

'Well, I'll go and get changed then,' he said, suddenly remembering their earlier plans. 'Shan't be a tick.'

Showing remarkable reserves of stamina, Giles turned towards the stairs and ran up them two at a time. Amanda could only admire him. Weakly, she turned round, pressed her back against the wall and slid down to a seated position on the floor.

'I'll wait for you here,' she managed to mutter rather faintly.

Miss Waites was consumed with the passion of fanatical zeal. Her telephonic rallying call to the godly had yielded surprisingly encouraging results. After fifteen minutes and some twenty calls, she already had a whole posse of pleasure-haters rounded up and converging on the Paradise Country Club to fight the good fight. An army of angst-ridden moralists, a platoon of passion-killers, a brigade of bigots. Already the volunteer vice squad numbered six spinsters, four lay preachers, three latter-day saints, two vicars and a defrocked Catholic priest.

But Miss Waites was not satisfied. She had hot fires of moralist conviction coursing in her blood, where they fuelled themselves on the highly combustible fumes. In short, Miss Waites was drunk with power, drunk with obsession and more than a little drunk with alcohol. It was a potent mixture.

Unfortunately, she was temporarily out of ten pence pieces.

'I need some more change,' she complained to Peter, waving her unfinished telephone list under his nose.

Peter saw his chance of escape. 'Why don't you go into the bar and help yourself from the till,' he suggested. 'Meanwhile I'll take a stroll outside to see if anybody has turned up yet.'

Miss Waites accepted the suggestion enthusiastically. Her excitement was already getting too much for her. Another medicinal brandy was most definitely called for.

Peter breathed a sigh of relief as she scurried off towards the bar. As soon as her back was turned, he was already making his own break for the front door. Leaping down the stone steps, he set off across the lawns towards the potting sheds at a loping run.

Miss Waites punched open the till and reviewed the contents of the silver drawer with glee. There was more than enough change to make twenty or thirty more telephone calls. Her heart surged at the thought. Happily, she scooped the coins into her open handbag and went to close the till again.

The corner of a piece of stiff paper sticking out from underneath the till caught her eye. It was a temptation which she was totally unable to resist, for, like most of her type, Miss Waites was an incurable busy-body. She glanced round furtively before starting to edge Andrew's photograph out from its impromptu hiding place.

Miss Waites' eyes bulged as she took in the graphic details of the pornographic picture. Her horror at the disgusting scene shook her to the core, but was only a prelude to the cold and savage jolt of cruel betrayal as she recognised Peter Blake advancing on the helpless girl with his stiff and angry-looking weapon jutting out of his trousers.

Miss Waites went weak at the knees and felt the blood hammering in her temples like a sledgehammer. Had it not been for the brandy already in her system, she might well have fainted again — but this time she knew the answer. Reaching for the nearest bottle, she uncorked it, lifted it to her lips, and drank greedily.

Several gulps later, she forced her eyes to return to the incriminating photograph, and a fresh wave of revulsion shook her sparse frame. Filth, decadence and licentiousness were everywhere. Sex and the sordid desires of the flesh were like a blight upon the land. Even the man she had dared to trust as her ally turned out to be a closet libertine. It was all too awful to contemplate. She took another couple of deep swigs at the bottle, as she stuffed the photograph into her bag.

One thing was certain, Miss Waites decided, as the alcohol surged into her system, firing her blood anew. Peter Blake must be punished for his wickedness. What was more, it was now total war. It was the apocalypse, the final confrontation of good against evil. No quarter, no Geneva Convention, no rules of combat. The Paradise Club, along with all its depraved inhabitants, must be destroyed by whatever means possible.

Staggering slightly from side to side, Miss Waites made her way back to the telephone to call in the heavy artillery.

'Oh, by the way — I've got a bit more information for you,' Giles said as they made their way towards the stables. 'Thought it might come in useful.'

'Do tell,' Amanda said. 'I'm all ears.'

Giles grinned, wrapping his arm around her shoulders. 'No, my dear Amanda. You are all cunt,' he said, not ungraciously. 'You are probably the sexiest, horniest, most totally vagina-orientated woman it has ever been my good fortune to meet — and I love it.'

Amanda grunted. 'I guess I'll take that as a compliment. So, what's this new information?'

'After you left this morning, I took the opportunity to look through some of Miss Waites' papers while she was out of the house. And among some of the correspondence relating to the land sales, I found this.' Giles fished in his jacket pocket and pulled out a sheet of paper.

Amanda took it, glancing at the letterhead. She had been half expecting the name of the Drummond Development Corporation to pop up, but this was even more intriguing.

'Associated Theme Parks of America,' she read. She looked up at Giles. 'Who are they, for God's sake?'

Giles shrugged. 'Who knows? But look, there's more.' He drew out another folded sheet of paper, which appeared to be some sort of plan. He pointed out one particular feature. 'Here — what do you think that looks like?'

Amanda studied the plan carefully. Although the area covered by it was mostly on Hadleigh land, the particular feature he picked out extended a good way beyond the boundaries of the estate.

'I'd say it was a rough plan for a gigantic roller coaster,' Amanda said after a while.

'Exactly what I thought,' Giles agreed. 'But look where it ends up.' He stabbed his finger down on the plan. 'Isn't that just about where your place stands now?'

Suddenly it all fell into place. The parcels of land which had been bought up on Giles' land were all starting points for various amusements and rides. But none of them could go anywhere without the complete takeover of all the grounds and buildings on Paradise land.

'So that's it,' Amanda muttered, as the full picture dawned. 'Basically, the Paradise Country Club is destined to become the tail end of a big dipper if Peter Blake and his cronies get their way.'

'Rather looks like it, old girl,' Giles commiserated. 'Pity all round, really. I'd have been more than happy to sell them my entire estate if they'd come to me with an open and reasonable offer in the first place. It sort of tickles my sense of humour to have the old family holding turned into one huge fun park. That would have a few of my blue-nosed ancestors revolving in their graves faster than a merry-go-round.'

'So why didn't they?' Amanda wondered. 'There

should be more than enough land on your estate to build the park and car parking facilities.'

By way of answer, Giles rubbed his finger and thumb together. 'At an educated guess, I'd say it all boils down to the old mazuma. These boys don't believe in spending out a penny more than they have to. So they probably figured a run-down club and grounds would be a lot cheaper to buy up than quality farming land. Which rather presupposes that they assume you'll be out of business fairly soon.'

'Or they're planning to make it happen,' Amanda murmured, suddenly remembering things which Andrew had told her earlier. How business had started dropping off soon after Peter Blake took over running the estate. How the local Anti-Vice people had started to become more militant, and how Peter seemed to be particularly close to Miss Waites all of a sudden.

They had reached the stables. Caroline came out to greet them, leading a ready-saddled skewbald mare. Amanda suddenly detached herself from Giles and ran across to the girl, grabbing her by the hand.

'We're going to have to forget the ride for the moment,' she said, tugging Caroline after her. 'Right now it's time to settle with Peter Blake once and for all.'

She called over her shoulder as they both started running back towards the club.

'Sorry Giles — have to rush. But thanks for the ride.'

Chapter Seventeen

Amanda and Caroline chose the shortest route back to the club across the fields, so they missed the first wave of Miss Waites' moral crusaders pouring through the main entrance and down the drive.

By the time they had let themselves in the back entrance and gone in search of Andrew and Sally, the Anti-Vice League's dirty tricks department was in full swing. Two members of the Animal Liberation Front had already tipped a sackful of live moles down the ninth hole of the golf course, a local redneck farmer had unloaded eight hundredweight of horse manure into the swimming pool and the defrocked priest was busy exorcising the erotic statues.

The main body of protestors were deploying themselves at key points around the estate, brandishing hastily made placards and banners.

It was this scene which greeted Cedric Drummond and his passenger as they cruised up to the huge iron gates in the Rolls Royce.

Randy Brandich III glanced up at the sign over the gates and roared with good-natured laughter. 'Say, I really like that, know what I mean? Paradise Cuntry Club. Kinda cute, huh? I gotta get a photo of that to show the guys back home.'

Jumping out of the car, he swung the expensive

Japanese camera around his neck into business position and started to shoot off a whole roll of film.

Sitting back in the plush upholstery, Cedric Drummond had to admit that Randy was a highly likeable, if somewhat stereotyped character. Although he had all the childlike enthusiasm which made Americans almost appealing, he appeared to have none of their abrasive, brash characteristics which Cedric found so infuriating.

He was, basically, a very agreeable young man, with a good sense of humour, apparently sharp business acumen and a remarkably sophisticated sense of taste and style.

He also had a seemingly endless fund of incredibly coarse jokes and stories, with which he had regaled Cedric for most of the journey down from Heathrow airport. All in all, he had proved to be an ideal travelling companion − and the fact that he came from an impossibly rich family was merely a bonus.

On several occasions during the journey, Cedric had found himself appraising the handsome, California-bronzed features of his fellow passenger and marking him down as absolutely perfect son-in-law material. Definitely a step up the ladder compared to Peter Blake, who although he might do quite well out of the Paradise deal, was never going to match the American in terms of serious wealth.

Randy looked up from his camera as a small group of placard-waving demonstrators appeared in the viewfinder. They appeared to be advancing on him with somewhat aggressive intent. He retreated quickly to the comparitive safety of the Rolls.

'Say, what the hell's going on, Drummond?' he

asked, as the small band of protestors came nearer.

Cedric didn't know — and more to the point did not want to hang around to find out. New paint jobs on a Roller came expensive. He leaned forward, slid back the dividing glass between him and the driver and barked instructions. 'Drive on to the house. And run those bastards over, if you have to.'

The chauffeur did as he was told, easing the limousine down the driveway towards the advancing horde. Surprisingly, they stood back meekly to let the car pass, content merely to wave their banners and placards at its side windows.

Miss Waites stepped out of the club to meet them as they arrived at the entrance. She was now well into her organisational mode, busying herself commanding her impromptu army and despatching them to various parts of the estate. She would have to find something for these latest recruits to do.

She regarded Cedric and Randy curiously as they stepped out of the Rolls. They didn't quite seeem like the usual run of Anti-Vice League members — but then, why else should they be here? Anyway, it hardly mattered. All volunteers, no matter how unlikely, were welcome. Miss Waites greeted them both warmly.

'Welcome, welcome. I'm so glad you could join us. Well, I expect you're both anxious to get to work, aren't you?'

'Excuse me, ma'am, but I'd sure like to know what's going on around here,' Randy started to say.

Miss Waites noticed the accent and cut him short quickly. 'Oh, an American,' she trilled, with obvious delight. 'How wonderful. Such a fine background of moral and religious convictions. You come from the Bible Belt, no doubt.'

Randy didn't get a chance to explain to her that he was actually from Los Angeles, where currently voodoo and satanism were probably the fastest growing religious cults.

'Well, no time to waste,' Miss Waites said briskly. 'Follow me and I'll take you to your posts.'

It was Cedric's turn to try and clarify the situation.

'Look, I'm not sure who you think we are, but maybe you've jumped to the wrong conclusion,' he said.

'Nonsense, nonsense.' Miss Waites dismissed him with a wave of her hand. 'You are here because you want to see this terrible club closed down and out of business, aren't you?'

Cedric nodded. 'Well . . . yes,' he admitted.

'Then let's get on with it,' Miss Waites said triumphantly. 'Now, follow me. We'll take the Games Room, I don't think anyone has been sent there yet. Heaven only knows what goes on in there. A den of gambling and drug taking, I shouldn't wonder.'

Miss Waites swept off into the interior of the club. Bemused, Cedric and Randy followed her, primarily out of curiosity.

In fact, although the Games Room did frequently host big-stake poker games at which substantial amounts of coke were snorted up various nostrils, it was not being used for this purpose at that precise moment. The room was, in fact, serving as a venue for one of Andrew and Sally's highly inventive sex games. So the scene which greeted Miss Waites as she threw open the door was not quite what she had expected.

Stark naked, Sally was seated on the green baize of the billiards table, her legs spread widely apart. At the other end of the table, an equally starkers Andrew was carefully chalking his cue before attempting to sink one of the red balls, using Sally's voluminous cunt as an extra pocket.

For the third time that day, Miss Waites let out a scream of horror and went weak at the knees. Muttering something completely inarticulate, she shot off in the direction of the brandy bottle.

Andrew carried on with taking his shot, but the sudden and unexpected interruption had ruined his concentration. He miscued badly, sending the ball skittering off the table to roll across the floor, stopping at Cedric's feet.

Cedric bent down and picked it up, more out of politeness than anything else. Randy plucked at his sleeve.

'I guess we'd better get out of here,' he suggested. 'I think maybe this pair would rather be alone, know what I mean?'

Cedric said nothing. His eyes were riveted by the sight of Sally's voluptuous body. Dumbly, he held out his hand holding the ball as Andrew trotted over to take it from him.

'Hi,' Andrew said, cheerily. 'Fancy a game?'

Cedric was torn with indecision. On the one hand, Randy's insistent tugging at his sleeve told him that he really ought to do what the man with the money suggested. On the other, Andrew and Sally's carefree attitude suggested that there was definitely some fun to be had — and since Mrs Drummond had entered the menopausal phase some three years ago, there had been precious little of that in his life.

Perhaps there was a compromise to be reached, he thought. He tore his eyes away from Sally to talk to Randy.

'Look, why don't you go and see if you can find out what's going on around here while I talk to these two,' he suggested. 'That way, we can both be gathering valuable information at the same time.'

To Cedric's surprise, Randy seemed to go for the suggestion. 'Hey, that might not be such a bad idea. You stay here and pump these two while I take a look around.'

Overhearing the conversation, Sally added her own comments.

'You're welcome to pump me anytime,' she said. 'But I'm not sure Andrew would go for it.'

Cedric's balls gave a definite twitch at the obvious double entendre. He glanced almost pleadingly at Randy, who seemed to get the message.

'Right — I'll go and dig up what I can. Meet you back here in, say, fifteen minutes?'

'Make it twenty,' Cedric suggested, confident that Sally could well be the sort of woman who might extend his somewhat modest sexual performance. There was something about plump women which invariably aroused Cedric to unusual stamina and particularly long-lasting erections. It was something to do with the way their flesh wobbled while they were being fucked.

Randy disappeared on his fact-finding mission, closing the door behind him. Andrew returned to the

billiards table and lined up another shot on his wife's
open fanny.

'So what is going on here?' Cedric asked.

Andrew looked up, abandoned the shot and lay his
cue down on the table. 'Oh, didn't I explain? This is
a little game I invented myself. I call it Sex Snooker.
The rules, as you may have gathered, are fairly
simple and obvious.'

The explanation wasn't quite what Cedric had
been looking for, but he let it pass.

'So, fancy a game?' Andrew went on. 'It's much
more fun if there are two players.'

Cedric swallowed. 'What are the stakes?' he
queried.

'First one to pocket a ball gets a blow job.' Sally
volunteered. 'The loser only gets to fuck me with the
blunt end of a cue.'

'So — are you going to play?' Andrew asked. It
was a rather pointless question, since Cedric was
already hurrying towards the cue rack on the wall.

He returned to the table with a freshly chalked cue.
'Right, who goes first?'

'No one does until you get your clothes off,' Sally
told him firmly. 'That's one of the rules.'

'That's the main rule,' Andrew put in.

'In fact, it's about the only rule,' Sally finished
off. 'After that, just about anything goes.'

Cedric needed no further encouragment. He
stripped off quickly and enthusiastically, dumping
his clothes on the nearby card table.

Sally appraised his body unashamedly. For a man
of his age, Cedric was in very good shape. Regular
sessions at the tennis club and the gym over the years

had achieved far more than just a good set of business contacts.

'You could have a real challenge on your hands here, Andrew,' Sally teased her husband. 'Something tells me you may be taking on a real hustler. He certainly has a professional-looking cue.'

Cedric followed Sally's admiring gaze down to his prick, which was already beginning to stiffen at the prospect of having Sally's generous and full-lipped mouth wrapped around it.

Andrew lined up his first shot, cueing up on the white for an angle contact with one of the reds, sitting close to Sally's left foot. He struck the cue ball hard, but slightly off centre, so that it clipped the red sharply, sending it to rebound from Sally's leg just below the knee, and trickle back down the table.

Cedric saw the chance for a good, straight cannon directly into the mouth of Sally's inviting cunt. He rolled the white ball carefully around the D until he was satisfied with its position, crouched into position and took his shot. The red missed its tempting target by only a few millimetres, slamming into the cushion of Sally's fleshy thigh and bouncing back into the centre of the table.

It was a perfect chance for Andrew. Taking the long rest from beneath the table, he cued up for a short, stabbing shot which would drive the red straight into the opening to Sally's slit. At the precise second that the white ball made contact with a very positive click, Sally lifted her arse from the table almost imperceptibly. The red shot directly on target to jam itself between the table surface and Sally's chubby arse, wedged there immovable.

'You cheated,' Andrew whined complainingly, robbed of what he had thought was a certain winner.

Sally shook her head in denial. 'No I didn't. I was getting cramp in my bum, that's all'

'So what do we do now?' Cedric asked, noting that the red ball was effectively out of play.

'Start again from the D,' Sally said. She fished the red ball out from under her arse and rolled it back down the table to baulk.

As Cedric fingered the cue ball into position again, Sally stretched the lips of her cunt open with her fingers, exposing the moist and succulent target.

'This one's a winner. I can feel it,' she announced confidently. She held her cunt open as Cedric bent over the table and sent the white ball scudding towards the red.

It made perfect contact. The red ball headed straight for the unusual pocket, looking like an ace every inch of the way. Just to be sure, Sally snatched it up at the very last second and thrust it into her cunt with a faint plop.

'Now that was definitely cheating,' Andrew muttered half-heartedly.

'No it wasn't. It was bang on target from the second the white ball left the cue. You've been fairly beaten, Andrew, admit it.'

Andrew dropped his cue on to the table in a gesture of submission. 'Fair enough, I concede.'

'Great! So now it's time for the prize-giving ceremony,' Sally said with great enthusiasm. She stretched herself out at full length on the table, with her head hanging over the end cushion.

Cedric saw the possibilities at once. His cock

jerked a few times and pumped into rigidity. Making his way up to the end of the table he stood by Sally's head as she bent her neck back as far as she could.

'Fuck my mouth,' she commanded. 'Fuck it as hard and as deep as you like, and don't stop even if I sound like I'm choking to death.'

Andrew had already picked up his cue again and turned it the wrong way round. 'If you can make her choke, then you're a better man than many,' he observed. 'My dear wife makes Linda Lovelace look like a beginner.'

Cedric moved in to claim his prize with mounting excitement. Holding his erect prick in one hand, he guided the tip towards Sally's parted lips as Andrew began to drill the blunt end of his cue into her waiting slit.

Sally rolled her wet tongue over her lips in anticipation as Cedric's thick cock brushed them gently. She opened her mouth wide, exposing the warm, wet tunnel of her throat.

Cedric thrust his thick cock deep into that enticing cavern, watching Sally's eyes roll ecstatically as the tasty tool slid into her. She clasped her lips around it, rolling her tongue around inside her mouth and working muscles in her throat to give the penetrating shaft of flesh a stimulating massage.

Cedric pushed in deeper, shivering with pleasure at the sensation. He held himself as long as he dared, worried that Sally would be fighting to breathe, before pulling back and letting his prick slide out again over those thick soft lips. A thin trickle of saliva ran from the corners of Sally's mouth as the head of Cedric's cock passed her teeth and nearly escaped. She jerked on the billiard table, gulping for the stiff flesh to fill her again. Cedric abandoned any worries about choking her and plunged back into her cunt-like mouth, fucking her lips and throat with furious enthusiasm.

Sally's huge creamy tits wobbled deliciously as Cedric rammed into her mouth. The mere sight of all that quivering flesh gave him an added thrill, sending a shiver of pleasure down his legs. Reaching forward, he took each soft mound in his hands, squeezing and massaging them with the tactile pleasure of a child with play-dough. He moved his fingers and thumbs to the large brown buds of her nipples, tweaking them until they were stiff and burning. Sally shuddered beneath his touch, pumping her mouth against his penetrating cock to swallow every available inch.

At the foot of the table, Andrew had pushed his cue as deep into his wife's cunt as it would go. He rolled the shaft of it between his fingers, rotating it in her deep and slippery hole like a drill bit. Sally's legs began to kick furiously as she abandoned herself to the rising sensation of orgasm, finally coming like a North Sea gusher.

Her large, fleshy body seemed to quiver all over as the racking waves of release tore through her. It was the final trigger for Cedric, who gave one last convulsive jerk and shot his full load of come deep into her throat. Sally's throat worked furiously to gulp it down, her lips and tongue pressing and squeezing against Cedric's pumping prick to milk out the last delicious drop.

Cedrick slid his wilting cock out of Sally's mouth,

suddenly feeling very foolish and vulnerable, like a little boy caught raiding the biscuit jar. Sally sat up, her eyes glittering brightly as if with anticipation for the next stage of the game. For some unaccountable reason, Cedric found this rather frightening. Remembering that Randy had promised to return to meet him, he hurred across to where he had thrown his clothes and began to dress.

Sally and Andrew looked disappointed.

'Aren't you going to play a rematch?' Sally demanded, somewhat petulantly. 'Give Andrew a sporting chance to even the score?'

Cedric shook his head wordlessly, hastily buttoning his shirt and stepping into his trousers.

'How about darts instead?' Andrew suggested. 'You know — the first one to score sixty-nine and all that?'

Cedric pulled up his zipper and reached for his jacket, feeling increasingly uncomfortable and embarrassed, but not quite able to pin down the reason for such feelings. There was a niggling guilt in the back of his mind that he had somehow taken advantage of the couple, although this simply didn't stand up in the light of rational analysis.

Later, when he had time to think about it, Cedric would come to realise the bizarre incident had represented a sort of cryptic encapsulation of his whole life and relationship with others. Stripped of their sexual context, Andrew and Sally's games were essentially innocent and uninhibited. They were like a pair of children, each with a child's naive enthusiasm and simple trust that the rest of the world both accepted and respected their uncomplicated rules.

Whilst he, Cedric Drummond, was a manipulator, a man of wealth and power, and always destined to be an unfair winner because of it. His own innocence had been lost a long way back on the road, chipped away by a dozen slightly shady deals, a score of subtle bribes and a hundred financial transactions which had exploited innocence or trust to his advantage.

But for now, Cedric Drummond only realised that he felt oddly out of place. He had stepped, temporarily, into a different world, and now it was rejecting him.

He finished buttoning his jacket and headed for the door, turning briefly to gape dumbly at Andrew and Sally. There ought to be something he should say, but he couldn't think of it.

Cedric scuttled out through the door, just in time to meet Randy coming up the passageway towards him.

'Well, did you learn anything?' Randy asked.

Cedric looked at him strangely. 'I think so,' he muttered. 'But I'm not sure what it is yet.'

Chapter Eighteen

Amanda and Caroline had finished searching the cellars without finding a trace of Andrew, Sally or Peter Blake. Amanda headed in the direction of the stairs leading to the bar.

'Come on, we'll search the whole bloody house if we have to. I'm going to find that bastard Blake and personally bite his balls off.'

Bounding up the last step, she was just in time to catch Miss Waites pouring the last drop of brandy in the bottle down her throat as if there were no tomorrow.

Amanda let out a roar of triumph, dived across the prostrate woman's throat, pinning her down.

'Good Lord, Amanda — what are you doing?' Caroline asked as she came upon the undignified scene.

'If I can't track down Peter, at least I have his co-conspirator,' Amanda said, grinding her foot down with a little more force than was actually necessary.

Miss Waites choked, gasped and let out a loud belch, which sent a wave of brandy fumes wafting up from the floor. 'You're too late,' she managed to croak. 'I've made sure every decent citizen for miles is here to close you down once and for all — and the police are already on their way.'

It was the first inkling that there was anything

amiss for Amanda. Having come into the house from the back, she and Caroline had completely missed the arrival of Miss Waites' troops, and the deep cellars had insulated them against the sounds of the pandemonium outside.

'Go and find out what this stupid bitch is blithering about,' Amanda snapped to Caroline. 'And make it fast.'

Caroline obeyed meekly, hurrying out to the reception area and the front door. One glance outside was enough. She ran back, squealing excitedly.

'She's right, Amanda. The whole grounds are crawling with assorted nutters and there's a police car coming up the drive.'

'Damn,' Amanda cursed. 'And I wanted a few minutes to choke some answers out of Lucrezia Borgia here.' She broke off, thinking quickly. 'Look, you go out and take care of the copper while I finish things off in here.'

Caroline looked blank. 'What do you mean — take care of him?'

Amanda sighed with exasperation. 'Well I don't mean mow him down with a Kalashnikov. Just use your initiative. In fact, use anything you've got. Just get him out of the way and pacify him for a while. Pretend to be me, for a start. That'll confuse things for a bit.'

Caroline started to catch the general idea. She grinned mischievously. 'And if I'm you, I'd be a totally immoral tart, I suppose?'

Amanda accepted the jibe in the spirit it was intended. 'You've got it in one, girl. Now get out there and do your worst for law and disorder.'

She turned her attention back to Miss Waites as Caroline hurried off to do her bidding. 'Now, you and I have a little serious talking to do, I think.'

Caroline appraised the good-looking young policemen who stood in the doorway. He looked rather naive and innocent, despite his uniform, and was a lot less threatening than Caroline had expected. In fact, he didn't seem very sure of his ground at all.

'Miss Amanda Redfern?' he muttered nervously, after a little cough.

Caroline noded. Somehow it didn't seem like quite so much of a lie, refusing to put it into actual words.

'Constable Harris, miss. I've had some rather disturbing reports that this place is being used for immoral purposes. Do you mind if I come in?'

'Not at all, constable,' Caroline murmured sweetly. 'In fact, I'm extremely glad to see you. One of those louts out there wrecking my grounds just assaulted me, and I think I might be injured.'

Constable Harris immediately looked concerned. The mob outside certainly hadn't looked at all friendly, and he was sufficiently new to the force to imagine that at least part of a policeman's role was to aid young ladies in distress. Especially young ladies as gorgeous as this one.

'Perhaps I ought to call for an ambulance, miss,' he suggested. 'I can radio from my car.'

'Oh, I'm sure it's not that serious,' Caroline assured him. She rubbed one hand over her swelling breast suggestively. 'It's just that I got punched rather heavily in the chest, and I'm afraid that one of my ribs might be cracked. Perhaps if you could be good enough to help me upstairs to my room, I can lie down and ease the pain. Then, of course, I'd be more than happy to answer any of your questions for you.'

Harris slid into the trap like an unsuspecting fly down the funnel of a carniverous pitcher plant. He jumped forwards, throwing a supportive arm around Caroline's slim waist.

She winced with pretended pain, lifting his hand up so that it was cupped against the softness of her left tit. 'Ah, that's better,' she murmured.

Constable Harris thought so too, but made no comment.

Caroline started to move towards the stairs, making sure that she pressed her body against him as much as possible. 'Now, if you can help me up to room eight,' she said, 'It's only on the first floor.'

Aware of a certain tightness in his trousers, Constable Harris began to ascend the stairs very slowly and carefully.

Moments later, Caroline was stretched out on her back on the waterbed, aware that its gently bobbing motion was an added turn-on in itself. Harris stood over her, by now acutely concerned that his rising erection was beginning to show. He shuffled his feet nervously, unsure of what to do.

Caroline lifted her blouse out of her skirt, slipping a hand up to massage her breast area. The movement made the blouse rise up, exposing the soft flesh of her belly and midriff to the young policeman's bemused gaze.

'Look . . . perhaps I'd really better phone for a doctor,' he mumbled awkwardly, starting to feel a little out of his depth. It wasn't a situation they had really covered in training school.

'Perhaps if you just massaged it for me?' Caroline breathed, hitching her blouse a little higher so that the swelling roundness of her breasts were clearly visible.

Harris took a couple of nervous steps back from the bed. He was now quite seriously concerned about the wisdom of his act of chivalry.

'Please?' Caroline prompted, putting on her best little-girl-lost voice.

It wasn't a particularly warm day, but Caroline noticed that Constable Harris was beginning to sweat rather heavily. He ran his tongue over his dry lips several times, shuffling his feet awkwardly.

'I'm sure a little massage would help,' Caroline pleaded, keeping up the pressure. 'It really does hurt.' She rolled on the waterbed, managing to hitch her blouse up another couple of inches as she moved.

Male instinct won out over police discipline. Hoping that his three-day course with St John Ambulance had qualified him for this particular type of medical emergency, Harris moved back towards the bed, flexing his fingers.

Caroline patted the side of the bed next to her. 'Sit down here,' she said. 'You'll find it easier.'

Harris perched himself precariously on the bed and reached out a tentative hand towards her. Caroline seized it quickly, thrusting it up under her blouse until his fingers were well over her breast.

'Just there,' she murmured. 'That's the spot.'

Harris began a slow, circular massage, trying desperately to look as disinterested as possible.

Caroline moved her body sensuously, letting out little cooing noises of satisfaction.

'Ooh, that's such a relief. So soothing. She reached up to grasp his wrist, forcing his hand to increase its pressures. 'Just a teeny shade harder, up a bit, to the left.'

Caroline lay back and relaxed for a while, letting the young policeman proceed at his own pace and actually taking a certain amount of genuine pleasure from his touch.

'You've got very soothing hands,' she told him, after a while. 'Did anyone ever tell you that before?'

Harris shook his head. 'No, miss, I don't think they ever did.'

'Well I'm telling you now.' Caroline patted him on the knee in a reassuring fashion, making sure that her fingers stroked gently across his thigh as she removed her hand. 'What's your first name, by the way?'

'David, miss,' croaked Harris. He fidgeted nervously on the bed as his stiff cock started to feel painful inside his pants.

Caroline reached up and began to fiddle with the buttons on his tunic. 'You look ever so hot, David. Don't you think you ought to loosen your collar?'

David gave a little shiver, and let out a weak, helpless groan. 'I really think I ought to go and call that doctor,' he said again, almost pleadingly.

'Shush, you're doing a wonderful job,' Caroline told him. She undid the top two buttons on his tunic.

David was trembling all over now. 'Look, Miss Redfern . . . I really don't want to get into any sort of trouble. I'm due for promotion soon.'

Caroline stared, rather pointedly, down at his

trouser front. 'You're certainly coming up for a rise, I can see that,' she said wickedly.

The policeman's eyes rolled in their sockets like a pair of demented marbles. 'I really shouldn't be here like this,' he said weakly.

Caroline knew that she had him on the run now. 'You're quite right,' she agreed with him. 'You most certainly shouldn't be sitting here with your trousers on, with a hard-on like you've got, it must be incredibly painful.' Caroline's fingers dropped to his zipper. 'You know something — I've always wanted to feel a policeman's truncheon,' she told him.

David groaned with total resignation. He was past the point of no return, and he knew it. 'I do hope you realise that I could arrest you for enticing a police officer?' he muttered, with a last desperate show of defiance.

'I'll tell you what, David,' Caroline breathed sexily, ignoring him. 'If you're really nice to me, maybe I'll blow your whistle for you. Do you think you'd like that?'

David groaned again, and all fight went out of him. He flopped back helplessly on the bed as Caroline's nimble fingers unzipped his fly and pulled out his throbbing manhood. She looked at it with quite genuine admiration.

'Oh boy — so it's not just the arm of the law which is long,' she said, sliding her hand lovingly up and down the stiff, twitching shaft. Sitting up, she bent over him and darted out her wet pink tongue, licking the smooth knob of his prick. The thought suddenly occurred to her that she had never sucked a man's cock before, even though she had fantasised about it many times. She felt rather glad that it was going to be with David, for Caroline felt that such a sweet and gentle man somehow especially deserved the ministrations of her virgin mouth. She just hoped she could come up with the technique to match her enthusiasm.

She ran her hot tongue over and under the blood-engorged helmet, and around the crease of his foreskin. A small bead of lubricant oozed out of the tiny slit at the top, and Caroline licked at it tentatively with the very tip of her tongue, rolling it around inside her mouth to savour the new taste. Pleasantly surprised, she took the whole bulbous head between her soft lips and sucked it as though it were a lollipop, hoping to coax more of the tangy juice out of it.

David's cock was twitching and dancing like a marionette controlled by a mad puppeteer. Caroline could feel it throb in her hand with every pulse of hot blood which was pumped up its thick length.

If she was going to suck it, she had better get down to it while she could, Caroline decided. She opened her mouth, running her tongue around to spread her saliva. Just before she swallowed it, she glanced up at its owner with a cheeky grin on her beautiful face.

'I'm taking you in now . . . but I don't promise you'll come quietly.'

Taking a breath, Caroline plunged her mouth down over the hot cock to begin her first blow job.

Phillipe was most disturbed by the wild goings-on around the grounds. Suddenly, it seemed as if his little haven of peace was going to be destroyed for

ever, and that the whole noisy, bustling world which
he had hidden away from for so long was finally
going to overcome and swamp him. He wondered,
idly, whether that was the price of his recent
awakening.

So far, no one had actually bothered him,
although Peter Blake had burst in to the potting
sheds earlier, taken a quick look around and then
left. But the crowd of strange people charging
around the grounds waving their flags and banners
might not prove quite so harmless, and they were
getting nearer to him all the time.

Perhaps now might be as good a time as any to go
in search of Miss Waites to make his declaration of
undying love, Phillipe thought. He tucked his pretty
plaything safely away in his trousers, remembering of
course that it wasn't a pretty plaything any longer.
The pretty blonde lady had told him the right word
for it. What was it she had said? Cock — beautiful
cock, that was it. Phillipe knew he must remember
those words for Miss Waites, and add them to the
short speech which he had prepared and rehearsed
several times over for her.

Pausing only to gather a small posy of flowers as a
love gift, Phillipe set out to find Miss Waites and
please her as he had apparently pleased the pretty
blonde lady and her friend.

Peter Blake was beginning to give up all hope of ever
seeing his dark-haired lady love again. In the last half
hour, he had looked everywhere, without catching so
much as a glimpse of her. Phillipe had been alone in
the potting shed, Andrew and Sally had the games

room to themselves, and Freda, having mended the fuses, was preparing the massage room for the imminent arrival of the Hon. Nigel for his cock-sucking therapy. And as far as the outside was concerned, Miss Waites' vice-hating vigilantes seemed to have taken over completely.

Returning to the house seemed the only answer, even if it meant bumping into Miss Waites again. Perhaps he could exercise some measure of control over her deployment of her troops. At the moment, things seemed to be getting totally out of control. Skirting around the side of the house to avoid the bulk of the banner-waving brigade, Peter headed for the front entrance, stopping dead in his tracks when he saw the Rolls parked outside.

Peter recognised it at once, by the distinctive Drummond Development logo emblazoned on the side door panels. A cold shiver of apprehension passed through his body. What was Cedric Drummond doing here? The fact that he had come at all, completely unannounced, could only mean that plans were not progressing smoothly as required. And that meant trouble.

Peter noted that Charles, the chauffeur, was in the car. They were at least on nodding acquaintance terms. He decided to see what limited information he could get out of the man. Approaching the Rolls, Peter tapped discreetly on the side window.

Recognising him, Charles wound the electric window down.

'Mr Blake, sir. What are you doing here?'

'More to the point, Charles, is what you are doing here. When did Mr Drummond arrive?'

'About half an hour ago, sir. Mr Drummond and an American gentleman we picked up at Heathrow airport.'

Peter's stomach lurched at the mention of the word 'American'. That meant the pressure was really on.

'Where are they now? Do you know?'

'They went into the house with a tall thin lady,' Charles informed him. 'She seemed to be in charge.'

Peter groaned. The description could only fit Miss Waites. He glanced sideways at the banner brigade, who seemed to be grouping together again and heading back towards the house. He nodded towards them for Charles' benefit.

'Are you having any trouble with that lot?'

Charles laughed, shaking his head. 'Good Lord no, sir. For some odd reason they seem to think that I'm one of them.'

'Even so, perhaps you'd be better off getting out of the way,' Peter suggested. A sudden idea struck him. Charles was a good-natured sort, and didn't get many perks in his employment with Cedric. He might appreciate a little treat. 'Look, why don't you go into the house and look for the Games Room? I think you might find you'd be made very welcome there.'

'Not a bad idea, sir,' Charles agreed with enthusiasm. He climbed out of the Rolls and set the central locking system. 'Perhaps if you see Mr Drummond, you could tell him where I am.'

Peter nodded. 'I'll do that.' He watched Charles head towards the front door and be narrowly beaten to it by Phillipe, who had just made a commando-like sprint from behind one of the azalea bushes.

* * *

In the bar, Amanda had given up any ideas of getting sense out of Miss Waites. Her massive consumption of brandy had finally caught up with her, and she was now hopelessly pissed. Inarticulate moans and repeated belches had now given way to a fit of the hiccups and schoolgirl-like giggling, no matter what Amanda did to her. Half-nelsons, Chinese skin torture and ice cubes down her sparse cleavage all produced the same effect.

Amanda had just decided to try a last desperate measure of squirting soda water up her cunt when Phillipe came bounding into the bar. He took one look at his beloved Miss Waites being tortured, let out a Tarzan-like roar, and swept to the rescue.

Scooping up the giggling, helpless woman in his powerful arms, Phillipe carried her off, giving a passable imitation of the famous scene from *King Kong* when the giant ape snatches Fay Wray. Deprived of a handy Empire State building to climb, Phillipe took the stairs instead, leaping up them two at a time despite his burden.

He reached the first floor landing and looked desperately around for a safe haven. The door of room nine was slightly ajar. Using Miss Waites' feet as a battering ram, Phillipe pushed it open and carried her inside.

He lay her gently on the bed. Having never seen a water mattress before, Phillipe was a little surprised to see the woman of his dreams bobbing up and down like a cork, but managed to take it in his stride.

Standing by the side of the bed, Phillipe drew himself up proudly and delivered the longest speech in the English language that he had ever attempted.

'Miss Waites, I love you and I want you to have my beautiful cock.'

Phillipe had not been quite sure what reaction to expect, but a particularly loud belch, quickly followed by a high-pitched giggle had not been on his list of possibilities. Unused to the mysterious ways of women, he took it to be some form of rapturous enthusiasm. Throwing himself to his knees at the foot of the bed, Phillipe shoved his head up Miss Waites' skirt, pulled off her thick flannelette knickers and began to nuzzle at her cunt like a pig at a trough. Miss Waites kicked her legs in the air wildly and attempted to scream. Coming out of her mouth on the same blast of air as another belch, it sounded something like the rallying cry of Red Indians on the warpath. With his ears firmly jammed between her muffling thighs, Phillipe heard only a faint yelp, which he assumed was one of delirious pleasure.

Taking a breath, he set about attacking the rather disappointing cunt again, which was nowhere near as moist and succulent as he had been expecting. However, he was not prepared to be deterred at this late stage of the game. Extending his tongue to its full length, he rammed it between the thin lips of the dry slit and began to waggle it about furiously, reaching down to unbuckle his trousers at the same time.

Miss Waites' frantic kicking subsided slowly, as a totally unfamiliar and not unpleasant sensation began to seep into her alcohol-befuddled brain. Somewhere, in the deep recesses of her memory, she recalled feeling a similar sensation as a young girl, when she had been persuaded to go behind the school

bike sheds with young Billy Jones. But that, of
course, had been before her Bible-thumping father
had found them, dragged her home and told her what
an evil person she was with every painful lash of his
leather trouser belt across her buttocks. Somehow,
Miss Waites felt quite confident that he would not be
spoiling things for her this time, since she had
personally tipped his cremated ashes down the toilet
some twelve joyless years ago.

Abandoning any further attempts at resistance,
Miss Waites relaxed on the bed, letting its sensuous,
slightly hypnotic motion quell her earlier feelings of
panic. She felt an electric tingle up her spine as
Phillipe's hot, wet tongue snaked in and out of her
virgin canal. Responding to a long-repressed instinct,
she lifted her buttocks, pressing herself against his
soft, sucking mouth. Phillipe's teeth ground against
her labia, nibbling at the soft folds of flesh which
were now starting to tingle and burn with their own
strange heat. Combined with the heady effects of her
unaccustomed alcohol consumption, it was all totally
overpowering. Miss Waites felt as though her whole
body was being turned into one coordinated pleasure
machine, with sensation being mounted on sensation,
thrill upon thrill. She drew her legs up, spreading her
knees so that Phillipe could bury his head deeper into
the valley of her thighs where the primary pleasure
source appeared to be located. She began to pick
feverishly at the buttons on her blouse, opening it to
expose her small, pinched breasts with their puckered
brown nipples which had never felt the warmth of
human lips.

Phillipe was beside himself with happiness. He

sensed, rather than felt, Miss Waites' body responding to his attentions – although the tight, arid cunt beneath his worrying lips was already more soft and swollen, and the pungent aroma of love-juice was starting to fill his nostrils. Suddenly, the material of the skirt above his head was whisked away, as Miss Waites unzipped its side fastening and threw it over the side of the bed. Phillipe looked up, briefly, from his cunt-feast, to drink in the full vision of his love in her total nakedness.

He hurriedly finished divesting himself of his trousers, and ripped away his shirt with a pop of buttons. As his mighty cock throbbed into stiffness, he raised his head and set about sampling the other delights of his fleshy prize.

Miss Waites shuddered as Phillipe's tongue traced a hot, wet line up her belly and lingered in the crater of her navel. Reaching up to grasp his head between her hands, she pulled it up to her breasts, letting out a thin squeal of passion.

Next door, Caroline was avidly licking off the last drops of come from the end of Constable Harris' still rampant prick. She gave the thick shaft one last hopeful squeeze in case there was a drop of the creamy nectar left for dessert, then dropped her hand to his balls, twining her slim fingers in their coarse, springy bush.

'Is this why they call you fellows the fuzz?' she asked jokingly, tickling his tight scrotum with the edge of one long fingernail.

David's prick jerked. To her delight, Caroline saw one final bubble of juice ooze out of the depleted reservoir and threw herself upon it, sucking the bulging head into her mouth once again and rolling her tongue over the bubbling slit. She savoured the last droplet for all she was worth, knowing that there would be no more until she could find another cock to suck.

And suck she most certainly would, Caroline decided. She had taken to blow jobs like a horse to water, revelling in the thrill of stiff, twitching meat against the highly sensitive flesh of her lips. In fact, she had taken so much pleasure from it that she was now aware of a further complication in her previously untroubled life. Having been thoroughly converted to the cause of the male prick, she was now unsure whether she preferred them pumping in her cunt or throbbing in her mouth. Perhaps the only way to really tell would be to have both at once, Caroline thought, and made a conscious decision to get herself involved in a threesome at the first opportunity.

Just thinking about that possibility made her feel impossibly horny again. She slid her hot mouth deeper down David's weapon, milking it gently with her lips and tongue. David rolled his arse, thrusting his hips upwards to meet her descending lips. His prick still throbbed, and felt as though it would never go soft again. Even though his actual sexual experience was still fairly limited, David was pretty sure that women with Caroline's sheer sexual power didn't come along too often in a man's lifetime. So it made pretty good sense just to lie back and enjoy it while he could.

The ecstacy of the moment was shattered by a loud

squeal from the room next door. David's police training came to the fore at once. He rolled away from Caroline, his stiff prick popping out of her mouth, wet and glistening with saliva.

'What the hell was that?' he asked.

Caroline pouted with frustration. 'I didn't hear a thing,' she lied, reaching for his cock again. She began to lick it up and down with long, lapping strokes as though it were a stick of seaside rock.

It was no good. The mood was broken. David scrambled off the bed and began to dress hurriedly.

'I heard a scream,' he told Caroline. 'I'll have to go and investigate.'

Caroline accepted the disappointing situation with a little sigh of resignation. It was the recurrent lot of every policeman's wife, she supposed. When duty called, everything else had to stop. Adjusting her own clothing, she waited until David was fully dressed and pointed to the interconnecting door.

'You can get into the next room through there,' she told him. 'But from the sound of that squeal, I'd say it was only Miss Waites.' It did not occur to Caroline to question what Miss Waites might possibly be doing in one of the club's bedrooms.

David looked even more concerned. 'Miss Waites? But that's the lady who made the complaint. Good Lord – perhaps someone is attacking her.'

He headed for the interconnecting door and threw it open. Caroline decided to play it safe, just in case there was anything nasty going on. Crossing the room to the two-way mirror, she switched it on and peered into the room next door.

Phillipe and Miss Waites were curled up on the bed

in *soixante-neuf* position, his mouth glued to her now bubbling and juicy cunt while she hugged his massive cock like a one-eyed teddy bear, pressing it against her breasts and planting hot, feverish kisses upon its smooth, circumcised head.

Caroline could only gape in disbelief at the totally unexpected sight. Fascinated, she continued staring as David came into view, charging in on the scene like a cross between Rambo and Inspector Morse. He stopped rather abruptly as the exact nature of the situation became apparent.

It was a little late to attempt a discreet withdrawal. David shuffled his feet with embarrassment, feeling that he ought to say or do something to justify his sudden intrusion.

'Are you all right, Miss Waites?' he finally muttered, in a rather weak and self-conscious voice.

Miss Waites jumped away from Phillipe's cock as if it had suddenly become electrified. Her brain raced, trying to come up with a plausible explanation, some dim memory telling her that she had once read that attack was the best form of defence.

'Of course I'm all right, you stupid young man,' she barked aggressively. 'Can't you see that I am just trying to help my young nephew with his yoga?'

'You made a complaint about immoral goings-on. So I thought you might be being attacked,' David said, defensively.

Miss Waites dived for her handbag on the floor. Scooping it up, she pulled out Andrew's obscene photograph.

'Here, young man. This is the disgusting sexual

pervert you should be looking for,' she said, stabbing a bony finger at Peter Blake. 'If I were you I would get after him right away, before he makes a clean getaway.'

David took the photo, feeling a hot flush of anger at the sight of Caroline's apparently helpless and tortured body.

'You're absolutely right, Miss Waites,' he said with total conviction. 'I shall get after the wicked scoundrel at once.'

David beat a hasty retreat, closing the door behind him.

Hardly had it clicked shut before Miss Waites threw herself upon Phillipe's rampant cock again, covering it with sloppy wet kisses. 'Phillipe, oh, Phillipe,' she murmured softly.

Phillipe pressed his face onto her chest, clamping his mouth around the nearest stiff little nipple.

'Miss Waites, oh, Miss Waites,' he responded, with the passion of total abandonment.

Miss Waites stroked his hair gently. 'Call me Desiree,' she crooned softly.

Chapter Nineteen

As Constable Harris shot off in pursuit of the notorious sex pervert Peter Blake, Amanda had just noticed him skulking through the reception area.

She screamed out at him. 'Blake, you two-faced bastard. I'm going to boil your bloody balls and feed them to you for breakfast.'

Not surprisingly, Peter made a bolt for it, hoping to lose himself in the club's maze of corridors before she had a chance to see which direction he had taken. Throwing open the nearest door, he ducked through it, just as the one next to it opened and Cedric and Randy stepped through. Cedric caught only a fleeting glimpse of Peter's face and then the back of his head.

'Blake,' he roared after the departing figure. 'You come back here and tell me what the bloody hell is going on?'

Constable Harris came tearing down the stairs, waving a photograph. Missing the last step in his hurry, he flew off the staircase, tripped on the hallway carpet and careered into Cedric, knocking him to the floor.

Apparently unconcerned about this slightly unusual way of eliciting information, he thrust the photograph under Cedric's nose.

'Have you seen this man?' he demanded.

Slightly stunned, and totally bemused, Cedric

studied the picture, recognising Peter Blake at once. There was also something oddly familiar about the girl, although Cedric couldn't quite place her for the moment.

Amanda came running out of the bar. 'Anyone seen that bastard Peter Blake? Which way did he go?'

Weakly, Cedric pointed to the door through which Peter had made his hurried exit. He addressed David and Amanda at the same time. 'He went that way,' Cedric announced, vaguely aware that he sounded like a character out of an old Roy Rogers movie.

David Harris scrambled to his feet, closely followed by Cedric. With Amanda leading the way, the three of them made a mad and undignified rush for the door.

Randy let them all go. It was all a bit too much for his basically laid-back character, and he was rapidly becoming convinced that all the Brits were hopelessly and utterly mad. Besides, he needed to use the bathroom. Assuming that the nearest one would be up on the first floor, he headed for the stairs.

Peter Blake's earlier worries about the deteriorating situation had by now approached the stage of blind panic. Suddenly, it seemed that the entire world was after his blood and that the fates had somehow conspired to stage his personal nemesis at the Paradise Country Club. In the last few minutes, he had more or less written off his half a million pounds. Right now, the immediate problem seemed to be one of survival. He hesitated in indecision for several moments, trying to think of a place to hide.

Behind him, at the end of the corridor, he heard the door being smashed open with a force that suggested an avenging mob. Glancing over his shoulder, he saw Amanda, Cedric and a uniformed policeman fighting to get through — all apparently intent on getting to him first. In desperation, Peter ran through the nearest door, which just happened to lead into the massage room.

Totally nude, a surprised Freda looked up from the manipulation table where she had been massaging the Hon. Nigel's prick between her massive tits and sucking him off at the same time. Having strapped him into position, it had proved more difficult than usual to get him erect enough for his therapy to begin, and she had been forced to resort to direct and intimate stimulation. It had obviously worked, since the Hon. Nigel's long cock jumped and quivered like a flagpole on a blustery day as Freda jumped back from the table, alarmed at the sudden and unexpected interruption.

Crashing into the room, Peter looked around desperately for a place to hide. Grabbing a couple of white towels off the wall, he wrapped them around himself and dived for cover underneath the massage table, hoping to disguise himself as a pile of dirty laundry. Hardly had he crunched himself up into a ball among the tangle of wires and cables left over from Freda's hasty and amateur electrical rewiring job than Amanda, Cedric and Constable Harris came bursting in through the door behind him.

With a little whoop of triumph, Amanda recognised Peter's patent leather shoes sticking out from underneath the manipulation table.

'Got you, you bastard,' she yelped, diving down to grab one of his ankles and giving a mighty heave. Peter kicked out furiously, scrabbling on his hands and knees to escape from her clutches.

Seeing a potential getaway, David ran round to the other side of the table to block any exit. Bending over, he attempted to get a firm grip on the struggling, towel-covered figure. The table rocked ominously, causing considerable alarm to its patient. Helplessly strapped down and totally confused by the sudden melee, the Hon. Nigel's mouth dropped slackly open.

Freda, backing away from the whole mad scramble, crashed into the control console and sat down on the starter button. The table started to whirr into life, gradually folding upwards at both ends.

Only Cedric remained uninvolved. He stood, stock-still, rooted to the spot and totally mesmerised by the sight of Freda's huge and wobbling tits. They were, for him, a perfect vision of heaven. At that precise moment in time, nothing in earthly life seemed of greater importance than burying his face in those mountains of soft, quivering flesh and sucking those ripe and juicy nipples into his mouth. Like a man entranced he shuffled into movement, advancing towards Freda with his lips drooling.

Beneath the table, Peter continued to struggle furiously as Amanda pulled his leg on one side and David tugged his arm on the other. His free leg snagged in a coil of cable, and he shook it vigorously, trying to extricate himself.

For all her formidable talents as a masseuse, Freda's efforts as an electrician made Heath

Robinson look like a micro-circuitry genius. Eschewing such irrelevant things as junction boxes and terminal connectors, her rewiring job was mainly held together with a combination of hairslides, bent paperclips and Sellotape. There was no way it could stand up to the sort of punishment it was currently taking.

A violent flash and bang from underneath the table was quickly followed by a yelp of surprise and pain from Peter. Amanda and David let go of his various extremities suddenly, both flying backwards to sprawl out upon the floor in shocked and crumpled heaps. The table, which had just received enough of a power jolt to light up the Blackpool Illuminations for a week, surged into high gear and folded up like a jacknife, taking its occupant with it. The Hon. Nigel had just enough time to let out a chocked scream of panic mixed with delight before his stiff cock was rammed into his open mouth. Making the most of this totally unexpected realisation of his life's ambition, he began to suck it with great relish.

Taking advantage of the confusion, Peter Blake managed to scramble out from beneath the table and make it to the door on his hands and knees. Before Amanda and David had a chance to clamber to their feet, he was out and running for his life, gaining a good twenty yard headstart before they managed to set off in pursuit.

Freda, never a girl to turn down any kind of sexual opportunity, grunted with passion as Cedric reached her and buried his head between her mighty mammaries. With her hands already clawing at his trousers, she dragged him to the floor, rolling him on his back. Yanking his trousers down to his knees, Freda rubbed her moist golden cunt against his rapidly stiffening cock and, squeezing her breasts together so that both red nipples were like a pair of Siamese twins, offered them to Cedric's greedy mouth.

Feasting upon the double delight, Cedric felt completely detached from his own dick. As far as he was concerned, the Swedish girl could do what she liked with it, just as long as he had her wonderful, wobbling tits to himself. He was hardly even aware as she fitted her oozing slit over its throbbing head and lowered her hot shaft on to its rigid length. Completely submerged in the fantasy land of his own breast fetish, his lips and tongue slavered over the two hot and stiffening nipples as Freda began to fuck him furiously.

Immersed in their own pleasures, neither of them gave a second thought to the unfortunate Hon. Nigel, still locked in the vice-like embrace of the concertinaed bed. His eyes rolling wildly, he had no other choice than to gulp down his own come as it spurted into his mouth.

Randy came out of the bathroom and stopped on the landing, pricking his ears to the rather odd sounds which were emanating from one of the rooms further along the corridor. Curious, and still anxious to find someone sane enough to tell him what was actually going on, he tiptoed along the passageway to the door of room nine.

The door was slightly ajar, and from behind it

Randy could hear a series of loud, guttural grunts, interspersed with high-pitched yelps and a regular, sharp, smacking sound.

Tentatively, Randy pushed the door, which swung open to reveal a near-demented Desiree Waites humping herself frantically on Phillipe's mighty prick. Flat on his back, the lad lay happily and submissively as she bounced up and down on its full, throbbing length, heartily smacking his thighs with the back of a hair brush which she had pressed into use as a riding crop.

Pulling the door closed behind him, Randy beat a hasty retreat. He was about to head back towards the stairs when Caroline walked out of the room next door.

It was, as portrayed in sloppy romance novels and TV mini-series, a classic case of love at first sight. They both froze, he totally entranced by the dark-haired vision of loveliness and exceedingly well-shaped tits, and she with the handsome sun-bronzed face, muscular physique and well-cut trousers which probably concealed a fair-sized cock. The pair of them stood, gazing into each other's eyes with unspoken passion, both waiting for a full string orchestra to swell into ghostly presence in the background. Instead, they had to settle for Desiree Waites' ecstatic yodelling as she finally came in a fountain of lust and sprayed her hot orgasm over Phillipe's youthful thighs.

Randy found his tongue at last. 'Hi, I'm Randy,' he announced.

Caroline's heart leapt at the sound of his voice. 'My God, so am I,' she breathed in a husky whisper.

Grasping him by the hand, she pulled him into the bedroom.

Like a man in a dream, Randy let her lead him to the foot of the bed. He felt strange and disorientated, almost breathless with the sheer intensity of the physical attraction he felt for this beautiful woman. It was like a force field all around them, bonding them together and at the same time completely shutting out reality and the world outside. It was as if his whole life had been merely a rehearsal for this moment — a meeting which had been preordained ever since his emergence from his mother's womb.

It seemed that there should be a million things they had to say to each other, yet mere words would be inadequate. Dumbly, Randy could only watch, entranced, as Caroline slowly undressed, exposing her lush young body for his personal and exclusive pleasure. So that was to be it, he realised. They would let their bodies talk for them, share the deepest and most intimate conversation of cock and cunt, mouth and lips, flesh upon flesh. As Caroline stood before him in all her naked glory, Randy undressed himself without hurry, sensing that they had all the time in the world. Finally, they stood silently regarding each other like a modern-day Adam and Eve, sharing a strange sensation of wonder and almost child-like innocence.

Reaching out, Randy cupped his hands under the swelling softness of Caroline's ripe, firm breasts, marvelling at the warmth and silky softness of her skin. His thumbs stroked the pink buds of her nipples with delicate precision, rolling them around in tiny circles as they stiffened under his touch.

Caroline stepped forwards, pressing her body against his and throwing her slim arms around his neck. She pulled his head gently down to her own, pressing her soft, full lips agains his mouth and running her hot wet tongue along his teeth.

It was a kiss apparently without passion, yet it triggered off a sudden and savage explosion of pure lust which shuddered through their entire bodies. Randy thrust his tongue deep into her inviting mouth, probing and licking in a pool of mingling saliva.

Caroline felt an electric thrill pulse through her body as the full power of their mutual attraction was suddenly released. Her body responded to it automatically, instantly flushed with a tingling, prickling heat. She pressed herself even closer against him, feeling a delicious shiver of pleasure at the hardness of his cock against her taut belly. Reaching down, she closed her slim fingers around its stiff and gently throbbing length, rubbing and rolling it against herself.

She drew back slightly, pushing Randy's prick down until it slipped into the cleft of her thighs. Holding it tightly, she began to rub it from side to side against her cunt lips and clitoris, stimulating the flow of her precious love-juices to welcome this lovely cock into its rightful home.

For Caroline no longer had any doubts that Randy's cock and her cunt were each other's natural partners. She had dimly sensed it when she had first set eyes upon him, but now, feeling its wonderful hardness against her soft flesh, she knew it for a fact. All her experiences and fantasies of the past couple of days were forgotten. There would be no more sexual experimentation because there didn't need to be. Caroline had found her man, and there was now only one prick she wanted and needed to fill her hungry hole. The thick, stiff shaft she could feel between her thighs would be enough. She wanted it in her cunt, in her mouth, and even in her arse, if that was Randy's pleasure.

Spreading her legs, she rubbed the smooth head of Randy's cock deeper into the oozing crevice of her hot slit. Randy gave a little shudder at the feel of her burning juices upon the sensitive tip of his organ. Flexing his knees slightly, he thrust his pelvis forward so that Caroline could guide the bulbous head into the moist softness of her fanny.

A warm and wonderful sensation of total satisfaction suffused them both as the stiff member eased into its silky sheath. Randy let his cock slide slowly and gently into place and shivered with pleasure as Caroline's tight cunt closed around it, sucking it in.

They clung to each other like that for several moments, each content just to feel the thrill of deep and intimate contact and the subtle transference of body heat. Finally, Caroline sank backwards on to the bed, pulling Randy down on top of her. She drew her knees up, spreading them apart as wide as she could to let him slip down the full length of her creamy tunnel.

Randy felt himself sink into her warm wetness, the juicy inside of her cunt sucking and massaging his stiff flesh with a sensuous, almost snake-like motion. He groaned softly, pressing his body against hers, and rocking his hips with a gentle, swivelling action. Caroline's lush lips parted in ecstacy, her hot breath panting against his throat.

'Fuck me, Randy,' Caroline grated out. 'Fuck me deep and slow. Fill my cunt and belly with your beautiful big cock.'

Randy felt his prick throb in response to Caroline's plea. He pulled back slowly, so that his tool almost popped out of her wet crack. With just the head of it poised against her portal, he made a whole series of short, fast, jabbing strokes which teased and vibrated against her quivering clitoris until Caroline was screaming for him to plunge into her again. Just as it seemed she would explode with sheer frustration, he obliged her, thrusting his hot prick the length and depth of her gaping cunt.

Caroline began to roll her arse around on the bed, adding to the delicious sensation of total penetration. She curved her spine, raised her hips and began to emulate the thrusting of his cock, slapping her belly against his with wet smacking sounds.

Randy's pace increased as he rammed into her and the mad fever of sheer animal fucking took over his mind and body. His cock vibrated like a machine, Caroline's wet cunt clasped against it with a burning, liquid heat which seemed to fuse their flesh together into a single, finely engineered unit.

With total abandonment, her legs rose and closed around his back, ankles locked together at the base of his spine. She pulled him down on her, revelling in his weight pressing down upon her body, his thick cock shafting into her and the furious intensity of his fucking. She could feel the head of his heavy cock ramming against the constriction of her cervix deep inside, shaking and racking her body with every shuddering stroke. She was completely fulfilled, her heart and body completely given over to this man who was fucking her with such consummate skill and artistry.

Caroline's orgasm rose in shuddering waves of pleasure from somewhere deep inside her belly. She stiffened, gripping him even tighter with her legs and contracting her abdominal muscles to squeeze his thick cock inside her.

Randy began to moan softly — a joyous, throbbing low note of pleasure made deep in his throat and torn from his open, panting mouth. The knowledge of his approaching climax was the final spur which pushed Caroline over the edge of the sexual abyss. Her fingernails raked his broad back as she felt herself losing all control. With her whole body quivering feverishly, Caroline let herself go and shuddered into the final stages of climatic release. As her hot juices broke like a crashing wave around his cock, Randy gave one last convulsive heave and spurted into her.

Caroline clenched her thighs, squeezing his body with her legs in time with the gradually subsiding waves of secondary orgasm which rippled her body. Then, finally, feeling completely and utterly fucked, she let them drop to the bed like lumps of leaden, dead meat. Randy rolled off her, laying on his back and staring at the ceiling.

They lay like that, unmoving and unspeaking, for a good five minutes. Finally, Caroline rolled over on to her side and threw her arm across his belly. Her fingers reached for his soft prick, stroking and teasing it into life again.

'Oh, Randy, fuck me again,' she pleaded.

To his surprise, Randy felt his sated cock quiver and twitch under her electric touch. Her sheer sexuality flowed from her fingers into his limp prick, willing it to rise again. It began to stiffen and swell, rearing into life again with renewed energy and hunger.

He leaned over to kiss Caroline's soft tits, licking her taut little nipples and marvelling anew at the sight and the feel of her young and vibrant flesh.

'Oh yes, I'll fuck you,' he murmured softly. 'I'll fuck you again now, and tonight and tomorrow and the day after that. I'm going to be fucking you for the rest of my life.'

Caroline drank his words in, a dreamy smile upon her lovely lips. It was a promise which she would make sure he kept.

Chapter Twenty

It was half-way through the evening before Randy and Caroline had finally fucked and sucked themselves senseless. Hand in hand like a couple of teenagers on their first date, they ventured down the stairs to face the real world once again, and to find someone to share their joyous news.

The reception area was an unusual hive of activity. Behind the desk, a beaming Sally happily greeted and handed out bedroom keys to a succession of extremely attractive young ladies and their escorts. There was no sign of any of the Anti-Vice League, although one of the clients bore a striking resemblance to the defrocked Catholic priest who had spent most of the afternoon sprinkling holy water in the fishponds.

'I think we both need a drink,' Randy said, leading Caroline towards the bar. They walked in to another scene of bustling activity, as the lounge was filled to bursting point.

Randy looked round in surprise. 'Gee, I didn't realise this place was so popular,' he muttered to Caroline. 'My information was that it was run down and practically derelict. But it's been nothing short of a madhouse ever since we got here.'

'We?' Caroline queried, suddenly worried. It had

not occurred to her that Randy was anything but a single highly eligible male.

Randy pushed his way towards the bar through the milling throng. 'I came down with a business partner. I guess he'll be in here somewhere.'

They were almost at the bar. With something of a start, Caroline recognised Charles, her father's chauffeur, helping Andrew to dish out the gin and tonics and pints of bitter. His afternoon in the Games Room had been more than enough to convince him that he was at a stage of career crisis in his life, and that there was alternative employment available which offered far more in terms of job satisfaction than driving a Rolls Royce around. And with Sally offering both the job and the satisfaction, he had jumped at the chance of becoming the Paradise Club's new assistant manager.

Charles recognised Randy, and came over smiling. 'Ah, Mr Brandich, sir. What can I get you?'

Randy ordered his drinks. 'Where's Mr Drummond?'

Charles nodded somewhere over the sea of heads. 'He's sitting over there, sir, with a rather large blonde masseuse. I believe she is just talking him into becoming a club member and enrolling for an ongoing course of manipulation therapy.'

Caroline heard her father's name and felt a twinge of panic. There was going to be some rather awkward explaining to do, and fairly soon. Gripping Randy's hand tightly for support, she steeled herself for the encounter as they began to ease their way through the crowds towards Cedric's table.

Cedric was in a wonderful little world of his own,

and hardly noticed them as they approached. Leaning across the small table, he was happily staring into the deep Scandinavian fjord of Freda's cleavage as he idly fingered her steaming cunt beneath it. Always a stickler for the social graces, Cedric had managed to convince himself that he was only following house rules, since just about everybody around him seemed to be indulging in some form of sexual foreplay under the cover of their tables. Freda purred contentedly, occasionally reaching over to stroke his stiff cock through the material of his trousers.

The quiet rapture of the moment was broken abruptly with the arrival of Randy and Caroline. Cedric's finger withdrew hastily from Freda's wet crack with a faint plop. She gave his prick a last gentle squeeze and placed her hands on top of the table, assuming a pose of genteel sophistication.

If Randy had noticed anything, he didn't make it obvious. He thrust Caroline forward proudly. 'Cedric, I'd like you to meet my fiancée,' he announced.

Cedric recognised the girl from the photograph at once, and was again struck by the oddest feeling that he knew her. Looking into her green eyes, he was sure that they too reflected a flicker of recognitiion.

Caroline sighed, and took a deep breath. It was time for the charade to end, she knew. Reaching up, she snatched off the black wig, revealing her blonde curls beneath.

'Daddy — it's me,' she announced, throwing her arms around Cedric's neck and planting a wet and sloppy kiss upon his cheek.

The full implications of the sudden transformation took a few seconds to sink in to Cedric's mind. When they did, and he realised that his only daughter had been the victim of Peter Blake's depraved attentions, his face went black with rage. He jumped to his feet, quite forgetting that he still had a rather sizeable erection from Freda's under-the-table ministrations. He banged his clenched fist upon the top of the table angrily. 'I'll make sure that swine Blake never works again,' he started to bluster, suddenly falling silent as he became aware of Caroline's eyes fixed on the prominent bulge in his trousers.

'Daddy, I never realised you had it in you,' she observed, in a voice which was a mixture of shock and somewhat awed admiration.

Cedric sat down abruptly, managing to partially cover his embarrassment with a sheepish smile.

Having dropped her minor bombshell, Caroline decided it was time to beat a temporary retreat. She smiled sweetly at Randy. 'Well, I'll leave you men to talk business for a while,' she said. 'I just want to go and talk to Amanda.'

She began to back away as Randy drew up a spare chair and sat down, confronting Cedric. 'What's this crap about you joining this bloody club?' he demanded immediately. 'I thought we were supposed to be demolishing this goddamned place, not becoming members.'

Caroline didn't wait around to hear the rest of the conversation. First, she needed to talk to Amanda. And if she heard what she wanted to hear, then she might well have a little compromise plan of her own to contribute to any business discussions. With a bit of luck, she could show her father that he wasn't the only wheeler-dealer in the Drummond family.

Searching the crowded bar, she finally picked out Amanda in the far corner, deep in conversation with a stunningly attractive redhead and a young Eurasian girl. Caroline fought her way across, after picking up a large vodka and tonic from the bar.

'Amanda — what's happening? Who are all these people? What happened to all the demonstrators?' The questions tumbled out one after the other.

Amanda greeted her with a gleeful smile. She seemed ecstatically happy.

'Isn't it marvellous?' she demanded, waving a hand around to indicate the throng of customers. 'Looks like the Paradise is back in business with a vengeance.'

Caroline could see all this for herself. It didn't really answer her questions.

'But how?' she wanted to know.

Amanda gestured to her two companions. 'It's all down to my friends,' she said. 'You remember I told you that I phoned some of the girls from my escort agency and invited them down for a weekend of frolics. Well, it seems that the word got around, and just about everyone in the business decided to bring their clients down with them. So right now, I guess that nearly every good-time girl in the south-east of England is here.'

'And the protest mob?'

'Ah — that's largely down to you.' Amanda beamed at her. 'I don't know what it was you did to that young copper, but it certainly worked wonders. After half an hour with you, he went berserk, running round the place and arresting everybody for disturbing the peace. And our dear Miss Waites did the rest,' Amanda finished happily.

Caroline didn't understand. 'Miss Waites? Where does she fit in?'

Amanda smiled. 'Well, she may have been an old prude in the past, but she certainly didn't turn out to be a hypocrite as well. To give her credit where it is due, once she realised that she had been thoroughly converted to the cause by Phillipe and his wonderful cock, she disbanded the Anti-Vice League at once. In fact, she's still around here somewhere, throwing brandy down her throat like there's no tomorrow.'

Amanda broke off to regard Caroline curiously. 'Anyway, where have you been all afternoon?'

Caroline smirked. 'That would be telling, my dear,' she said. 'Let's just say that I sort of worked my way through this place and back again. It gave me something I needed, and I shall always be grateful for that. But somehow, I don't think that the Paradise Country Club is quite suitable for the extremely rich and elegant Mrs Randy Brandich III.'

Amanda sensed a moment of parting. She embraced Caroline like one of her oldest and dearest friends. 'You know you'll always be welcome here, don't you?' she said.

Caroline nodded, grinning. 'Yes, of course. But somehow, I just don't think I will ever need the peculiar sexual magic of the Paradise again.'

Caroline paused, thinking about the words she had just used. It was true — the Paradise Country Club did have some special quality. Perhaps it was something to do with all the cocks which had throbbed and spurted here over the years. All the hungry cunts that had been filled, all the secret desires and fetishes which had been realised, and all the sexual games that had been played. It was as if all this sheer sexual energy had somehow been absorbed by the very walls of the building itself, charging the whole place with an aphrodisiac quality which affected anyone who stepped into it.

But for her, it was time to leave. She had found her freedom, tasted all the delights of pure lust, and now she was liberated. She had come full circle, discovered her true female self and realised that, in the final analysis, she was essentially a one-man woman. It didn't mean that she was any better, or worse a person than someone like Amanda, or Sally, or Freda. She was just different, with different needs and a different attitude to life.

She gave Amanda one final and affectionate squeeze. 'I've got to go,' she said, almost regretfully. 'I just need a bit of time to arrange the favour I owe you, and I'll be on my way.'

She detached herself, smiling up into Amanda's rather confused face.

'Favour? What favour?' Amanda started to ask. 'You don't owe me anything.'

But Caroline had already started to walk away, back towards Randy and her father.

'You'll see,' she called out over her shoulder to Amanda, and then she was lost in the crowd.

Chapter Twenty-One

Amanda and Giles lay together in bed, masturbating each other gently and unhurriedly. In the other bedrooms all around them, the rest of the overnight occupants were fucking themselves crazy, creating a minor symphony of sloshing waterbeds and smacking flesh. In couples, trios and even copulating quartets, pulsating cocks plunged in and out of cunts, mouths and arseholes. Lips sucked on nipples and pricks, tongues darted in and out of wet slits and fingers dug into soft flesh.

For those weekend revellers who had not yet retired to their beds, there was still a wild party going on downstairs in the bar. Freda and Amanda's red-headed friends were giving a spirited and enthusiastic lesbian show on the counter, their heads buried deep in each other crotches as they sucked greedily at each others flowing cunts, lapping up the copious juices on lips and tongues and gulping it down with relish.

Their demonstration was watched by a small, but appreciative audience of male customers who stood in a line, cheering them on. On the floor, Angie and Carol scrambled about on their hands and knees, pausing at regular intervals to pull a rigid cock out of a fly and stuff it in their mouths, plating furiously until they were rewarded with a throatful of hot come. Then it would be time to move on to the next

305

throbbing member and the next sticky treat.

Behind the bar, Charles the ex-chauffeur was revelling in the perks of his new job. Still marvelling at his luck, he contentedly pulled fresh pints as Sally, sitting impaled on her prostrate husband's prick, nibbled at his dangling balls. As Andrew began to writhe beneath her, she lifted her face and took Charles' wonderfully fat cock between her thick lips, swirling her hot tongue around the smooth and shiny head. Charles thrust against her, driving his cock deeper into her mouth and throat. Sally accepted the face-fucking happily, more than content that she had finally found the ideal partner to share her and Andrew's sex games.

At one of the tables sat a totally drunken Desiree Waites, with a beatific grin all over her face. It was not entirely due to the brandy, since underneath the table, the defrocked Catholic priest had his head up her skirt and his tongue up her cunt, lapping away for all he was worth. Miss Waites accepted his oral ministrations through an alcoholic haze, and vainly tried to concentrate her mind upon a schedule for the course of English lessons she was planning for Phillipe.

On the bar counter, Freda suddenly gave a loud shriek and convulsed into wild orgasm, demonstrating to all and sundry why she had been given the nickname The Sprayer. Floods of juice poured from her Vesuvius-like cunt, her frantic kicking legs and bucking hips sending it splashing and gushing across the counter top in steaming waves.

Angie and Carol both finished off the last stiff

cock simultaneously and stood up, sperm dribbling from the corners of their mouths like a pair of venereal vampires.

But for Amanda and Giles, all this was a world away. After the frenzied activity of the day, it was good just to relax in eath other's company, sharing the pleasures of their bodies in a quiet and gentle manner.

Giles moved three fingers slowly in and out of Amanda's wet cunt, rotating them from time to time so that his knuckles bounced over her slick and throbbing clitoris, eliciting a tiny shudder of pleasure.

'You know, it's been one hell of a day,' he said quietly, taking his mouth away from her tits for just long enough to speak.

Amanda nodded thoughtfully, her slim fingers tracing up and down the length of his gently throbbing organ.

'Yep, we've certainly seen some action here,' she agreed, thinking about the whole strange chain of events which had taken place in the past twenty-four hours.

A roar of raucous, drunken cheering reached her ears from the bar downstairs, as the customers expressed their appreciation of Freda's orgasmic display.

'And from the sound of it, we're in for plenty more action in this place for the foreseeable future. There's no doubt about it — the Paradise Country Club is most definitely back in the pleasure business.'

Amanda fell silent, running it all through in her mind, and trying to work out how differently things

might have turned out. If Peter Blake had managed
to get his way, the future would not be looking quite
so rosy. Right now, she might have been saddled with
a closed-down and defunct business, instead of a
thriving proposition.

But Caroline had made good on her final promise
to pay back her imagined debt. Using her feminine
wiles on Randy and her father, she had managed to
convince them both that there was a real need for
purely adult pleasure parks like the Paradise Club
along with the swings and roundabouts and
rollercoasters of the theme park. More to the point,
Cedric Drummond was willing to inject some capital
into the place, to restore it to its former glory and
finance much needed improvements.

And with her new-found source of clientele,
Amanda was sure that it would soon become a Mecca
for tired and jaded businessmen for miles around.
Now that the local Anti-Vice League was officially
disbanded, there would be no more opposition to the
Club's continued success.

Yes, she had to admit, things had turned out pretty
well all round. Amanda toyed with Giles' cock
playfully, stroking the thick shaft between her thumb
and finger.

'Mind you, you've not done so badly out of the
deal,' she said to its owner.

Giles stretched luxuriously, running the flat of his
hand up and down the crease of Amanda's dripping
slit.

'No, not bad at all,' he conceded. This was
something of an understatement, since he was now
roughly two million pounds better off than he had

been in the morning. With the Paradise Country Club saved, there had been only one place left to buy up land for the theme park. So when Randy Brandich III had made him an offer, he had accepted it gratefully.

Giles smiled to himself, thinking of his family home turned into the centrepiece of 'Mediaevalworld', as Randy had put it. Complete with clanking suits of armour, serving wenches in period costume and a host of special effects to provide everything from jousting tournaments to headless ghosts, the old place would soon be echoing to the screams and gasps of delighted children. Remembering his father's almost reverential worship of the old house, Giles found this particularly amusing.

'Yes, everything turned out very well indeed,' Amanda was saying. 'The only thing which still puzzles me is what happened to Peter Blake. He seems to have disappeared from the face of the earth.

Giles sat up in bed with a sudden jerk, his face creased into a frown. 'Oh, Christ, I completely forgot to tell you,' he muttered. 'I found Blake skulking around my place earlier this afternoon. Knowing that you wanted to talk to him, I locked the poor bugger up in the stables and forgot all about him.'

Amanda started to giggle, remembering how Caroline had told her about his pathological fear of horses. 'The bastard is probably a gibbering imbecile by now,' she said to Giles, explaining the situation.

Giles looked concerned. 'Do you think one of us ought to go and let him out?'

Amanda shrugged. 'Let him sweat. It'll do him good.'

The continuing noise of the party downstairs still drifted into the room. Amanda slid down the bed and stuck her head between Giles' thighs to shut out the intrusive sounds. She licked Giles' cock lovingly.

'God only knows what it's going to be like next week, when we hold your Hunt Ball,' she said. 'I reckon that will make tonight's little shindig look like a vicar's tea party.'

Ah, yes, that will be another story, I'm sure,' Giles said, agreeing with her.

Amanda chuckled. 'You'd better believe it. That will most certainly be another story indeed.'

Then her hot mouth clamped over the end of Giles' rampant cock, and she didn't say anything more for a long, long time.

Headline Delta Erotic Survey

In order to provide the kind of books you like to read - and to qualify for a free erotic novel of the Editor's choice - we would appreciate it if you would complete the following survey and send your answers, together with any further comments, to:

> Headline Book Publishing
> FREEPOST 9 (WD 4984)
> London
> W1E 7BE

1. Are you male or female?
2. Age? Under 20 / 20 to 30 / 30 to 40 / 40 to 50 / 50 to 60 / 60 to 70 / over
3. At what age did you leave full-time education?
4. Where do you live? (Main geographical area)
5. Are you a regular erotic book buyer / a regular book buyer in general / both?
6. How much approximately do you spend a year on erotic books / on books in general?
7. How did you come by this book?
7a. If you bought it, did you purchase from: a national bookchain / a high street store / a newsagent / a motorway station / an airport / a railway station / other........
8. Do you find erotic books easy / hard to come by?
8a. Do you find Headline Delta erotic books easy / hard to come by?
9. Which are the best / worst erotic books you have ever read?
9a. Which are the best / worst Headline Delta erotic books you have ever read?
10. Within the erotic genre there are many periods, subjects and literary styles. Which of the following do you prefer:
10a. (period) historical / Victorian / C20th / contemporary / future?
10b. (subject) nuns / whores & whorehouses / Continental frolics / s&m / vampires / modern realism / escapist fantasy / science fiction?

10c. (styles) hardboiled / humorous / hardcore / ironic / romantic / realistic?
10d. Are there any other ingredients that particularly appeal to you?
11. We try to create a cover appearance that is suitable for each title. Do you consider them to be successful?
12. Would you prefer them to be less explicit / more explicit?
13. We would be interested to hear of your other reading habits. What other types of books do you read?
14. Who are your favourite authors?
15. Which newspapers do you read?
16. Which magazines?
17. Do you have any other comments or suggestions to make?

If you would like to receive a free erotic novel of the Editor's choice (available only to UK residents), together with an up-to-date listing of Headline Delta titles, please supply your name and address:

Name...

Address..

....

....

A selection of Erotica from Headline

FONDLE ALL OVER	Nadia Adamant	£4.99 ☐
LUST ON THE LOOSE	Noel Amos	£4.99 ☐
GROUPIES	Johnny Angelo	£4.99 ☐
PASSION IN PARADISE	Anonymous	£4.99 ☐
THE ULTIMATE EROS COLLECTION	Anonymous	£6.99 ☐
EXPOSED	Felice Ash	£4.99 ☐
SIN AND MRS SAXON	Lesley Asquith	£4.99 ☐
HIGH JINKS HALL	Erica Boleyn	£4.99 ☐
TWO WEEKS IN MAY	Maria Caprio	£4.99 ☐
THE PHALLUS OF OSIRIS	Valentina Cilescu	£4.99 ☐
NUDE RISING	Faye Rossignol	£4.99 ☐
AMOUR AMOUR	Marie-Claire Villefranche	£4.99 ☐

All Headline books are available at your local bookshop or newsagent, or can be ordered direct from the publisher. Just tick the titles you want and fill in the form below. Prices and availability subject to change without notice.

Headline Book Publishing PLC, Cash Sales Department, Bookpoint, 39 Milton Park, Abingdon, OXON, OX14 4TD, UK. If you have a credit card you may order by telephone – 0235 831700.

Please enclose a cheque or postal order made payable to Bookpoint Ltd to the value of the cover price and allow the following for postage and packing:
UK & BFPO: £1.00 for the first book, 50p for the second book and 30p for each additional book ordered up to a maximum charge of £3.00.
OVERSEAS & EIRE: £2.00 for the first book, £1.00 for the second book and 50p for each additional book.

Name ....

Address ....

....

....

If you would prefer to pay by credit card, please complete:
Please debit my Visa/Access/Diner's Card/American Express (delete as applicable) card no:

Signature .... Expiry Date ....